Histress

A Novel By

Crystal Lacey Winslow

http://www.melodramapublishing.com

Histress
Copyright © 2007 by Crystal L. Winslow

All rights reserved. Printed in the United States of America. No part of this book may be used or reproduced, stored in a retrieval system, or transmitted by any means, electronic, mechanical, photocopying, recording, or otherwise, without written permission from the publisher. Although every precaution has been taken in the preparation of this book, the publisher and author assume no responsibility for errors or omissions.

For information address:
Melodrama Publishing
P. O. Box 522
Bellport, New York 11713-0522

Web address: www.melodramapublishing.com
e-mail: melodramapub@aol.com
author's email address: **melodramaticbrat@aol.com**
Library of Congress Control Number: 2007900802
ISBN 1-934157-03-1
First Edition

This novel is a work of fiction. Any resemblances to actual events, real people, living or dead, organizations, establishments, locales are products of the author's imagination. Other names, characters, places, and incidents are used fictitiously.

10 9 8 7 6 5 4 3 2 1
First Paperback Edition

Histress

Married women have affairs, too

Prologue

Summer 1987

THE LOUD, BLARING SIRENS WERE INDICATIVE OF THE trouble he'd gotten himself into. He held onto his new bride tightly in an attempt to give her the protection and security that he had failed to do only moments earlier. The end results were tragic, but there weren't any other options. He was a man. And he was going to stand behind his decision. When her hysteria slowed to a soft whimper, she pushed his strong arms from around her waist and glared at him. She wouldn't speak. His heart broke as he looked at her, his wife, disheveled and battered. Her once vibrant eyes were now swollen and sullen. Her tear-streaked face was puffy and accusatory. His guilt made him look away.

He drew a long breath. "I'm soooo sorry, baby. I should have been here to protect you—"

"Police! Open up!"

"I'll never let anything like this happen ever—"

"I said, open the fucking door!"

"Please don't cry…I love—"

BOOM!

"Baby, look at me—"

BOOM! BOOM! The battering ram pummeled the front door, breaking the locks and ripping it off its hinges.

"POLICE! DON'T NOBODY FUCKING MOVE!"

Instantly his hands flew up in surrender. A nine-millimeter revolver was pointed directly at the back of his head.

"Get on the fucking ground, asshole. Now! Lie down, face first!"

"Officer, I can explain," he pleaded, still in compliance.

"We have six witnesses that state you just murdered a Mr. Emmanuel Morales in cold blood."

They were right. He did murder a man. He chased him out of his apartment and shot Morales once in the back, and when Morales dropped to the ground, he unloaded his security-issued .357 Magnum into the back of the dying man's head and neck. He felt no remorse, and wouldn't make any apologies. What they didn't know was this:

"He raped my wife!" the man yelled.

"Hmmm," the other officer snorted while his partner tightened the silver bracelets on the suspect's wrists, digging his knee deeply into the suspect's back. "Tell it to the judge."

"He raped my wife!" he screamed again.

"You have the right to remain silent. Anything you say—"

"Baby, please tell them. They're taking me to jail for murder!" He looked at his wife and she looked past him, wide-eyed and frozen.

"Officer, please, just get her some help. She needs to go to the hospital and get treated. Look at her. She's in shock, for God's sake!"

One

Anthony Cross
Winter, 2007

I KNEW IT WAS OVER THE MOMENT SHE ASKED TO borrow $7,500 because she was behind in her rent. There was nothing more unattractive than a sexy, successful black woman who was unable to handle her finances. I watched as she pouted her plump, scarlet red colored lips and lowered her naturally sleepy eyes toward the ground.

"I really hate to ask you this, but I'm in a situation, you know," she said.

No, I don't, I wanted to reply dryly. But what would be the point? I knew I wasn't giving her the money. She was using our as-yet lack of a sexual relationship as a bargaining chip. Probably thinking that $7,500 wasn't going to break the bank for a man in my position. Correct. But where she went wrong was putting too much value on her pussy. Yes, she was pretty. Gorgeous, to be more exact. But sex was sex, and looks faded. And if anyone knew that, I did. I was one of the very few successful black plastic surgeons in New York. My practice has been open for over a year and my clientele was steadily increasing.

I took another quick look around at "the setup." She'd invited me over for dinner and drinks. Fresh white lilies decorated her mantel, and large scented candles illuminated her dining and living room areas. All other lights were off. During dinner she purposely drank too much, no doubt so she could later pretend to be intoxicated while I fucked her pussy numb. That way, in the morning, she could make believe she was the all-American good girl she'd been portraying these past two weeks. This whole seduction night probably cost two to three hundred, easily. Again, nothing more unattractive than a sexy, successful, black woman with bad finances. The money she'd invested in tonight should have gone toward her crisis. It made me wonder how many of these setups she pulled each week. Some other schmuck must have shelled out the cash for her to seduce my dick, and she wasn't even getting that.

Fuck! The weight of the world was now on my shoulders. During these past two weeks I thought that she could be the one, that I may have found something genuine in this woman, some pure qualities other than a money-hungry, grubby, gold-digging, scandalous bitch. In my profession, they came out the woodwork in droves. I couldn't dodge them quickly enough before they tried to get into my deep pockets. This bitch needed to realize that her problems were not my problems. Jeez, I needed to start dating *white* women. Well, let me not get ahead of myself. It wasn't *that* serious.

I decided that I could either make up some excuse and pull a quick exit, or simply tell her to fuck off.

"Is that why you called me over for dinner?" I asked.

"What do you mean?"

"It's like this. Why didn't you ask me for the money over the phone? Did you think it would be harder for me to say no in person?"

"Baby, I didn't have a clue what your response would be."

Straight-faced, I decided to get to the point.

"No."

"No?" she shrieked. "Why?!?"

"I don't need a reason why. It's just no."

"Did you not just hear me say that I'm in a situation?" she pressed on. "I would really, really appreciate it if you could help me out of it."

"Laura I'm not even going to pretend that I'm remotely concerned about your situation."

Her eyes stretched open, "Are you serious?"

"This situation is really beneath you."

Her eyes burned with fury. Pursing her lips tightly together, she cleared her throat while straightening her dinner napkin on her lap.

"I understand your reservations. Really, I do. But I never asked you for anything—"

"You're not supposed to!" I exploded. "I hardly know you!"

She shook her head and gesticulated wildly. "You know me enough to want to fuck me!"

I peered into her eyes. "Are you kidding me?"

"I mean, you would fuck me, right here, right now!"

"What kind of stupid-ass statement was that? I could have *fucked* you on our first date. But where I went wrong was trying to *court* you. Treat you like you're more than an object but," I paused and let out a sympathetic sigh, "Forget it. You're just like everyone else. A waste of my fucking time."

At that point I had my light-bulb-shining moment. As a man, you could always assume women held their pussies on a pedestal, but this chick was holding her pussy on a seventy-five-hundred-dollar pedestal.

"What about my time? And the fact that I was feeling some sort of connection to you, and thinking that you felt the same way. Now that money has come into play, you've turned into this different person in a matter of seconds. You would think I asked for a fucking Porsche!" Laura began a roof-shaking temper tantrum.

"Listen, listen, listen, I'm not going to sit here and entertain this a moment longer. I'm so sick of this shit. We, as men, are sick of this shit. Women see a fucking dick and think it's an ATM. Do you really think that your burnt-ass steak dinner was going to be worth my hard-earned coin?"

"Get out!" she roared as her face distorted into several levels of ugliness.

After a few tense seconds, I got up to leave.

"People always have expensive tastes when it comes to someone else's budget. The T-bone steak was a nice gesture but if I were you, I'd stick to what I could actually afford. Chinese takeout, perhaps," I said, getting in a last jab as I exited her place.

I was fortunate enough to live five blocks from my Upper Eastside practice. I owned a modest, two-bedroom apartment in the upper Sixties that cost me a hefty $3.9 million. My mortgage was obscene, but real estate in New York was always a smart investment. At 33 years old, my practice was growing due to the fact that more African Americans and Latinos were getting plastic surgery. To tap into the market, I did a lot of advertising on the radio stations that had large African American and Latino audiences. At the moment, tummy tucks were most popular with black women, whereas most of my non-minority patients opted for breast implants. This morning I had a butt-implant consultation.

I strolled into my office in an upbeat mood, despite the pathetic situation that had unfolded the previous night. I laughed to myself as I remembered how Laura tried every trick in her book to get that money from me as if I was some sort of trick. One part of me wondered if she really needed the money for her crisis, but the other part of me—the cynical side—thought she might have used it for a pair of the latest Christian Louboutin stilettos.

The brisk winter air had put pep in my step, and I'd gotten to the office earlier than I'd planned. When I walked in my trusty receptionist, Anika, was already there with her signature Starbucks Caramel Macchiato, and her cell phone glued to her ear.

"That'll kill you," I said and gave her a sly wink.

"I'm shutting off my service tomorrow!" Anika joked, referring to her cell phone.

Inside my office I noticed that Anika had brought me lunch, neatly packaged in her Glad Tupperware. She cooked for me at least three times a week and would also pick me up what I'd call *care packages* when she was at Duane Reade or CVS, which would consist of a bag of Mentos candy she knew I liked, or a six-pack of Gatorade, or something as random as Condoms. I could smell that she'd prepared my favorite baked macaroni and cheese and turkey chops. The aroma put a smile on my face. That girl was really a sweetheart. On occasions such as these, I would always remind myself that I needed to reciprocate her small, yet thoughtful gestures. I wanted her to know that I didn't take her for granted. But then I would get so inundated with work—I never followed through. I

went into my calendar on my Blackberry wireless phone and put a re-
minder to order her a bouquet of *thank-you* flowers and perhaps I'd take
her to see a Broadway play.

I took a quick look at my calendar—three consultations, one breast
implant, four patients for BOTOX injections, and one tummy tuck. I had
a full schedule and probably wouldn't make it home until after nine o'clock,
and my day still wouldn't be over. I had to make a follow-up call to each
surgical patient to make sure that there weren't any complications.

Soon the office was buzzing with my staff, and it wasn't even eight
o'clock. I peeked my head out the door and everyone jumped to attention. No matter how much I tried to lead a staff- and customer-friendly
work environment, it seemed that everyone was always on pins and needles
when I was around, except Anika. She was always too busy flirting with
me to be intimidated.

"Dr. Cross, your eight o'clock is already waiting for you inside exam
room one," Samantha, my RN, stated. Samantha was a stiff-looking, older
white woman. She had paper-thin lips, silvery white hair that was oily and
tassled and a frail, undernourished looking body.

"Okay, cool," I said while inching over to Anika. "Whew, I have to
tell you about last night," I said to her.

"Long legs, sleepy eyes, big boobs," Anika said while rolling her eyes.
"I bet she was stiff in bed."

"Would you believe that nothing happened?" I asked, laughing.

"No."

"I'm too sexy, right?" I joked. "How could a woman ever resist me?"

"Pah-leeze, punk! You ain't that fine," she retorted while twirling her
fingers dismissively in my face. I leaned in real close.

"You know I'd eat your pussy until you came in my mouth, and then
fuck you to sleep," I said softly. "You're waiting for the day I break you off
a piece."

Her round eyes got really low and seductive as she gave me a throaty
whisper.

"You couldn't handle this…"

"Don't want to," I said and gave her a soft punch on her shoulder.

"Stupid!"

"Hussy!"

"Womanizer!"

"Cunt!"

With that last remark, Anika's jaw dropped and I won our little childish battle by default.

Anika was a nice girl who I knew was madly in love with me the moment she came in for an interview. Even though we talked shit and our conversations, taken in the wrong context, could lead to sexual harassment, I'd only push the envelope with Anika. I trusted her and I was not that stupid to get that familiar with my other staff. In all honesty, I'd grown to love Anika in a brotherly-sisterly way. That could be mainly because I was not attracted to her. She was a nice-looking girl, but a little undernourished for my tastes. I liked my women voluptuous, and if they weren't, then BAM! That was what I was there for. My hands could sculpt any body into a masterpiece, but Anika wasn't having it.

One day I suggested that she should consider having her As increased to full Bs and she almost chewed off my head. She walked around giving me the cold shoulder for almost a month before she cooled down. I realized that I had hurt her feelings and her silent treatment taught me a lesson. Out of all my staff, she and I related the most with each other. We liked to laugh and talk shit, maybe because we were close in age. She was 24, and I was 33. Well, maybe we weren't that close, but the other staff members were well into their forties.

My first consultation that day was a petite Mexican woman with naturally large breasts and a flat, pancake-looking ass. When she turned around, her ass was saggy with cellulite dimples and the elasticity was virtually nonexistent. She was looking to get buttock augmentation. I grabbed her chart and leafed through it.

"Mrs. Rodriguez, nice to meet you," I said.

"The pleasure is mine," she replied as she gripped my hand. "So strong and handsome."

"Thank you. When we're done, I'm going to take you into my office and show you sample sizes of the implants. Do you have an idea of what size you're looking to get?"

"*Sí, sí,* yes. I have pictures of Jennifer Lopez. I want to look like J.Lo."

I smiled, but it wasn't toward her. I wished I could personally thank J.Lo for her naturally big ass. My first surgery was for a woman who wanted

Jennifer's voluptuous ass.

"Mrs. Rodriguez, I want to give you a brief overview of what your surgery will entail. I can make an incision either where the butt cheek meets the back of the thigh, or down the buttock crease." I used my finger to trace her body as she stood looking in the mirror. "I prefer to make the incision in the buttock crease, where scars are not noticeable. But let me warn you: this area does carry a high infection risk."

"Don't worry, doctor, I'm clean," she commented, and then added, "I don't have any diseases. No HIV, no herpes, no nasty woman tings."

"Okay, great," I replied and when I looked up, she was staring directly at me, eyes unwavering. Then she smiled, as if I'd just read her mind and we were on the same page. I continued. "I'll create a pocket large enough to insert the butt implants. For a more natural look and feel, I'll place the implants under the *gluteus maximus* muscle, make sure they're symmetrical and look natural, and then you're done. You'll be under general anesthesia and the surgery should take just under three hours. Do you have any questions?"

"Why aren't you married?"

I laughed.

"Because you're already taken."

Two

Gracie Lane

I WALKED AROUND MY ULTRA POSH, 6 -BEDROOM, 6 ½ bathroom, apartment, located in the Time Warner Building at Columbus Circle. The former home of celebrity moguls such as Jay-Z and Ricky Martin. I was putting the last finishing touches on the party arrangements for my husband, Ed. We were celebrating our tenth wedding anniversary and I thought it would be a nice gesture to do something unexpected and throw him a surprise dinner.

Ed was a simple man who didn't indulge in the high-end lifestyle that I was afforded. In fact, he still opted to work at Verizon telephone company, although, I was worth, thanks to my deceased husband, Phillip, well over one-hundred million dollars. Our marriage worked because I allowed him to be a man. Not a *kept* man. He paid all the utilities in our apartment and I always allowed him to pay for dinner when we dined out. Of course I took care of the larger tickets such as the mortgage and condo maintenance fees. Most times when we traveled, at his behest, we split the costs. When we dashed off to more exotic locales, such as the South of France where the menu consisted of *foie gras* or *escargot* then I always picked up the costs.

Today's menu consisted of a red velvet cake from the illustrious Cake Man Raven of Brooklyn, soul food from B. Smiths, and top-shelf liquor, which included Hennessy, Bacardi, Moët, Dom Perignon, Bailey's, and

Absolut vodka.

I had decided on a small, quaint setting consisting of a few very close friends, family, and Ed's colleagues from work. I didn't allow a lot of people to know where I lived and I allowed even fewer people inside my home. I felt like my house was my personal, private space and I don't know if it's the selfish side or cautious side of me that protected my whereabouts by any means necessary. I had just under an hour before everyone was due to arrive.

Doing a slight gallop up my winding staircase, I stripped off my clothes in a frenzy leaving a trail of designer garments behind. At that point, my nerves began to overwhelm me. I desperately wanted everything to be perfect. Careful not to stay too long inside the shower, I timed myself by bathing to track number 14, *"Father in You,"* on Mary J. Blige's latest CD. The Bryston Surround Sound speakers in the ceiling belted out Mary's soulful voice as I identified to the words in the song. I knew all the words and also knew that the song was roughly four minutes long.

The basic black, form-fitting, Diane von Furstenberg dress that I was wearing cost $3,000. It was the most expensive dress I owned. Not that I couldn't afford expensive garments but sometimes designers could be insufferable with their prices. If it was worth it then it was mine but there just weren't a lot of things out here in the fashion industry I felt worth my money. Besides, I looked good in anything. I splurged on certain things such as jewelry, coats, shoes and real estate. Those things, if rocked properly, could make the right "I'm rich-bitch" statement while wearing a pair of jeans. It's all in the attitude. I'd purchased the dress four years ago to accompany my husband to a fundraiser held at City Hall. Ed had plans on getting into politics, and I always supported his endeavors.

After I was dressed, I took another look around downstairs and was doing last-minute touchups when the doorbell rang. I told the doorman there wasn't a need to announce each guest since we were having a party. I gave instructions that all my guests had to do was give my name and apartment number and in turn, they should be allowed entrance. To my surprise, the first guest to arrive was Ed's sister, Tamara. Taking a deep breath before exhaling all my anticipated stress, I opened the door.

"Hello, gorgeous," Tamara beamed.

She's such a phony bitch, I thought.

I managed a tight smile. "Hey, Tamara, come in. The other guests should be arriving any minute," I replied, before looking my sister-in-law up and down. "What have you got on?"

"What's wrong with my clothes?" Tamara asked, looking down at her outfit as if she was seeing it for the first time.

I took a long look at Tamara's slinky, see-through shirt with her non-existent, exposed breasts, micro-mini skirt, and newly bleached blond hair, and wanted to choke the life out of her. Tamara was awkwardly tall like her brother with long limbs, a now bleached-blond short Afro, and dark chocolate skin. She had fine facial features and a gorgeous smile with an over-the-top personality that I despised.

"Tamara, you knew this was going to be a formal dinner, and you waltz through here as if you're going to a nightclub!"

"I don't remember you stating the dress code," she whined.

"Of course you don't. You have a selective memory. Why should I be shocked?" I sarcastically replied. "You're always doing this to your brother, after everything he does to help you."

"Lighten up, Gracie. You're too uptight. I got an extra joint if you want to relax a little before your guests come."

"Don't you light that up in here!" I bellowed, playing directly into Tamara's hands. Tamara thrived on irking my nerves. She knew that I didn't indulge in drugs, and also knew that I would burst a brain cell if she lit up her joint during the party.

Two hours later, the dinner table was bursting with laughter as Ed sat at the head of the table like a king. He was genuinely surprised when he walked in and saw only familiar faces. He barely relaxed his face; his smile seemed permanent.

I beamed in my role as hostess.

"Would anyone like more Champagne?"

"Yes," Tamara replied. The remainder of guests all shook their heads.

"While I'm up, what about more dessert? Anyone?"

"Yeah, bring me more of that cake, too," Tamara blurted out. "I don't turn down anything but my collar. Yes, yes, yes, to any and all your shit."

I glared at Tamara.

As the night began to wind down, the festivities were interrupted by the incessant ringing of the telephone. I made a quick dash to the phone and had to put my index finger into my ear to tune out the jazz music that was playing.

"Hello?" I asked.

"He's dying," the familiar, husky voice replied. The optimism of the night suddenly became tempered by my bleak reality.

"H-h-how did you find me?" my voice personified my fear.

"Bad move being photographed at that fundraiser last summer. You still look good…you've aged…but you're still recognizable. Again, bad move."

"How did you find me!" my voice personified my anger.

"Calm down I'm not your enemy. We fam and I'm here to tell you that you should stay out the papers. Your telephone number was listed under your husband's name. If you're trying to hide from folk I'd suggest trying a non-published number. I reread that newspaper one-hundred times. *The wife of hopeful New York councilman, Edward Lane, Gracie, sat supportively by her husband's side…*"

"Are you kidding me?"

"I'm calling you, right? And I haven't seen you in two decades," Benjamin snickered.

"You won't see me for the next two, either."

"Funny. Your joke…funny," he replied, sarcastically.

My voice was a husky growl, "You think I'm playing games here?"

Ignoring my question he asked, "I got something to ask you. Your face looks a little different. Did you do something to it? Have it altered? I can't put my finger on it…Don't matter…I still recognized your ass—"

"This is too much to take right now. Listen, I would really appreciate it if you didn't call—"

"I'm not calling to catch up on old times. I'm calling because the old man is on his death bed."

"So bury him!"

"Come on, sis, stop being like that. I just said that the old man is dying, and he keeps asking about you. It's time that you let go of the past before it's too late."

My brother Benjamin went on to tell me that our father had been diagnosed with a brain tumor that was malignant. The doctors didn't expect him to live much longer.

"Well, what can I do?" I probed.

"All he wants to do is see you, to make things right before he goes."

My mind couldn't help but drift to the past and thoughts of my father.

"Daddy, my friend Kim's parents bought her those new leather sneakers for her birthday. And I was thinking that since my birthday is next week, and also since I made the honor roll again, that maybe I can get the same ones. Everyone says we look just alike. She's like the sister I never had. So please, please, please, can you buy me a pair for my fifteenth birthday?" I asked.

"Girl, I don't care what your friend's parents done bought for that nappy-headed, ugly gal. If I hear you say one more time that you two look alike, I'mma put my foot so far in your backside, I'll tear you a new asshole. You hear me?"

"Yes, sir. But what about the sneakers?"

"You must be crazy. Those sneakers cost nearly fifty dollars—"

"But you bought Benjamin a pair!" I protested, interrupting my father.

"Benjamin needs a good pair of sneakers to practice in. All those basketball scouts are always out looking to draft young kids, and your brother has a shot. Benjamin needs the best sneakers so he can do all that dunking, just like Mike," he reasoned.

"What about Andre? You bought him a pair, too!"

"Don't be questioning me, chile. I got good reason to do what I do for my boys. Do you know how hard it is for a black man in America?"

I rolled my eyes. I'd heard it all before.

"Do you want your brother busting someone upside his head and stealing his money to buy those sneakers? My boys are not gonna be victims of society. They're gonna make me proud one day!"

"What about me? All you care about are your sons! It's not fair!"

"How old are you?"

"Fourteen," I screamed.

"You about one year too old to be coming in here asking me for expen-

sive shit. All these boys out here, and you asking me? When your mother was with me I gave her the world . . ." His words drifted off as he thought about his wife of sixteen years, who'd ran off and left him with three kids. He missed her so much, his heart hurt. "Go on and get outta my face! And I better not hear you crying, 'fore I give you something to cry about!"

"Is it safe to come around?" I cautiously asked, snapping out of my daydream.

"It should be." Benjamin paused and then continued. "No one's been around in a while. Years in fact. But don't take any chances. Come at night and through the back door. The spare key is still in the same spot."

My forehead scrunched into tight folds. "I'm not promising you anything. You know how I feel about George—"

"He's Daddy, not George," Benjamin corrected.

"He's never been my daddy. He and I only share DNA!"

The morning after the party and the disturbing phone call, I was beginning to feel a little stressed. I was contemplating taking the day off from where I did volunteer work at the Adults and Children Community with Learning Disabilities otherwise known as ACCLD. I volunteered as a developmental aide for mentally-challenged adults living in a residential home. It was my way of giving back to society. We took them on trips, helped them develop social skills, cleaned up after them and we also dispensed a few medications. The state doctors prescribed so many medication to the mentally handicapped adults that it was a curse and a blessing. Either they walked around like zombies and stayed out of your way all day, or they were violent and had vicious outbursts whereas you had to ultimately fight for your life. So along with the job came defensive class training. That wasn't too bad because the perk for me was being around my dysfunctional coworkers. There was always some drama going on, and I loved drama as long as it didn't involve me or my household.

I awoke and stared at my calm-mannered husband. At 30, Ed was significantly younger than me. I'm 39.

"Thank you so much for last night," Ed said while kissing me on the nape of my neck.

"Are we talking about the party, or *last* night," I teased.

"Both." He smiled. "Now, it's time for your present."

"Ed, you didn't have to get me anything."

"Of course, I gotta get you something. It's our tenth wedding anniversary. Are you kidding me? Who's luckier than me? I got the most beautiful wife in this world, and I want to give her something she's been contemplating," Ed exclaimed.

"I can't take the suspense. What did you buy me?"

"Well, I've been listening to you and Anika talk crazy for weeks. And I know that you want to go in to see the doctor she works for, about a tummy tuck. That's your gift. You can go in and have the procedure done. That's if you still want it."

"Ed, don't be silly. You don't have to pay for such an expensive gift. I'm not really sure I want the procedure and if I decide to have it, I can pay for it. No big deal."

"This isn't a debate," he snapped. "I said I can afford to buy my wife a nice gift for our tenth wedding anniversary and that's what I'm going to do."

"All right. You don't have to get upset."

"Why are you always telling me what you can afford as if I don't know? Don't you think I know what you can or can't afford?"

I knew the question was rhetorically so I remained silent.

"For once I'd like to do something nice for you without you feeling sorry for me. I hate hearing the pity in your voice."

"That's not fair at all. Don't be like that...mean and all...I'm sorry," I said and nuzzled his neck and put my hands tightly around his waist. Instantly, he relaxed.

"If you want me to be the gold-digging hoochie I was born and raised to be just say the word."

"I want you to be my gold-digging hoochie." He kissed my lips.

"Good. You can start by leaving your credit card by the bed on your way out."

"My credit card, huh? I dunno...I wasn't satisfied with your services last night," he joked. I began tickling him and we wrestled around on top of the bed until he had to leave for work.

I sat back and thought about how Ed had promised me the world when we first met, and slowly he was making all my dreams come true. I'd come to New York as an escape. Never did I imagine that I'd meet someone as innocent, gentle, and loving as Ed. Yet he'd always managed to make me feel safe and secure. I was newly widowed and just had inherited a large estate. I had met Ed while I was married to a millionaire who gave me a monthly allowance that was barely enough to get my hair washed and a descent manicure. He was cold, disrespectful and thrifty. Life with him wasn't a fairytale. I began taking long walks in central park to get away from my husband's smothering ways. That's where I first met, Ed. I pretended to be dirt poor and Ed really was—but we talked for hours about our aspirations and dreams. Ed did most of the talking, and I was a great listener. I told him I didn't have any family and he accepted my "truth". When my husband Phillip had died from a fatal asthma attack, I practically ran into Ed's arms. We'd been having a mental affair in the park, twice a week, for two years. I told him that I'd never marry again, and he accepted me. He told me that I was too beautiful to marry a guy like him, and I accepted him.

Soon we were both riding on a love high when the bad news came. My kidneys weren't functioning and I was in dire need of a transplant. Of course, I thought that my newfound wealth could buy anything—it couldn't. I had to be put on a donor list as everyone else. I panicked. Surely I didn't want to die. I was 28-years old and finally ready to live my life to the fullest. At first I thought it was just a kind gesture to ease my anxieties. Ed said that he wanted to get tested to see if his kidney would be compatible. I swatted him away and he came back even more aggressive. Finally, I allowed him to give me the best gift in the world—life. Ed and I married on my hospital bed. That was ten years ago and we're still happily married.

Over the years I contemplated telling him about my past, but my love for him prevented me from getting him involved. I thought that the less he knew the better off things would be. He'd never be forced to choose sides, nor would he have to live with the burden that was mines to carry.

At first, being older than Ed scared me. Was I too old? Would some younger woman one day come along and take my husband away? But as the years passed, and our bond grew, Ed had never so much as looked at another woman in a lustful manner. He told me on the night we married that he pledged his eternal love to me, and that he'd never allow another woman to break our bond. I, in return, said nothing.

Three

Anthony Cross

MY WEEK STARTED OFF CRAZY AND HAD NOW TURNED mundane. I decided to take off a couple hours between clients to go to the New York Sports Club in Harlem, where all the pretty sisters worked out. Also, it was great networking. Even though most of the women were being proactive in either maintaining a great shape or striving to get a great shape, no one was perfect. During these sessions, I passed out a lot of business cards and met a lot of potential future wives. I knew I'd never get married before I hit my forty-fifth birthday, but that didn't stop me from dangling the possibility in front of every woman I'd ever dated. Women ate up that shit. Not that I didn't want a life partner, but I didn't have one faithful bone in my well-toned body.

I jogged the three miles up to Harlem listening to my Apple iPod. I had 10,000 songs programmed; mostly upbeat tunes. I took a shortcut through the park, crossed a thicket of bushes, and then did power walking down a cobblestone path. I made it there in less than 40 minutes.

The instructor for the kickboxing class was no joke. He went hard. Male or female—no one was exempt. He had an in-your-face attitude, and loved interacting and pushing everyone to the limit. Sweat poured down my skin as I paced my breathing, taking large gulps of my Smart Water. I could actually hang out here all day. They had a host of classes that I wanted to delve into, but I had to make it back to the office for a tummy tuck consultation in less than an hour.

But not before I played into her hands. She'd been eyeing me the whole class, vigorously kicking her long legs, throwing strong left and right jabs, and keeping up with the instructor's two- and three-piece combinations. Her legs were toned, her ass was firm, and her stomach was washboard. Her small waist and shapely hips would look better, though, if she had C-cups to complement her assets.

"That was a great workout," I said casually as I wiped sweat from my face.

"Yeah, he's amazing," she stated, breathing heavily.

"Dr. Anthony Cross." I extended my right hand. "Pleasure to meet you."

What could I say? I was shallow.

"Cynthia Rowley," she replied, barely containing her huge grin. "You look so young to be a doctor."

"It's in my genes."

"What type of doctor are you?"

"I'm a board-certified plastic surgeon. I have my own practice on the Upper Eastside, 72nd Street."

"Oh, my gosh, I've heard about you!"

"Is that a fact?" I asked knowingly. This one was going to be easy.

"Well, I mean, I've heard your ads on the radio. This is really cool," she exclaimed.

"Is it really?" I replied. She was savvy enough to detect my sarcasm.

"I must sound foolish. Please forgive me."

"Don't be silly."

My eyes scanned her body one last time and decided she was worth a shot, but I didn't have much time for small talk.

"Listen, Cynthia, here's my business card. Give me a call and perhaps we could get together."

"I'd like that." She took the card and quickly read it. "I'll give you a call this week."

Cynthia then licked her luscious lips and sauntered away. She didn't realize there wasn't a need to continue flirting. I'd already chosen her within the first sixty seconds of conversation.

Back at the office, I felt great. The workout had given me momentum and I was on an adrenaline high.

"Where were you?" Anika asked as I walked through the door.

"Mother, I'm getting too old for a curfew," I joked.

"Funny. Your two o'clock has been waiting. And she isn't just any two o'clock. She's my best friend I've been telling you about. It's Gracie. Remember, I told you she wants abdominoplasty."

"Oh, yeah, yeah, I remember. Tell her I'll be there in five minutes. Which examination room is she in?"

"Room three."

Over the past year, I'd heard so much about Gracie that I felt as if we were old pals. What Anika failed to mention was that she wasn't bad looking. Just my type.

As I glanced at her chart, it noted that she didn't have any allergies, was married, had a kidney transplant, and was 39 years old. *That's odd,* I thought. Anika was 24, so why would she be best friends with someone Gracie's age? The better question was, what did a 39-year-old woman have in common with a 24-year-old? Gracie certainly didn't look anyone's definition of 39, though. She was definitely well preserved.

She sat on the exam table with her medical gown opened in the back and her legs dangling like a child. Her hazelnut-colored skin, round, expressive eyes with long eyelashes, and pouty lips were sexy. She looked as if she stayed in sexy mode all year round; as if she walked around with a garter belt, thigh-high stockings, and stilettos all day, every day for her man. I took another look at this old cougar and got a little turned on. Not much, just a slight tingle. I was jolted back to reality when my RN, Samantha, began speaking.

"Dr. Cross, this is Mrs. Lane. She's interested in a consultation for a tummy tuck."

"Hi, Mrs. Lane. My name is Anthony. How are you doing today?"

"I'm doing well. Thank you."

"Good, good. Well, I like to tell my patients what I'll be doing. That way, there won't be any surprises. I'm going to lift up your gown just above your belly button, and take a marker and draw lines so that you can see what I'll be removing and sculpting. Are you nervous?"

"Nervous? You're not the first man to see my goodies," she teased.

When she smiled, she had two delicious dimples in her honey-colored cheeks. The dimples made her look deceptively innocent. Briefly I wondered if she was telling a blatant lie about being 39.

"Not about that, Mrs. Lane. I'm talking about your tentative surgery."

"Oh that." She let out a soft chuckle and displayed pearly white teeth. "Not at all."

As I sat in front of her and peeled up her gown, I noticed a hideous sight. Her stomach was splattered with stretch marks and she had what I'd describe as a kangaroo pouch belly. Quickly I glanced back at her file and she'd put zero for kids. There had to be some mistake.

"Mrs. Lane, it says here that you don't have any children."

"That's correct."

"Okay, good," I replied as I began to make my drawings on her stomach. I didn't probe further, but there wasn't any way she'd get these stretch marks if not through childbirth.

My silence gave her reason to explain. "As a child, I was overweight. My stomach is the last remnant of my fatso past. I'm hoping you can remove all traces."

"I'll do my best," I replied. Guiding her to the mirror to take a look at the diagram I drew across her stomach, I continued. "I will make a long incision from hipbone to hipbone, just above the pubic area. The second incision is made to free the navel from surrounding tissue. I will then separate the skin from the abdominal wall all the way up to your ribs, and lift a large skin flap to reveal the vertical muscles in your abdomen. These muscles are tightened by pulling them close together and stitching them into their new position. This provides a firmer abdominal wall and narrows the waistline. The skin flap is then stretched down, and the extra skin is removed. A new hole is cut for your navel, which is then stitched in place. Finally, the incisions will be stitched, dressings will be applied, and a temporary tube may be inserted to drain excess fluid from the surgical site."

"Sounds like it's a bit much, but I'm game," she said and then flashed her warm, seductive smile.

"You don't have to have any reservations," Samantha piped in, "Dr. Cross is one of the best."

"So I've been told."

"While I'm in there, you may want to consider having liposuction to take away the fat deposits that are resting around your waist and your lower back."

"Liposuction?"

"Yes. I could take a little from here"—I pinched her excess fat on both sides of her waist—"and sculpt you a new figure. Suck a little out of your back where fat has built up, and you'll be looking like you're twenty again."

"Why would I want to do that?"

"The liposuction?"

"Go back to being twenty. I dreaded those years," she said, looking aloof. "I'm comfortable in my skin. I say I'm 39 with great pride. In fact, I can't wait to celebrate my fortieth birthday. I didn't come here to run around and pretend to be some little teenybopper."

"That's not what I meant—"

"That's what you said," she snapped.

My mind quickly raced back to see if that was indeed what I'd said. I was used to patients being cuckoo for Coco Puffs, and this one was definitely a candidate.

"Please forgive me, Mrs. Lane, for being presumptuous. You're right. You're perfect as you are. Let's just stick to what you came here for. Shall I have Samantha schedule you in for surgery?"

"Do you always fold so easily?"

"Pardon me?"

"Well, as a plastic surgeon, isn't your job to sell a patient more than what they need? Isn't that how you stay in business? I'm only asking because I'm truly curious."

"You're being a bit presumptuous now, aren't you? I didn't go to Harvard Medical School to end up being some kind of used-car salesman. I don't force, persuade, or manipulate my patients into getting surgeries they don't need. I simply suggest all options so that they can leave here aware and informed." I tried to keep a level head at her offensive remark. The nonprofessional side of me wanted to scream on her judgmental ass, but I knew better.

She flopped back down on the examination table and stared me directly in the eyes.

"Anika never said you were self-righteous," she mockingly replied.

"I'm sorry, Mrs. Lane, but is there a problem?" Samantha intervened.

"Only if you want one," she challenged.

I was dead silent as I stared at the woman with the haughty personality. I was just about to reconsider taking her on as a patient when she said, "I'm joking…seeing how you hold up under pressure. How much will it cost for the extra surgery? With the lipo, how much will it all cost? Of course, I'll have to talk it over with my Ed. You know, he's paying for this. Isn't that sweet, y'all? He's such an amazing man."

"Mrs. Lane, it's not exactly two separate surgeries. You won't have to pay for the anesthesiologist twice, so you'll only be charged for my services which, of course, will be combined. Anika will fill you in on further details. Talk it over with your husband and let us know."

"Done."

"Without further discussion?"

"I have my ways of persuasion."

"Very well," I said.

After I left the consultation with Mrs. Lane, I was drained. When Anika came in to chat, I really wasn't in the mood, but I indulged her briefly.

"So what do you think about Gracie?"

"Oh, her," I remarked dryly. "Is she a friend or family member?"

"She's a friend. Why do you ask?"

"Get rid of her. She's too old for you, and too uptight."

"Gracie? Uptight? Never."

"You know, you two look a lot alike. She could pass for your cousin or aunt or something."

"We get that all the time."

"And why is she your friend, again?"

"Most of my friends are older than me. That's why I'm so cultured."

"Cultured, my ass! Your ghetto ass has got to be kidding me. And let's not mention your old cougar girlfriend with the nice face and banged-up body. What's wrong with her? I think she's bipolar."

Anika and I burst into gut-twisting laughter that lasted a few minutes. Tears streamed down my cheeks as I thought about why I called her a cougar and what Gracie would say if she heard me ripping into her.

"Cougar, huh? You just mad 'cause she wasn't flirting with your over-sexed ass."

"Are you stupid? She was all over me the moment I walked in the door. Oh, doctor, you're so handsome," I said, putting on a show.

"Boy, pah-lezze. Gracie doesn't have eyes for any man other than her husband."

"How long has she been married?"

"She just celebrated her tenth wedding anniversary."

"What does he do?"

"He has a good job. He works for Verizon."

"That's decent."

"Decent? They making bank over there. I wish I had a piece of that," she said longingly.

"Then go get it," I replied. My tone got serious. Although I would hate to lose Anika, she was a smart girl and could do much better than being my or anyone else's receptionist.

"Really? I heard the entrance test is almost as hard as brain surgery."

"You're not giving yourself enough credit. All you have to do is study. If you get the book, then I'll help you."

"You'd do that for me?"

"Of course."

"But why?"

"Why?" I was perplexed by her question. Why wouldn't I want to see her better herself?

"Why would you take the time to help me?"

"Jesus, because anything I can do to get you out of my face every day . . ."

"Yeah, right. You love me and you know it."

"As you would say, 'pah-leeze.'"

"You do the girlie impression a little bit too well," she joked.

"Ooh, for real?" I replied, in a flamboyant, effeminate voice and began prancing around, doing vogue hand movements made famous by Madonna. Anika was laughing so hard, holding her stomach while her eyes slanted shut. I only did this because no one was in the waiting area and also I got a kick out of acting silly. It relived my stress. After she calmed down, I went back to my line of questioning.

"What does Gracie do?"

"Huh?" she retorted, trying to catch her breath.

"The woman, your friend, what does she do?"

"Watch soap operas," she replied, dramatically rolling her eyes.

On that note, I decided to call it a day.

Four

Gracie Lane

HERE SHE GOES AGAIN, I THOUGHT AS VANESSA, A coworker, came strolling into work wearing a full-length mink coat that swept the ground as she walked. The female skins were at least four inches thick in diameter, which represented an expensive cut. Vanessa was a new member of the 40/40 club, which meant she'd just turned 40 years old and was in constant competitive mode with me. Vanessa despised the fact that I was married and she'd only managed to be another man's mistress. Her string of affairs were just a BAND-AID® to cover what she really yearned for, which was the love and stability of a husband. That, coupled with the fact that I bragged about Ed all day, made for a healthy serving of jealousy. But we were too old to ever voice our differences.

"Girl, look at you," I said, realizing that I *had* to make a comment. Vanessa kept her coat on for a full five minutes. "That's a gorgeous mink."

Straightforwardly, Vanessa replied, "This *is* a gorgeous mink. You'll never be able to afford it," and sashayed past me, leaving my mouth momentarily gaping open. Inwardly, I snickered. No one at my job knew of my wealth or that I was working as a volunteer. That's the way I choose my situation to appear from the onset. I would never walk in all jeweled up nor did I drive any of my luxury vehicles here. Out front sat my Honda hybrid. My rationalization was to do something good—from my heart—

to make up for my past. Not use the opportunity to do good as a platform to upstage anyone. I knew I could let that bitch have it! But common sense superseded any thoughts of revenge.

I continued, "Who bought you that? Robert?"

"Robert has just about gotten on my last nerve," Vanessa said, finally removing her coat. "This was a blackmail move on my part."

"What? Give me the dirt." I suddenly perked up.

We were inside the living room of the home where we both worked. John and Lisa, two other staff members, were inside the kitchen dispensing medication to the mentally handicapped adults. It was me and Vanessa's job to clean up the house after the school bus came to pick up the clients.

John strolled into the living room and flopped down on the sofa right next to me.

"What's up?" he asked.

I turned up my nose.

"John do you have any gum?"

He reached in and pulled out a stick.

"No *you* need it, not me."

"Huh?" he asked through lips that were dry and cracked.

"You heard her," Vanessa snapped. "Everyday you come in here smelling like you got a dead body in your throat! Like it's a fucking funeral in that bitch," she exclaimed and everyone burst into laughter. Everyone was sick of John's tart breath. He refused to get help for what we thought was halitosis.

"Don't start this early in the morning, Vanessa," John said while kicking off his Timberland boots and putting his feet up on the coffee table. Our supervisor wasn't in yet. It was just nearing seven o'clock in the morning.

"Well, I'd like to tell my story before Jessica, the Wicked Bitch of the North, comes in," Vanessa said, referring to our supervisor.

"What's up?" John asked.

"Well, as I was telling Gracie, Robert thinks he's so slick. Do you know I caught him almost cheating on me with a girl half my age?"

"Almost? How can you *almost* cheat?" I asked.

"He almost cheated because I busted him before it got any further. The other night I kept calling his cell phone and it was going to voicemail, so I knew he was up to something. So around two in the morning, I couldn't take it any longer and decided to get in my car and drive to Tiffany's house."

"Who's Tiffany?" I asked.

"My daughter's best friend."

"Why would Robert be at your daughter's friend's house? And why when he didn't pick up didn't you just suspect that he was in for the night? I mean, he is a married man," I probed.

"First things first. I'd seen Tiffany eyeing Robert whenever he was over at my house, and second, his fat-ass wife doesn't hold any weight. When I call, he answers!" she exclaimed.

Don't hold any weight? I wondered. *She's his wife.*

"So get to the point," John commented, already bored with Vanessa's theatrics.

"Just as I suspected, I drove over there and his car was in the driveway. I went ballistic. I told Tiffany that if she didn't open the door, I was gonna whip her ass old-school style, and she knew I meant what I said. Robert came skulking out with his tail between his legs, proclaiming that nothing happened. Two days later, I got this." She smiled as if her reward was the end that justified the means.

"And you believed him?" John asked.

Vanessa gave him a look like, *how dare you even ask such a stupid question.*

"Of course I do. Did you not hear the part about me getting there in the nick of time?"

"Are you telling me that you think they didn't fuck?"

"He said that it didn't happen," Vanessa responded through clenched teeth.

"It's like this. If I was on Tyson's jury, he woulda walked. The only reason a chick rolls home with a guy at four in the morning is to get fucked. The only thing that could convince me otherwise is the videotape. If you're saying you rolled over to her house at two in the morning and he said nothing happened, that's what he's supposed to say. That doesn't mean you believe him." John shook his head at her dumbness. "I wish my ex-girl was as stupid as you. And your ass is mad old."

I needed to intervene.

"Whether they fucked or not is neither here nor there. Bottom line is that you are sharing Robert. Whether with one or ten women, it's just arithmetic," I reasoned.

Our female bonding became acrimonious in seconds, and the claws came out.

"Why would you say something like that?!" Vanessa exploded. "You come in here as if you're better than me, each and every day. Ed this, Ed that. I'm so sick of fucking hearing about you and Ed's perfect little house, with the white picket fence, that I wanna throw the fuck up each time I hear his—"

Our little powwow was stopped short when our supervisor walked in. Tension was halted as we began picking imaginary lint off the sofa, prodding and plumping pillows, and dusting already clean surfaces.

"Good morning, Jessica," we all sang in unison. Jessica barely acknowledged our greeting before she started in.

"Whose car is blocking the driveway?" she asked. Everyone was speechless. "Vanessa, don't you drive that gas-guzzling BMW X5?"

"Yes, but I know for a fact that I didn't block the driveway," Vanessa retorted in a gruff voice. Often she contemplated whipping Jessica's frail, white ass, but held back for two reasons—she was too old to be fighting, and the Suffolk County racist police department would lock her up and throw away the key.

"John, come look and tell me what you see." Jessica called her "yes" boy to settle the dispute. John jumped to attention and ran to the window.

"Oh, I see what you saying. Vanessa, you could have moved back a little. Your front end is partially in the driveway."

Vanessa rolled her eyes and scowled at John.

"Well, I'll move it later. I got work to do," Vanessa sneered, walking upstairs and out of sight.

"I suggest you move it within the hour!" Jessica barked with false bravado.

I was a little pissed that I didn't get a chance to brag about Ed paying for my tummy tuck. I'd have to save that tidbit for tomorrow.

Ed crept upstairs carrying a plate of turkey sausages, egg whites, and apple juice squeezed from a juicer, in an attempt to surprise me early this morning. The aroma from the food made it to me before he did. I got a whiff of the breakfast and began to smile.

"Hey, babe," he said and gave me a wet kiss on my cheek. "Get up."

Slowly turning over, I did a languorous stretch and then yarned.

"What's all of this?" I asked, clearing the phlegm from my throat.

"Just a little something, something I whipped up for you, before I headed out to the gym to work on my stubborn belly fat."

"Maybe I should go with you. I really want to work on my thighs before I go into surgery."

"Not today," he stated. "I don't want to wait for you. I'm ready to go. Besides, I need you here."

"Need me here?" I asked as I stuffed the turkey sausage into my mouth. "For what?"

"My sister, Tamara, and her loser boyfriend finally broke up. She'll be moving in with us for a few weeks to save money. I told her she could have the guest bedroom, and that she wouldn't have a problem from you."

"Ed, please don't do this to me."

"Gracie, don't start. She's my sister and I can't see her out on the street."

"This is the second time in one year that she's lived with us. All she does is drive a wedge between us, and I can't allow that. Not this time! Tell that bitch she can't stay."

Ed, who was non-confrontational yet always stern and unwavering in his responses, simply said, "There's nothing more to discuss. She'll be here in a couple hours."

Five

Anthony Cross

"YOU WANT THIS..." SHE PURRED AND SEDUCTIVELY sauntered toward me. Little by little, she climbed on top of me as I admired her nakedness. Her ripe nipples dangled provocatively. She began kissing me from the base of my ankles up to my calves, behind my knees, and once she began licking between my thighs, my penis stood at attention. She purposely kissed around my dick because she didn't give head.

"I love this dick," she stated while vigorously jerking my dick with her hands.

I dug my hands into her massive hair weave and pulled her up. Dakota allowed me to flip her over, spread her legs wide, and began to taste her pussy juices. I sucked on her clit until it was swollen and I heard her moan in pleasure, then I began to gently nibble and bite down on her clitoris, while finger-fucking her. Dakota began to grind her hips slowly, while softly digging into my shoulder blades.

"Your pussy tastes sweeter than honey," I breathed. "All wet, hot, and sticky."

"Eat it all up, Daddy."

"Emmmmm, hmmmmmm," was my response as I continued to eat her tasty pussy until she reached her peak.

"I'm cumming!" she screamed as her legs began to tremble and her juices began gushing out. I continued to eat her out.

"Fuck me, baby," she purred. "I want your big dick! Fuck me…"

"Fuck you!" I said as I pushed my dick deep inside her warm, wet pussy. She wrapped her sexy thighs around my waist and I began to give her strong, steady strokes until we both climaxed, again. I collapsed on top of Dakota until we both regained our composure.

I was ready to go again.

"I got something for you."

Groggily, she pulled her tired eyes open, but remained silent. She watched me go inside my drawer and pull out a small dildo.

"Anthony, what are you gonna do?"

"Shhhh, relax baby," I coaxed. Gently, I turned her over to lie down on her stomach. I parted her legs and rubbed K-Y Jelly on her ass.

"Daddy, nooo," she pleaded. "I don't wanna."

Only she did.

I purposely bought a smaller version of my dick to open her up before I entered her. I tried gently to insert the dildo and she began to squirm and try to wiggle free.

"Baby, relax," I calmly replied, not allowing my voice to reflect my aggravation.

"I don't wanna," she stated in a baby-like voice, which at that moment annoyed the hell out of me.

I turned her back around, tossed the dildo on the floor, and rammed my dick into her resisting pussy. I began to angrily fuck her, and only got more excited as she protested.

As her legs began to quiver and she realized she didn't have any control over her movements, she tried to get up, but I wouldn't let her. I pushed her back down and made her handle it.

"Is this what you want?" I continued to give her angry thrusts, "*Only* this dick!"

Strong waves came cascading down through our bodies, and we screamed out in pleasure.

We both came.

Usually I would have knocked out and gone to sleep, but Dakota decided she wanted to talk. And I wasn't prepared for what she had to say.

"Anthony, do you notice anything different about me?" she asked as she snuggled up under my arm and began to stroke my belly with her small hands.

"Dee, please not tonight. I got a heavy morning ahead of me."

"Baby, I've been holding this back for too long."

"Holding what back?"

"I'm pregnant," she blurted out.

The color drained from my face and my mouth went dry. I pushed her off me as I bolted straight up in bed. I glared at her as my eyes adjusted to the darkness.

"What happened to your birth control?" I asked in disbelief.

"Remember I told you that I had missed a couple of consecutive days, so I had to wait and start over," she lied.

"What?" I flipped. "You never said any such thing!"

"Ummm, I did. Well, I thought I did." She began biting her bottom lip and I knew that was an indication that she was lying. We were now facing each other, and it was beginning to become a hostile environment. "It was a mistake."

"Mistake? I don't make mistakes. You know how I feel about having children without being married. I want my children to live in a stable environment, just like my parents gave me."

"So why can't we get married?!" She pouted.

"Don't do this."

"Do what?"

"Be a sneaky, conniving bitch! Don't force my hand, because you won't like the outcome."

"I would never deceive you," she persisted.

"D-d-don't do that," I stuttered. "Pretend to be all innocent. That act got me, but it won't keep me."

"It's not an act."

"Furthermore, your innocent *act* has turned me off," I stated, ignoring her. "You can't even fuck straight. When are you going to suck my dick! Get rid of that baby! Now!"

Dakota leaped from the bed, hysterical and in tears, and began dressing frantically. She couldn't get her clothes on fast enough. I sat and watched her—amused, relived, and angry, all at once.

After she was dressed she lingered around wanting attention. "You're not going to take back what you said?" she screamed, throwing a childish tantrum.

"What sense does that make? *'Take back'* what I fucking said! Are you an idiot? Learn how to speak properly. How are you going to be someone's mother and you can't even form a proper sentence. I wish your child luck—"

"I HATE YOU!" she screamed like a maniac, folded in half and then fell to the ground. After I ignored her shenanigans for a while, she got up the gumption to lunge toward me. I blocked her angry blows with my elbows until she got tired and then I jumped up and grabbed her scrawny little ass by the back of her collar and tossed her out of my front door!

I lay back on my bed and only hoped that I could reason with Dakota in the morning. There was no way that I was ready to have a baby, especially with her.

Six

Gracie Lane

I WALKED IN AFTER A LONG DAY OF VOLUNTEER WORK, to find my house in disarray. Tamara was lying on the sofa, getting her beauty rest. Meanwhile, all the lights were on, including a television that Tamara obviously wasn't watching. And Tamara had cracked each massive window in the living room in the middle of the winter, letting all the heat escape. The house was an icebox.

"Tamara!" I exploded. "Get up."

"What's wrong?" she asked, jumping up in surprise and holding her chest.

Our eyes met solidly.

"What did I tell you about opening up the windows and letting all the heat out?"

"It was baking in here," she replied, wide-eyed and frozen.

"So turn down the heat. Do you realize that our heat bill has tripled since you moved in?" Tamara always took for granted that her brother married wealth. What she didn't realize was that my money was just that— mine! And I wasn't going to throw it out an open window.

"I'm so sorry, Gracie," she lied as she ran to shut the windows. "It won't happen again."

"That's what you said the last time."

While my hands were full with groceries, I walked into the kitchen and listened intently as Tamara got on her cell phone to make yet another appointment to get a facial. This was the second facial she'd had in six weeks. For someone who was supposed to be on a budget and saving money to move out on her own, Tamara sure was splurging. From weekly colonics, hot stone body massages, manicures, pedicures, facials, body waxes, cocktails at the W Hotel, shopping excursions at Saks, and lobster at Mr. Chow's, she was doing just the opposite of saving. I was tired of complaining to Ed, who couldn't see how his sister was using us. Tamara always put on this syrupy-sweet voice, opened her eyes wide like a cherub, and lied through her straight, big teeth whenever Ed was around.

"You're going to get another facial?" I called out.

"Umm, yeah, you should come with me," Tamara replied, walking into the kitchen to face me. The granite island was full with groceries and she didn't even give a weak attempt to help me put them away. "I really don't have the money, but I don't have a choice. Do you see these fine lines appearing on my forehead?" She pointed to imaginary lines. "Can you believe it? I'm only 28 and already I'm getting wrinkles."

I didn't even bother to look.

"I really wish I could, but I got better things to spend my money on," I sarcastically replied.

"Yeah, I know what you mean. But unlike me, you don't need it. You have great skin. I wish I had skin like yours."

I wouldn't allow myself to fall victim to Tamara and her bullshit game. She thought she was a grade-A con-artist, but she was amateur at best. The only person her tactics worked on was Ed. Everyone else saw straight through her, including all of her ex-boyfriends.

Ignoring her fakeness, I prepared myself to clean up the house before my husband got home. What irritated me most was that Tamara was a slob. She was just nasty. She was the type of person that would drop another piece of paper in an already-full wastebasket. Emptying it wasn't an option in her mind. She bathed sporadically, and when she did hop her funky ass in the shower, she wouldn't even contemplate taking a capful of Clorox to disinfect it before or after she used it.

"What the fuck—" I yelled as my bare feet stepped into a sticky residue plastered on my kitchen floor. One more step backward gave me a small gash into the sole of my right foot as I stepped into a pile of something sharp. "Ouchhhhh!"

"What happened?" Tamara asked. She was back on the sofa watching the 60-inch LCD television.

"I don't know," I responded as I flopped to the floor to get a better look at my foot. While down there, I noticed that there were small shards of glass on the kitchen floor, and what appeared to be dried-up juice. I followed the trail, looked in the garbage, and noticed that yet another dish had been broken. And, of course, it was the expensive china.

"Tamaraaaaa," I said in a long whine, "you broke another dish!"

"Oh, yeah, I'm sorry," she said nonchalantly.

"Sorry?!" I yelled, "Come here."

Tamara took her time walking back into the kitchen.

"When is it going to stop? Every night we come in here and you've broken something. By next week, we won't have a dish to eat on. And why didn't you mop up this slop on the floor?"

Calmly, Tamara's eyes glanced at the floor.

"I don't see anything," she replied in an even, unfazed voice.

I looked at my cream-colored marble tile with the purplish stain and gave up. I gave a disappointed sigh, then glared at Tamara as I dropped to my knees and began scrubbing the dirt out of my floor. Meanwhile, my foot was throbbing and my nerves where shot. Unaffected, Tamara grabbed the can of cashews I had just purchased, and excused herself.

"She has got to fucking go, or so help me, I'mma whip her ass in here!" I screamed.

"Lower your voice. Do you want her to hear you?"

"I hope she does hear me! Maybe she'll get the fuck out!"

Ed was spent. The constant bickering between the only two women, besides his mother, he loved was wearing upon his sanity. He couldn't understand why we couldn't just get along?

The drive on the New Jersey Turnpike heading south was one filled with anxiety. I decided to drive my Honda hybrid in order to not alert my family about my financial situation. The article that my brother had read was just about a blue collar worker being active in his community. That's it. Nothing on me. In fact, you could barely see my face. It was a side profile shot which amazes me that Benjamin would be able to recognize me.

I wasn't happy about seeing George or revisiting my past. As I drove up to the old, decrepit house, which had seen better days, I was shocked. The white house with burgundy shutters and a white picket fence no longer existed. There, in front of me, stood an off-white, dirty exterior, and missing shutters. Flowers that used to decorate the pathway were no more. Huge patches of missing grass were sprawled sporadically throughout the yard, while in other parts weeds were overgrown.

I shut off my headlights and pulled around to the backyard. I could barely see as I crept up the chipped concrete, formerly known as stairs. I felt around underneath the huge ceramic flower pot and found the spare key. It had been almost two-decades since I'd run away from here and vowed to never return.

The screen door creaked as I pulled it open. I peered into the house from the opening of the back door, and my heart palpitated wildly.

Once inside, the pungent smell that permeated the house stopped me in my tracks. Immediately my hand covered my nose and I held my breath. The smell was so strong; it felt as though it was literally burning my nostrils. For a split second, I wondered if something or *someone* had died.

"George," I called. "George, are you here? It's me . . ."

I stepped farther into the house, only to notice that there was barely any furniture. George was sleeping soundly in his lazy chair by the window, with a shotgun propped between his legs. Garbage, broken furniture, and flies occupied the once-immaculate residence.

How could this be? I wondered.

"George!" I yelled, startling the old man, who had begun to drool. Without a second thought, he aimed his shotgun directly at my heart.

"It's me, your daughter."

"I know who you are, gal."

"Then why are you still pointing that gun at me?"

"Whatchu doin' here? In my house? Didn't I tell your scandalous ass that I didn't eva wanna see you no more?"

"I had the same sentiments, but Benjamin called and said you asked for me to come." He thought for a moment.

"Oh, I did, didn't I?"

"What do you want from me, George?"

"Those honkies at the bank tryin' to take my house. Damn crackers! I told them that I'll shoot up the whole town before I let that happen! That cracker-ass sheriff will be the first to go if he comes around here trying to kick me out!"

Since there wasn't anywhere I could sit, I continued to stand.

"What are you talking about?" I asked, wondering if George was on any medication for his brain tumor and if so, whether it was making him delusional. "This house has been paid off for years."

Even though my mother had left us when I was young, my parents never divorced. When my mother died in a car accident, her life insurance policy was payable to my father. Back then, $150,000 was a lot of money. I never saw a dime of that money, though. George paid off his house and then splurged the rest on his two prized possessions—his sons.

"That was 'fore Andre ran into some trouble and needed to pull the equity out of the house to save his ass. White folk 'round here won't let him keep a job."

"Is that what he told you?" I snapped. "And you fell for his bullshit, as usual."

"You better watch your mouth! I'm still your father. I don't care how old you are, you're never old enough not to feel my foot in ya ass!"

I shrugged off his threats. They meant nothing.

"Again, what is it that you want from me?"

"Is you stupid?" he barked. "I want you to save my house and pay off my mortgage!"

My stomach knotted in disgust. I looked at my DNA donor and got physically sick. His leathery skin had pockmarks from years of bad acne, four rotten teeth remained in his yuck mouth, and his once virile body had shriveled up like an overcooked pea; but he still had the strength and energy of a bull. He thrived off hate.

"What the fuck is wrong—"

My outburst was interrupted by my brother Benjamin. He was a pitiful sight. His body had clear signs that it had been ravaged by drug use.
His body was no bigger than a Blow Pop, with a big head to match. His
clothes hung from his body as if it were a hanger, and he smelled like a
mixture of piss and shit.

"Hey, baby girl, you made it," he said and tried to embrace me, but I
took a step back and used my hands to put up a barrier.

"Benjamin, how could you let this happen?" I accused.

"What?" he replied, oblivious to their living conditions.

"What do you mean, 'what?' This house is disgusting. We weren't
brought up like this!" I retorted.

"Come on, now, it's not that bad."

"Are you crazy? I could, would, never live like this."

"You think you so high and mighty, like you're better than somebody," her father chimed in.

"No one's talking to you!" I took his shit when I was a little girl, but I
refused to take it now as an adult.

"Pops, I got this. Sis, let me speak to you in here." Benjamin led me
into the funky kitchen. "Look, we fell on hard times after Andre did his
bullshit."

"Yeah, George told me he refinanced the house."

"Did Pops also mention that Andre took all the money and ran?"

"No way," I said as my jaw hung open.

"True story. Now we gotta come up with $20,000 before the fifteenth
of this month, or we gonna get thrown out on the street. And you see I ain't
got that kind of money. A brother is fucked up right now."

"If I had it, I wouldn't give it. But my conscience is clear because I
really *don't* have it," I lied with a straight face. "Maybe you can stay with
one of our relatives and put the old man in a nursing home. He's dying,
anyway."

"Nah, he's not dying. That old dude is gonna outlive all of us. I just
said he had a brain tumor to get you to come. No matter how much you
pretend not to care about him, I knew you'd show up."

I didn't even pretend to be relived at his admission. "Oh, you're a
psychoanalyst now?"

"Something like that," he replied and nudged my arm. "Listen, let me hold something."

"Hold what?" I asked, clueless to his request.

"That means, in layman's terms, to give me a couple dollars so I can bounce."

I stared directly into Benjamin's eyes, but he couldn't hold my stare. I knew my brother was strung out on drugs, but I chose not to mention the obvious. I gave him all that I had in my wallet, which was $110 dollars. Before I could say another word, he was gone. I strolled back into the living room to bid a final farewell to my cantankerous father.

"Listen, I'm about to leave."

"You were never invited," he replied, not missing the opportunity to take one last stab.

"Look, I checked inside your refrigerator and you don't have any food. I'm going to send nonperishable groceries in a box overnight, via FedEx. Make sure you answer the door when they come."

"So that's it, huh?"

"That's all I got to give."

"You're worthless. That cat-trap coochie you got can't save my house," he stated and let out a hearty cackle. I had figured out a long time ago that my father treated me badly because he never got over the fact that my mother broke his miserable heart, and I looked just like her.

"You're nothing but a bag of noise, old man. A miserable, self-righteous, depressing old devil!"

"Oh, you talking big and bad now! Wait until those people get ya."

"George they won't *get me* because I've made like the gingerbread man, and ran. Bye-bye," I sassily replied, and with that I was gone.

Seven

Anthony Cross

MY BOYS AND I WERE ON OUR WAY TO SUE'S RENDEZvous strip club to celebrate Kevin's one-year anniversary. After one year of faithfully fucking only his wife, he deserved a little break.

Kevin was meeting us at the club, but Chris came by to get me. He came upstairs instead of calling because he knew that I took a long time getting ready. He often joked that I was metro-sexual, because I liked to look good. I stared in the mirror at my ensemble. I was wearing dark blue True Religion jeans—which looked a little gay, but I was confident with my manhood—a black, red, and green Gucci knitted hat with a matching sweater, and black Gucci loafers with the gold buckle. My caramel-colored smooth skin, husky shoulders, broad back and deep baritone voice, combined with my six—foot, one-inch stature, ensured that I looked good in almost anything. All of my suits were tailored and I only shopped at the high-end stores and boutiques such as Barney's New York and Saks Fifth Avenue. I hate to admit this but fashion was a passion of mine. Secretly, I TiVo'd Project Runway. I loved that show.

Chris came through, looking more street. He had on an oversized, goose down, cream-colored jacket; baggy Sean John jeans; a matching sweater; and Timberland boots. Chris was always going through an identity crisis. In school, he got beat up constantly because of his lean body, soft voice, and wimpy attitude. Now, as a grown man, he was living the life he thought he should have lived in his youth. His scrawny body had been replaced with all muscle, and only 10 percent body fat. His speech, although he still had a light voice, had been replaced with street vernacular.

"You still in the mirror?" he joked in his effeminate voice. "Just like a girl."

"Yeah, well, at least I don't speak like one." Hey, he asked for that one.

"Don't get fucked up in here tonight," he threatened. "I promise you, I don't hit like a girl. I'll bust your whole shit open."

I gave him a stern look.

"Don't get carried away with that tough talk. I'll put you over my knee and spank you like my bitch," I barked back. Chris and I had a love—hate relationship. It was a man thing. We were very competitive, always trying to show who had bigger balls. "Come on, let's go!"

Chris, Kevin, and I rolled in the place shortly after midnight. As we sat back in the VIP area, sipping on Armand de Brignac — also known as Ace of Spade Champagne — this sexy, petite, black girl came slinking over. She was wearing a white and baby blue bra, G-string panties, and white thigh highs with a baby blue garter belt. On her small feet was a pair of stilettos. I loved the way her dark chocolate complexion contrasted against the white outfit. I motioned her over.

"Hey, baby," she greeted and smiled. "You want a lap dance?"

"Yes, but not for me. I want you to dance for my man right here. He hasn't been out in a year."

She took a look at Kevin and immediately obliged. I watched as she straddled him and began to grind on his dick. As I sat back, drinking in the scene, I didn't notice at first that another man had joined us.

"Anthony, this is my man, Gabriel," Chris said.

"What's up?" I asked, acknowledging the newcomer while giving him a firm handshake. His name sounded familiar because he was all Chris had been speaking about for the past month. He was some sort of investment guru. I looked at his watch—Audemars Piguet; shoes—alligator;

fingernails—manicured. Okay, so maybe he was someone I should listen to. I couldn't tell whether Gabriel was Italian or Greek. He had naturally tanned skin; thick, jet black hair; a sculptured jawbone; and stood around 5'7" with shoes on.

"Nothing much. So, I hear you're a hotshot plastic surgeon."

"Yeah, something like that," I replied and took another sip of my Champagne.

Before the night was over our tab was nearly five grand, and Gabriel picked it up. When we left, he offered to drive us home, and I couldn't help but notice he was driving a Bentley Phantom. I was impressed. Kevin and I declined the ride and jumped into a Yellow taxi, but Chris took Gabriel up on the offer since he was going Gabriel's way.

"Are we still on to watch the game at your house tomorrow?" Chris asked me as Gabriel waited for him in his car.

"Yeah, yeah, no doubt. Listen, bring your man. I may want to pick his brain with this investment situation. He looks as if he's doing well for himself."

Chris and I embraced, gave a quick handshake, and parted ways. Kevin and I went uptown, and Chris and Gabriel headed downtown.

The next morning, I prepared for the abdominoplasty on Mrs. Lane. Our first encounter kept going through my head, and I was praying that she didn't start any shit this morning. I decided to go and mess with Anika. She always cheered me up.

"What's up, hussy!" I joked.

"What's your dweeb ass smiling about?"

"Shit. Truthfully, I don't have anything to smile about. My week has been shit. Dakota and I aren't speaking, and its got me stressed."

"Drop that needy bitch!"

I laughed at her forwardness.

"Speaking of bitches, I hope Mrs. Lane isn't on her period this morning!"

"Why do you care?" she asked suggestively.

"She better care. Hope I don't skim on the anesthesia. Give her local instead of general, and she'll be feeling every nip and tuck."

"You freak!"

I stuck my tongue out my mouth and flickered it rapidly, as if I was eating pussy.

"All day!" I said.

Mrs. Lane was unusually cheery as she lay in the hospital bed wearing the cotton shower hat and cotton gown that she was given.

"How are you this morning?" I asked, glancing at her chart.

"I'm doing well. Very well. A little nervous, but excited too."

"You should be. You're going to come out looking like an eleven, since you're already a ten." I shot some corny-ass game her way, trying to loosen her up. For some reason, she had me on pins and needles, and I wasn't sure if my statement would cause her to react crazy. But she just grinned.

"Me? A ten? You think so?"

That was an "A-ha!" moment. A little narcissistic, were we? Loving the praise.

"Of course I do," I replied and then focused my attention on the anesthesiologist. "She's ready," I told him.

"You're looking handsome this morning," Mrs. Lane said, apparently not wanting to let the moment fade. "I can see why Anika is always talking about you. Did you just get a new shapeup—"

Lights out. The anesthesia had taken over and she was knocked out.

"Let's roll," I said to my staff.

That day had been a long, exhausting one, and I wasn't in the mood for any interruptions while I did a little paperwork. Dakota had called, screaming and sobbing heavily, asking why I was doing this to her? She accused me of ignoring her and playing mind games. Mind games? That was exactly what she was playing with her planned pregnancy. How could I have been such a fool? If she didn't get her pregnancy terminated, I was looking at at least $5,000 a month, easy. And although I wasn't cheap, that was too much money for child support. Jesus, the thought made me sick to my stomach. I was a new surgeon trying to maintain my practice in a plush neighborhood, a new condo, and an asshole full of student loans. Now just wasn't the time to add pampers and baby formula to my long list of debt.

The office building that I leased my space from had other practitioners as tenants, some of whom I'd grown to like, and some I didn't. Arthur was one of those doctors that I didn't enjoy speaking with, and he was always calling every second of the day.

"Hey, you busy?" he asked as he breathed heavily into the phone receiver. His weight had gotten out of control.

"Yes," I abruptly stated.

"Well this will only take a minute," he replied, oblivious to my annoyance. "I don't know what happened, man, but Eric got fired today."

"Eric who?"

"The LPN that works with us."

"For what?"

"He didn't say. All he said was that the supervising RN told him that he had 20 minutes to leave the building. I feel really bad for him. I mean, what could he have done?"

"He knows what he's done! He could have been downloading kiddy porn or stealing computers. Getting food stamps in bogus names, does it fucking matter? They fired his ass, bottom line."

"Poor Eric," he empathized.

"Does he have any kids?"

"No."

"Does he have a wife or sick parent?"

"No."

This guy was dumb as the day was long. I didn't have the patience to tolerate him much longer.

"Listen, Arthur, I gotta go. Someone just walked into my office."

For at least two seconds, I was lying. That was, until my office door flung open and in waltzed Elizabeth. She and her best friend, Gwyneth, were tenants in the building who co-owned and operated a cosmetic podiatry practice.

"I am so busy," she said while plopping down in the empty chair.

"Then what the fuck are you doing in my office?" I asked.

I looked at Elizabeth and realized that she was always exhausted; not from work, but from trying to get as many free dinners per week as possible.

"He decided to break it off," she stated.

"Who this time?"

"Michael. Remember him? The firefighter."

"Did you sleep with him?"

"Yes."

"Are you surprised that he kicked you to the curb?"

"Of course I am," she shrilled.

"'Of course I am,'" I mocked. "Come on, you're forty-five competing with thirty-five-year-old women. Even Jordan isn't in the NBA anymore. Don't fool yourself."

"Screw you!"

I was stumped. I looked at Elizabeth and wondered where she went wrong? She was a raven-haired, intelligent Jewish woman who owned a nice apartment on the Upper Eastside, parents who were about to kick the bucket and leave her a boatload of inheritance, and she was whoring herself out almost every night to losers. She had a Jones for black men in uniform, preferably firefighters who — after the third or fourth date — would drop her like a bad habit. For some reason, she couldn't keep a man. I kept telling her to stay in her lane, try dating a nice Jewish man whose age was compatible to hers but *nooooo*, she wanted men in their twenties who weren't interested in settling down and having babies with an old, white, Jewish woman.

"Okay, I'm sorry for being obnoxious. I'm going out after work with my boys. You're welcomed to join us."

"Where are you going?"

"Most likely downtown, either in the Meatpacking District or Soho, to club Chaos."

She took a moment to think.

"Nah, I think I'll call Wayne and see if he wants to come over."

"Of course." I laughed. "Why pass up definite dick for a maybe?"

"I so hate you!"

"You do not!"

Just as I was about to make up some lame excuse to kick her ass out of my office, my Blackberry vibrated with a text message from Chris, saying that our plans tonight had been canceled. No explanation. Suddenly, I didn't feel like getting rid of Elizabeth.

"Listen, let me ask you a question," I began slowly, "My girlfriend is pregnant but I'm not ready to have any children. And before you state the obvious, I thought she was using birth control."

"Do you love her?"

"Not at all," I replied, truthfully. "Maybe one day I could...but for now, I just like our time together."

"So it's just casual but let me guess, she thinks differently."

"Precisely."

"You're a pig," she griped.

"I'm not letting you in on my personal life for you to judge me. I need a woman's point of view. If you were in her situation, what could I say to make you have an abortion? I've tried everything in the book! I'm afraid her little girlfriends will get in her head and the next thing she'll be saying is, '*I don't need you to help me raise my baby. I can do it all by myself,*' bullshit."

Shaking her head, she responded, "If she loves you and thinks that you truly love her and that the only thing blocking her from running off into the sunset with you is this pregnancy, then she'll have an abortion. If she feels that she doesn't have you, that maybe another woman has your attention, or that there isn't a possibility that you and her have a future, then she'll keep the baby. As a keepsake. Something to forever keep you in her life. It's all mental. You hold the key on whether she keeps the baby or not. Unless," she paused, "she's wholeheartedly against abortions."

My talk with Elizabeth was enlightening. She was cool, after all. I was now prepared on how to move forward with Dakota.

It had been weeks since I'd hit the town, but tonight was a night to celebrate. Dakota had finally given up and had the abortion, and we were right back at it as if we had never stopped. Of course, I bagged up every time now. Sometimes I even doubled up. But it was all good.

Chris, Mike, and I ended up at Butter with the after-work crowd. We rolled downstairs to the bar area to listen to the music. There were a few sexy sisters in four-inch stilettos, tight jeans, and glossy lips that had desperation written all over their faces. They were on the prowl, which I liked. As I sat in a corner booth, I had the waiter ask the ladies what they were drinking, and told him to put it on my tab. He casually walked up behind the most petite of the trio and whispered in her ear. At first she had a look of shock on her face until what he'd said registered. A huge Colgate grin splattered across her face as she turned to find out who the generous stranger was. When I was pointed out, we made brief eye contact and I decided that she was pretty cute. She looked to be around 27 with full lips. Her entourage came over to our table and we started with the small talk— names, occupations, do you have kids, are you married—stuff like that.

During the night, someone decided that we should all start taking shots of Patrón. I should have used better discretion since I had a surgery planned for noon the next day, but I didn't. The full-lipped girl, who I later found out was named Candy, had attached herself to me and already told me she was coming home with me. She now looked on the verge of a coma.

"Let me go and get some bottled water. I think we all need to detox a little," I said. At that point, I was sweating profusely. As I strolled over to the bar, I noticed a familiar figure hop up on a table and begin a slow grind to "Hit it Shorty" by Lloyd. And, no, it wasn't Paris Hilton. She dropped it like it was hot and did a sexy grind back up. She was cheered on by her friends and bystanders. I walked over and got caught up in the moment. I stared at her as she seductively mesmerized me. I drank in every curve of her now—flawless body.

I climbed on the low table and positioned myself behind her. She began to give me a private dance, as if there weren't hundreds of people in the room watching. Her reckless behavior pulled me in.

As we slow danced to about five fast songs, the alcohol began to get to me and I realized I was toasted.

"I bet you got banged—up feet," I joked. "Pretty girls always got ugly feet."

To my surprise she kicked off her shoe, thrust her newly pedicured, sexy foot in my face, and said, "Now what?!"

I grabbed her big foot in my hand and instinctively began to massage it. "Damn you got some big ass feet." I remarked.

"I wear a size ten!" she belted out, apparently not embarrassed by her unladylike feet.

"I heard women with big feet will walk all over your heart."

"That's bullshit. Just like the rumor that men with big dicks all know how to fuck."

I liked her forwardness, but maybe it was the liquor talking.

"Now suck my toes," she demanded.

I looked in her eyes and realized she was serious.

"Not here," I replied and gave her a sly wink.

Eight

Gracie Lane

ANTHONY'S APARTMENT WAS VERY PLUSH. HE HAD beautiful parquet floors sanded to a pale beige, and a huge, Sony flat screen, 50-inch LCD television with Surround Sound, which hung on his wide wall. A very expensive, large brown leather sofa with huge suede pillows — embroidered with the initials A.C., a round, granite coffee table, and a high-tech CD player completed the décor. His dining room set was a masculine maple wood with a beautifully decorated table. His bedroom door was closed, and his apartment smelled of a combination of warm cinnamon and vanilla.

He had huge candleholders everywhere lamps should have been. Obviously, the doctor had done very well for himself. His Upper Eastside address and doorman facilitated my admiration. I was *somewhat* impressed. My apartment was three times as big and cost four times more but at least he'd earned what he had and for that he earned my respect.

I walked farther into his apartment in my stiletto heels. I purposely took languorous steps, and as I walked my ass jiggled slightly, in my form-fitting dress and thongs.

"May I?" I asked as I slowly turned the knob to his bedroom door.

"Do you," he replied.

One by one, I stepped out of my shoes and left them by his bed. I was too drunk to think about consequences and too horny to care. I wanted to fuck some new dick tonight, and the doctor was the usual suspect. He grabbed me by my small waist, pulled me in close, and began passionately tongue kissing me. Expertly our tongues intertwined and he seemed to enjoy how I playfully bit and sucked his lips. I pulled back to see how badly he really wanted me.

"Come here," he said, reaching out to pull me back in so I could feel his hard dick. The lust in his eyes took away any uncertainties I may have had. I inhaled his cologne and began to taste his skin.

Gently he put his hand behind my neck and kissed me passionately. His kisses slowly moved down to my earlobe, and then he began to gently suck my neck—not aggressive enough to leave any marks, but assertive enough to make my pussy moist. He sucked and then blew, sending a tingly sensation through my body. In an effort to speed things up, I pulled up my skirt, revealing my bald pussy—no low Caesar, no landing strip, nothing. Just all pussy was staring in his face just like a porn star. Anthony began to take off his boots.

"You can leave your boots on!" I exclaimed. "I came here for one thing."

"Relaxxxx," he soothed. "We got all night."

"You got all night. I'm married and I got less than an hour, baby."

"Mrs. Lane," he joked, "may I call you Gracie?"

"Shut up and *fuck*!" I demanded and grabbed his bulging dick. "Come to Mama."

"As long as you call me Daddy."

"Daddy, what's your pleasure?" I asked.

"Everything."

I stood back, pulled off my blouse, and let it tumble to the floor. My skirt went next. Following my lead, Anthony pulled his shirt over his head and let it hit the ground. We stared at each other in silence. He pulled off his jeans while kicking off his boots. Taking one last look at my now-perfect body, he shoved me onto his bed.

"Do you want me to fuck you, or make love to you?" he asked.

"If I wanted to make love, I'd be home in bed with my husband," I purred. "I came here to fuck."

He grabbed the K-Y Jelly. I was talking his language.

"Turn around, and you better not say no!" he commanded.

Eagerly I turned around and assumed the position.

"Be easy now," I whispered.

"I got you."

Anthony began to massage the cool jelly between my ass cheeks while sucking and licking my back.

I began moaning my pleasure and almost pleading for him to enter me, I was so aroused. Quickly he grabbed a condom from his nightstand and wrapped his dick before steadying himself. He gently began to ease into my juicy ass, pushing through my resisting flesh. As he began digging deeper into my anal cavity, the tightness had him ready to explode prematurely. He had to slow it down to gain control again. He pulled me into the doggy style position and I began throwing it right back at him.

"How it feel?" he asked as he slapped my ass, leaving a pink version of his hand on my honey brown butt cheeks.

"I want you to go hard," I demanded through clenched teeth. "I want you to fuck me like you own this!"

Anthony dug his hands into my hair and pulled back as he continued to pump his ass rapidly into my resisting flesh. "Like this..."

". . . oooh, yes, baby, like that."

"I see you like it rough..." he assessed.

We fucked liked minxes—hot and sweaty—but I wasn't done.

Naked, we moved into his bathroom. As we stood on his cold, tiled floor, we continued to kiss each other. Deep, sloppy, passionate kisses had us both excited. He put his hands around my small waist and hoisted me up onto his sink. I slightly parted my legs and took Anthony's bulging dick and guided it toward my moist pussy. I then began working my hips, gyrating them until his dick made its way all the way into my snug pussy. While working my hips, I grabbed his neck and simultaneously wrapped my legs around his waist. He gripped me by my butt and slowly lifted me up and down on his dick until he hit my G-spot.

"Damnnnn, this dick is so good," I crooned.

We fucked until we came a second time. When Anthony pulled out of me, instinctively, I turned around because I wanted to do it from the back. I bent over, holding the wall for support, and reached in between my legs to grab a hold of his dick and slid it into my pussy, which by this time was extremely wet. To help ease into this position, I lifted my left leg up and put it on his toilet. As we fucked, I looked over my shoulder at Anthony and moaned seductively. This drove him crazy and he began thrusting harder. This time, when Anthony came, he pulled out and squirted his juices on my back.

I sensed he was now ready for me to leave, but I had other ideas.

"Go back in your bedroom and wait for me," I commanded as I ran into his kitchen and began fumbling through his refrigerator. "Ah-ha!"

I waltzed back into the bedroom with the energy of a child. Anthony lay face down with his head buried into his pillow, snoring loudly. I smacked him hard on his firm ass, startling the tired and weary doctor.

"What's going on?" he panicked.

"Shhhhhh," I said, sheepishly, as I covered his lips with mine and gave him a soft kiss. "Let me wake you up."

Slowly, I poured chocolate syrup on the tip of his dick and watched the gooey liquid slide down his shaft. I looked up to see if he was into it. His smile gave me confirmation. I teased him by licking the chocolate from his shaft and then nibbling on his now tasty tip. His pickle-shaped dick glided in and out of my mouth, and he moaned his pleasure. I enjoyed sucking his dick and began slobbering all over it and making slurping noises. I arched my neck and opened my jaws wide to deep throat him. He encouraged me with his moans.

"Ummm, yes baby, that feels soooo good," he murmured. "Damn, it feels good."

I went to his chocolaty balls. I continued to jerk his dick with my right hand while my warm mouth took in both nuts. My tongue flickered rapidly like an expert while pulling them in and out of my mouth. When Anthony started talking gibberish, I knew he was ready to release his semen. I took him fully into my mouth and sucked until he exploded. His cum erupted into my mouth, and I eagerly swallowed his sour-tasting liquid.

"Come here…I want to taste your pussy," he murmured. "I want you to sit on my face and cum in my mouth."

I moved up and assumed the position, pussy gaping open, while Anthony slid his long tongue into my throbbing, moist cave. As I rocked my experienced hips, his strong hands gripped my shapely thighs while I fucked his face. Anthony could not believe the stamina I had, which only pushed him to keep up. This time, I was silent as I came in his mouth.

I slid back up and lay on my back in the missionary position. I was extremely aroused as I remembered how much I enjoyed casual sex. We both laid there for long moments, contemplating our next move. When Anthony began stroking my stomach, I tensed up.

"I've got to go," I exclaimed, pulling away.

"But you just got here," he said, already half asleep.

"You'll see me again."

He perked up.

"Really? When?"

"In your dreams," I sassily replied. "Goodnight."

"Girl, do you have any Neosporin? I got fucked something awful last night. My pussy was pulled, ripped, split, licked…," I stated as I walked through the door of my volunteer workplace. Vanessa was making coffee, unenthused by my remark.

"Since when does Ed put it down like that?" she asked, taking a sip of the hot cup of French vanilla coffee.

"You don't know the half of what's been going on," I replied while contemplating whether I should confide in Vanessa about me and Anthony's escapade. I didn't have anyone to talk to about how good the doctor's dick was. I couldn't talk to Anika, who would normally be my first choice with whom to share juicy gossip, because I knew that Anika was secretly in love with Doctor Good Dick and wouldn't understand. She just wouldn't.

"Oh, so please do tell," Vanessa encouraged, hoping to get a little piece of dirt to hold over my head, something she could dangle every now and then to keep me grounded. Or, use the dirt to kick me off my throne when I was feeling happy and complete with Ed.

The desperation in Vanessa's voice made the decision for me.

"Ed has always put it down. Why else would we have celebrated ten wonderful years of marriage? Did I ever tell you about how he proposed?"

"More times than I can count," Vanessa remarked dryly. "Here comes this bitch."

"Hi, Jessica," we both sang in unison.

Ignoring our greetings, Jessica began to randomly pick in each nostril, as if she was in deep thought.

"Gracie, Human Resources called yesterday, saying that the social security number you gave is incorrect."

"Incorrect? That's been my number for thirty-nine years. There must be a misunderstanding."

"Yeah, maybe. I'm just telling you what they said."

"Well, what do they want me to do to straighten this out?"

"I'll need to follow up with a telephone call. They just left that message on our machine."

"Okay, thank you."

I went home that night and soaked in a long, luxurious bath before getting out admiring my new figure. I did look just as I had when I was twenty. Doctor Good Dick was right. As I began dressing for bed, my phone rang. Hoping that it was the doctor I was a bit disappointed when Anika's name flashed across my screen. I allowed Anika to go to voicemail and then dialed Anthony.

"Hello?"

"Hi, this is Gracie."

"How are you?" he replied. I felt I detected a little reservation in his voice. My mind quickly wondered which approach I'd take to ensnare Anthony. There wasn't any way I only wanted him for a one-night stand. I felt that I needed to allow him to be the aggressor. Men loved the chase.

"I'm not doing too well after last night."

"Really?" his voice rose with skepticism. He sounded guarded. "I thought we had a good time."

"Well, yes...I mean, I'm so embarrassed. We were both intoxicated and I should have never crossed the line. I'm married, happily, and I want to apologize and assure you that you don't have to worry about me telling Anika or trying to take this further. It was one time—"

"Hey, wait a minute. Do I have a say in this?"

"What are you talking about?"

"You're calling me to end something that hasn't really started."

"I'm calling to apologize for what we both know was a mistake and should never happen again."

"I don't know about you but after last night I really want to see you again. I haven't felt like that in a long time...the way you made me feel."

"I can't...I'm married—"

"Did I mention how sweet your coochie juices are," he breathed, getting me aroused as he spoke.

"Did you . . . did we . . . I can't remember everything. I was a bit intoxicated," I lied as my mind quickly replayed every juicy scene.

"I *did* eat you out, and I can still taste and smell you like it was happening right now," Anthony exclaimed.

I blushed.

"Stop it," I purred.

"I can't stop it. I'm already hooked on your wet, tight pussy."

"I mean, we can't continue like this. My husband...I've never done anything like this before in my life."

"I know you're a good woman." He paused and then continued. "And I'd never do anything to jeopardize your marriage. But I can't get you out of my mind. I'll give you my word, your husband won't ever find out about us. I have to see you again. All you have to do is say yes. Trust me, no one will ever find out. I don't kiss and tell."

Nine

Anthony Cross

LIFE WAS FULL OF SURPRISES, BUT NOT LIKE GRACIE! In all my years of conquests, I never would have imagined that I'd meet Mrs. Stuck-Up in a club, take her home, and fuck her pussy dry. And she was good, too. Any man's dream fuck. A perfect one-night stand. I sat in my office with my feet up on my solid oak desk, contemplating last week's events. *Gracie* . . .the name surreptitiously crept through my mind repeatedly.

I heard trustworthy Anika stroll into the office, and when I came out she was sitting there, sipping on her coffee and yapping away on her cell phone. Impatiently, I waited for her to hang up. Finally she got the hint and ended her nonsense.

"Who was that?" I asked, the nosey side of me winning.

"None-ya," she replied.

"Fuck you. Listen, what's up with your friend?" A level of anticipation had developed. I tried to keep my voice monotone and casual.

"Who? What friend?"

"The married pain in the ass."

"Gracie?"

"Yeah, her."

"What do you mean, what's up with her?" she asked, and I could feel her pressure going up.

"How's she recovering?" I lied, sensing tension.

"Oh," she replied, exhaling. "You can ask her yourself. She's in examination room two."

"Right now?" I asked, panicking. "She's not due for her final checkup until next week."

"Well, she's here early."

"I can see that."

Briefly I wondered how I looked. Was my tie on straight, haircut clean, did I choose the right shoes? My insecurities had me baffled. I was a don. I shouldn't be behaving this way.

"Okay," I continued, "I'm going to check on her."

"Alone? That's against the rules. I'll go with you—"

"You'll do no such thing," I insisted. "She's a friend of yours. I doubt she'll be accusing me of a sexual assault. I'll have her in and out in a few minutes. I need you out front."

I tapped lightly on the door before gently pushing it in. Gracie sat conservatively, on the examination table, and her stern face immediately unnerved me.

I stepped in, leaving the door slightly ajar, grabbed the chair, and positioned it right in front of her.

"Mrs. Lane, how are we doing today?" I formally asked her.

"Very well, doctor," she replied, and to my amazement she parted her legs to reveal a panty-less pussy. "You've got to apologize to her for the other night."

Nervously, I looked over my shoulder.

"Really?"

"Yes, really."

"What does she want from me?" I asked, enjoying this dangerous game.

"She wants you to kiss it," she purred.

"That can be arranged," I said, immediately positioning myself in front of her sweet-smelling coochie.

Roughly I stretched her legs open as far as they could maneuver in her form-fitting skirt. I leaned in close, placed my wet tongue on her ripe clit, and began to suck her juicy clitoris as if I were sucking on a peach. She stifled a moan as I licked her nether lips and began to finger fuck her. Just as her hips began to grind my finger, I heard someone coming. Their heavy feet galloped—*click clack, click clack.* Quickly I backed away from Gracie, just in time as the door swung open.

My RN, Samantha, flung open the door in an attempt to catch something gratuitous.

"Dr. Cross, am I late?"

"Of course not. We're early. And we're done. Mrs. Lane, you're all done."

"My pleasure."

"Likewise."

When Gracie left, Samantha whispered in a low, annoyed voice, "What's going on?!" Her porcelain complexion turned beet-red with fury.

"Get back to work!" I snapped, and pushed past her. I guess she didn't know who buttered her bread. I made a mental note that if she challenged me—ever—in my office—her ass was gone!

She'll be easy, I thought. The girl from the gym—damn, what was her name?—oh, yeah, Cynthia. She was coming over that night for dinner and a Blockbuster movie, or so she thought. Little did she know we'd be making our own movie. My housekeeper had already cleaned the apartment and made my favorite pan-seared salmon marinated in balsamic vinaigrette, with a side of Caesar salad. Nothing too fancy, but it still made a statement.

After I showered, I stood naked in front of my full-length mirror located inside my small, walk-in closet. I admired my biceps and triceps and began doing my routine ego boosting, flexing my muscles in the mirror. Next I looked at my svelte waistline, masculine thighs, and eight-pack stomach, and I realized I was every woman's dream. You couldn't get any better than me.

I decided to play it casual, so I put on a pair of dark blue Antik Denim jeans, a Polo button-up shirt, and Bond No. 9 cologne, and I was ready for the sexy lady.

Moments before she arrived, I added a blank tape to the hidden video camera system I had installed in my bedroom. This expensive, high-tech system wasn't for protection against burglars; I was a voyeur. Call me foolish, a freak, an asshole, or just plain stupid, but I've been videotaping my sexual liaisons since I was in high school. It started out as a way to fit in. I had been going to St. John's Preparatory, a private high school in Astoria, Queens, when I started hanging out with a few students on the other side of town. These guys grew up in Baisley, a housing project where gun shootouts were an everyday normalcy and the streets were littered with drug dealers and drug users. In any event, it was rumored that they were videotaping having sex with girls and those same videotapes were circulating around our five boroughs. One day I was inside a small, three-bedroom home in Jamaica, Queens with my newfound friend Mike. Mike was slightly older, at eighteen, and had two girls in there from my high school, Tina and Michele. Their faces weren't anything to talk about but they both had bodies that would rival most women.

Before they'd gotten there, Mike took me in the bedroom and showed me the hidden video camera. I was excited and scared at the same time but played it off like I was cool with it. All I kept thinking about was getting busted and what would my parents think. Needless to say, we didn't. We all fucked clumsily and fast as we experienced our first orgy. When the two girls left we watched the tape over and again, cracking jokes and pointing out the highlights. The thrills and adrenaline high that secretly videotaping the girls gave me has carried over into my adult life. I still get the same rush that I'd gotten back then. Have I ever considered telling my sexual encounters that I want to tape them? Negative. The pleasure comes from each woman being unaware of what's going down. I didn't need anyone playing up for the camera, only wanting to be fucked on the right side because they felt their left side wasn't as attractive. Any nonsense like that would take away from the raw, uncut footage. Even though what I did was wrong, I have never—and won't ever—share my tapes with anyone. They were my personal stash, and I kept them under lock and key.

Just as I slammed the camera shut, the front desk called.

"Mr. Cross, you have a Ms. Cynthia Rowley here to see you."

"Please send her up," I replied.

Cynthia came sauntering in, wearing fuck-me pumps, and her skimpy, cheap dress barely covered her plump ass, not to mention her boobs, which were oozing out. The six-inch stilettos and dress were hardly appropriate for a dinner date, but who was I to complain? She came here knowing what she wanted. I must admit that I was a little shocked, though. Her nighttime attire was quite different from her daywear.

"Hey, babe," I said as if we'd known each other forever. "You look great."

"Thank you," she replied. "I wanted to look good for you."

"You did all this for me?" I complimented her while grabbing both her hands in mine.

Later, after dinner, we sat in the living room to watch the movie. Being presumptuous, I thought we'd only watch the first ten minutes before we'd be fucking. But to my surprise, our small talk turned into long, stimulating conversation.

"I had no idea that you were a lawyer," I said, not allowing my voice to mask my surprise.

"Why do you sound so shocked?" she asked.

"Actually, I really don't know."

"Well you're not the only one who seems a little stumped once they ask my occupation. Truthfully, being a lawyer was my destiny. When I was eleven years old my brother, Richard was falsely accused and convicted of rape. He was sentenced to 25 years to life in a maximum-security prison. My family didn't have any money, so he had a public defender that was overworked and underpaid but most importantly, the attorney believed that my brother was guilty."

"Did you ever question his innocence?" I asked.

"Never!" she replied defiantly.

"What about your parents?"

"We *knew* he was innocent. I still remember sitting in the courtroom when the verdict was read. Three correction officers all huddled around him in anticipation of the guilty verdict. When the judge asked him to stand, and the guilty verdict was read, I still remember the look in his eyes as he turned around and told my mother not to worry about him. Can you imagine being sentenced to spend the rest of your natural life in prison at only twenty years old, and you tell your family not to worry about you?"

She was so passionate as she spoke about her brother. You could sense that it was an intimate matter that still troubled her.

"Anyway, my first year at law school, I wrote to the Innocence Project about my brother's case. I told the organization that when my brother was convicted, DNA testing wasn't yet developed. Not only did the Innocence Project agree to take on my brother's case, but the attorney working the case allowed me to assist. Needless to say, my brother was freed four years ago and now lives a productive life."

"That is quite a story," I told her as I refilled her wine glass.

"Enough about me. Tell me more about you."

"Well," I said and kissed her lips softly, "I like to party like a rock star." We both laughed, and then I continued. "I basically got a secure career, no kids, no wife—"

"What about a girlfriend?" she asked.

"None of those."

"Are you a womanizer?"

"My girlfriend and I broke up."

"I'm sorry to hear that," she lied. "Was it recently?"

Good lawyering, lawyer, I thought, *making sure you're not a rebound.*

"A little over a year," I lied.

"Was it serious?" she probed, and I got turned off. I didn't want to have serious conversation anymore, especially about a phantom ex-girlfriend.

"I'm over her. It's all about you now," I said and she melted. I leaned in, kissed her neck, and led her to my bedroom. I stood behind her and slowly slid her dress over her head. Maybe I did it a bit too slowly, because she took this as a sign to unclasp her bra. Her large breasts fell into my hands as I nestled behind her. I pressed my dick against her lower back and she began to grind slowly, making my penis grow. She turned around to face me. I bent down and began to lick and suck her pink nipples. I paused for a minute to admire her hot pink areolas.

"You have prefect breasts," I whispered and continued to suck on her nipples.

We made our way to my bed and playfully fell on it, my body resting on top of hers. I removed my boxers, slowly slid off her panties, pushed two fingers inside her wet pussy, and twirled them around. Hot juices seeped onto my finger and we both got excited.

"Play with your pussy while I watch," I demanded.

She began masturbating on my king-sized bed while I watched. She finger-fucked herself feverishly, while simultaneously massaging her ample breasts. She continued moaning sexily and chanting my name.

"Anthony, you feel sooooo good," she crooned as she ground her hips into her own fingers. "I love your big cock!"

My dick almost went soft the moment this black female said *cock*, but I revived it and decided to get on with the deed.

I stood over her and began to jerk off on her face and chest. Cum squirted everywhere, and she wasn't even embarrassed. She began moaning even louder. The kinkiness of the moment was sexually gratifying.

I slid on my Magnum and then slid inside her with ease. It was too easy! And I prided myself on being a big guy with a big dick. What was this world coming to? After a few deep thrusts I contemplated changing condoms and taking a chance on her letting me put it in her ass, but I was turned off. I pretended to cum, which was a first for me, and collapsed on my bed, burying my head in my pillow from frustration.

Visions of Gracie kept going through my head. Sexy, uninhibited Gracie.

"That was good, right, baby?" she asked.

"No."

"I said that was good, right?" she repeated, clearly perplexed.

"I heard you, and you heard me."

"Seriously?"

"Have you ever thought about having labiaplasty?"

"What? What are you talking about?"

"It's a cosmetic procedure that tightens your vaginal walls so that there will be more friction for your partner. It's a non-evasive procedu—"

"You're an asshole," she screamed as she leapt from my bed. In one swift movement she put her hooker clothes back on and was gone in sixty seconds.

Jeez, what a waste of a good meal, I thought as I hopped up and hit rewind on the tape. I needed instant replay of her facial expression when she called me an asshole.

The next Sunday, Chris and Gabriel came over to watch the game. It was supposed to be just a guy's day in, but I had other plans. Gabriel was being tight-lipped about his power moves, and I intended to pry them out of him. Chris came to the party fully loaded with Heineken, pizza, chips, and cocaine. Personally I didn't do drugs, but Chris liked to indulge occasionally. He was his own man. I gave him my opinion about his drug use one time too many a few years back and he went berserk. He was coked up, had the energy of a bull, and wanted nothing less than a street brawl. His first punch caught me in my left jaw and I whipped his ass. But that one lucky punch he landed knocked the sense in me that I needed to mind my own business. Since then, we've had an unspoken understanding.

As we gulped down beer and got hyped from the game, I sporadically took sneak peeks at Chris. He had a platter of uncut, pure cocaine, a razor blade, and determination in his eyes. As early as a year ago, Chris would do three-inch lines. Now, he's superseded his previous limit and had cut four lines at least twelve inches in diameter. He was officially out of control. At first I thought that Gabriel didn't indulge, since Chris had been at it for almost an hour and Gabriel, as I, had only watched. But soon enough Chris passed the plate to Gabriel, and he began his ritual of holding one nostril closed while inhaling the powdery, white substance with the other.

The game had long been over, but those two were like glassy-eyed zombies sprawled out on my sofa. They looked like two pimps. Both had on three-piece suits, but Chris sported a fedora hat and Gabriel rocked a pair of pink alligator shoes. Ten years ago during the Gianni Versace era, the pink alligator shoes would have been fly, now they just looked gay.

Chris was obviously being heavily influenced by Gabriel. I could see that in his new wardrobe and demeanor. He was a one-dimensional, jean-and-boot type of guy, so it surprised me to see him in wing-tip shoes and tailored suits.

I took this opportunity to crack on the information I so desperately wanted. Financially, I knew that in five years I would be well off. My practice will continue to get a steady clientele and I'm certain I'll have a household name. In fact, I'd hired a publicist and entertainment manager to pitch a reality show to Lifetime, VH-1 and BET following me and my growing practice. I wanted to be the black Dr. 90210. But until I got my big break, I needed to steadily build my practice, make wise investments so that I could maintain my lifestyle and pay back my student loans.

"So, Gabriel, Chris was telling me about this top secret investment deal you're putting together."

Before answering, he sucked on his teeth and dug in his left ear while his eyes rolled back in his head, as if he was about to have an orgasm. The scene was annoying. Finally, he answered.

"Yeah, that deal is a win-win."

"I thought there wasn't any such thing?"

"You've been socializing with the wrong people."

I laughed a superficial snicker.

"Yeah, I guess you're right. Tell me about what you're working on."

"Anthony, let me find out—" Chris sniffed, "that you're trying to get in on this deal."

"Nah, I'm just asking questions. What's wrong with that?" I asked, pretending the moment was innocent.

"He just wants to be informed, that's all," Gabriel said in my defense. "Chris, if I didn't know any better, I'd think you were trying to keep your man in the dark, that you're trying to make all the money without putting him on."

"Yeah, put me on!" I cosigned.

"Don't you have enough money?" Chris sneered.

I was caught off balance by Chris's demeanor. He was a bails bondsman and owned his own company and made quite a lot of money himself. The only thing was he didn't know how to manage his own money. He splurged on unnecessary things, I guess. What? I don't know. He didn't have a car, didn't have a steady girlfriend, didn't buy expensive clothing; but again, he just didn't manage his money right.

"C'mon, man, you can never have enough money. I may want in!"

"Well, it's like this: I got this deal I put together where you'll get 20 percent return on your investment within thirty days. The minimum you'll need to get in is $20,000, and there isn't a max."

Skeptically, I listened.

"United Oil International Liberty is an investment that allows you to buy units at $10,000 per unit. Within the first 30 days of your initial investment, you'll see a 20 percent return. I can have my lawyer forward you copies of our periodic letters and brochures outlining the actual proceeds from the oil and gas properties. He'll explain in depth the respective prospectus regarding United Oil International Liberty acquiring rights in various oil and gas producing properties, located in Missouri, Texas, Louisiana, Oklahoma, Mississippi, and Belize."

As Gabriel went into details about how I was going to gain on my investment, I thought about how much I was willing to invest when he answered that question for me.

"If you want in, I'll need your cashier's check no later than next Friday. Also, I don't know how much liquid you have, but you can't come in on more than the $20,000."

"That's it?" I asked.

"Yes."

"But you said that there wasn't a maximum."

"Had you got in earlier there wouldn't be a maximum, but you're the last one, and there's only room for that investment."

Twenty-thousand dollars was hardly a great investment. I could lose that in one minute in the temperamental stock market. When investing they teach you that you should only invest what you're prepared to lose. Meaning, don't invest your mortgage money. At the moment, I didn't have "fuck you" money. I wasn't any where near broke but I was on a budget. I had a lot to take into consideration. My practice employed eleven people who garnered large paychecks, not to mention the building lease and all the amenities it takes to run an office of that magnitude. And what about my lifestyle? I had purchased a 1300 square foot, Upper Eastside apartment with a hefty price tag. And my maintenance fee was obscene. Even though I had liquid assets, one false move could bring me under. Truthfully, I did have a small amount of money that I could risk if my investment went sour because the flip side of the gamble is that it could actually pay off. I decided to sit this one out and do more research on Gabriel and his company. I didn't quite trust him, his expensive suits and flashy lifestyle.

Yes, I'll definitely sit on the sideline and watch to see how Chris' situation will unfold.

Ten

Gracie Lane

THAT NIGHT, ANTHONY INVITED ME TO A QUAINT, romantic, restaurant where I wouldn't have any fears about getting caught by one of my husband's colleagues. When I asked him where he was taking me, he was vague. I guess he wanted me to be surprised.

"Gracieeeee," Tamara called out. The mere sound of her voice almost swayed my mood.

"What is it?" I snapped.

"Anika's on the phone!" Tamara obviously detected the annoyance in my voice. Hurriedly, I walked over to my home phone just to make sure everything was all right with Anika.

"Hey, are you all right?"

"Yeah, why you ask that?"

"Because you're calling the house phone. You usually call my cell first."

"I did but it kept going straight to voicemail."

"Really? That's odd." I was only half-listening. I was checking out my curves in the mirror.

"So what's up for tonight? What are you doing?"

*If you only knew…*I thought. *You wouldn't like it…*

"I'm going out with a few women from my job," I lied.

"Thank you for not inviting me," she laughed. "Okay, really quickly and then I'll let you go. What do you think of him?"

"Him?"

"Anthony…my future husband." Her words stung.

"Umm, well, I guess he's all right. A little insufferable though. I can't see how you can stand to work around him. He seems as if he's in the mirror all day."

"Yup, that's Anthony."

"And he seems chauvinistic…not to mention a womanizer—"

"A womanizer? Why would you say that? Did he make a pass at you?" Her voice had elevated as she panicked.

"Of course he didn't. He knows we're friends. He just seems as if he has a lot of lady friends. He's successful, in his early thirties and not married. That's a combination of a womanizer." I hoped my explanation would suffice.

"Gracie he's not a womanizer. He's just trying to find the right woman. He's so sweet, and funny, and cute. I have the biggest crush—"

"Anika, sweetheart, I have to run. I have people waiting on me. I'll call you tomorrow."

"Oh, ok. Have a good night."

"You do the same."

I heard Anika talk longingly about Anthony numerous times but tonight it felt strange. In the past, I hadn't met him and we hadn't fucked. I feel so sneaky and low and a little sorry for her being in love with someone who doesn't want her. If I knew one thing I knew that Anika could never find out about me and Anthony's affair.

I slipped on my same Diane von Furstenberg black dress that I'd worn to my husband's anniversary dinner and a pair of sexier high heels with black leather straps. I stood back to see my reflection in the mirror. I looked regal. I applied a little foundation, gold eye shadow, and Christian Dior copper lip gloss, and was pleased with the end result.

I looked alluring in my all-black get-up, but I felt there was something missing. I walked over to my dresser, opened my jewelry box, and pulled out a beautiful brooch that Ed had given me for our eighth wedding anniversary. It was gold-plated with faux ruby and emerald stones. To compliment the costume brooch, I adorned my small wrist with an eight-karat, diamond tennis bracelet and five-karat, emerald-cut diamond earrings my late husband, Phillip had purchased. I told Ed that I was invited to have dinner with Vanessa to celebrate her 40th birthday, but Tamara felt that she needed and explanation as well.

"Going somewhere…again?" Tamara's voice dripped sarcasm as she watched me put on my finishing touches of makeup.

Ignoring her sarcasm, I decided to be on the offensive. As I puckered up my pouty lips and dabbed on another layer of lip gloss, I casually replied, "You're still living here?"

Tamara gave me a once-over. "And she's wearing her *one* good dress…I hope he's worth it."

"Perhaps you should put on your *one* good dress and go out as well…oh, I forgot, you have no friends."

Tamara knew that if I wanted I could buy a million of these dresses but what frustrated her most was that I didn't. She couldn't understand how I choose to spend my money. It annoyed her that I shopped in Target or Wal-Mart and also cut coupons on the weekends. She didn't have any idea how I amassed my fortune and I didn't tell her because it wasn't her business. I didn't feel a need to tell her that before I married rich that I lived off Ramen Noodles and pizza so I know how it feels to not have any money and I wasn't ever going back to that lifestyle. Now, I live off the interest of the money I have in the bank. My late husband was a financial guru but when he unexpectedly died it's not like I had the business savvy to continue to pull in multi-million dollar mega deals. I hired a financial advisor, invested a lot of the money into conservative mutual funds and began doing volunteer work.

I grabbed my Hermés purse and pushed past Tamara, leaving her scowling in the hallway.

The Buddha Bar restaurant was upscale and cozy. I decided to bit my tongue because I'd been here on several occasions with and without my husband. But I wasn't a regular. Its earth-tone colors beset the huge, gold-plated Buddha statutes. It had huge tropical plants in every corner and brick stucco on the walls. There were high-back, eloquent chairs with an array of round tables. Anthony led the way through the crowd and I followed close behind, one leg extending after the other with the grace of a panther. My hips swayed one way; my head the other.

We were led to the V.I.P area in the far right wing of the restaurant.

"Take your pick. You can choose any table you'd like." Anthony boasted. He had paid to have the whole area for only us.

I beamed. "Then I choose this one right here."

Our table could easily have sat fifteen people. When I looked down underneath the table, I pretended to be surprised with the aquarium. The clear blue water was bursting with exotic fish. You could literally look down and see fish swimming under your feet.

"Oh my gosh, how spectacular," I squealed.

"Yes, it is. If you want, I could have the owner open it up and you can dip your feet in the water."

"Really?"

"Yes, really."

I thought for a moment. "Nice gesture, but I think I'll pass."

Anthony couldn't take his eyes off of me. "You look absolutely stunning."

"Thank you."

His eyes zeroed in on my jewelry. "That's an impressive bracelet. Let me see."

His strong, masculine hands quickly grabbed my wrist and began to inspect my trinket.

"And those earrings…wow."

I snatched my wrist back. "Thank you."

"Those are…" his voice trailed off.

"Real?"

"Are they?"

"Of course."

He nodded. "A gift?"

"From my husband."

"Really? I thought he worked for Verizon."

"How would you know that?" I asked, annoyed for two reasons: One, he was prying into my personal life and two, Anika was running her mouth about my situation and she should have known better.

"Oh, I think you mentioned it."

"No, I didn't." My voice was stern and unwavering. Anthony looked away and I sensed he wanted to change the subject. He cleared his throat in hopes to cut the tension that had suddenly built up.

Suddenly, I thought I spotted Ed's supervisor, Michael, at a table. He was having a conversation with a woman. It looked as if she had asked him something and then he leaned in real close and gave her a kiss on the cheek.

My heartbeat accelerated and my palms began to sweat. This always happened when I was nervous. As I continued to stare intently, I could see that it wasn't my husband's boss after all, and I was immediately relieved.

The candle that sat in the middle of the table flickered playfully and cast a golden, seductive light upon Anthony's face. I thought he looked picture-perfect.

"How was your day?" he asked. He took my hand and snugly placed it in between his.

"It was pleasant enough. Nothing to discuss. And yours?"

"It's always a good day for me when there aren't any complications during my surgeries. Other than that, it was all pretty much humdrum."

"I guess you haven't read the newspaper?" I asked.

"Was I supposed to?"

"Well, when you're in it, you should."

"I was in the papers today?"

"Don't act as if you didn't have a clue," I teased.

"I honestly didn't. What did they say? How I'm the number-one, most sought-after bachelor in New York?" he asked cockily.

"Nooo!" I laughed. "There were two sentences on the *Page Six* column of the *New York Post,* saying that you're about to be a father."

His expression turned to stone.

"Are you serious?"

"As a terrorist attack."

"Jeez, where do they get this information?" His annoyed tone complemented the sudden fuchsia tones in his dark complexion.

"Who cares? It's free publicity."

"I guess you're right," he commented. "But it's not true."

"If it were, it wouldn't change anything with our arrangement. Well, at least not for me, it wouldn't."

Changing the subject, Anthony asked, "I'm glad that you could get away tonight. I really wanted to see you. How were you able to sneak away?"

"Ed is at a fundraiser tonight, so I told him that I was having dinner with the girls."

He looked deep into my eyes and then stuck his index finger into my dimpled smile.

"You have the cutest smile."

"Of course I do, I'm an eleven, remember?"

He laughed, "Right, right...the day of your surgery...you remembered."

"My memory is long."

"I hate to be the barer of bad news but I was lying!"

Playfully, I punched him on his shoulder. "You were not."

"No, I wasn't lying. You're that and more." He leaned in and gave me a soft kiss on my lips. "Tell me about yourself."

I tensed up.

"Not much to tell."

"What was your childhood like?"

"It was okay." I looked away, detached.

"What about your parents? Do you have any siblings?"

"Really, my life isn't worth your time. How about you tell me about you and your parents and siblings? How did you decide to become a surgeon, and a plastic surgeon at that? I haven't met too many black plastic surgeons."

"Who you kidding? You haven't met *any*," he joked. "But to answer your questions, my childhood was great. My father is an open-heart surgeon, and my mother was a stay-at-home parent. My parents have old-fashioned values and I really had a wonderful upbringing."

"Really? No skeletons in your family's closet? Daddy didn't get caught fucking the nanny?"

"Of course he did." Anthony laughed. "But the nanny was my mother."

"You really did have a great childhood."

"Yeah, so being close to my father and admiring him for years, I knew

I'd follow in his footsteps, and my parents couldn't be more pleased. The only thing left to do is get married and have a family."

"How close are you to that goal? Anyone special in your life?"

"Gracie, I'll answer in a moment. Our *maitre'd* is here. May I take the liberty of ordering for you?"

"Please do." I loved his take-charge attitude. It was a turn-on.

"For our appetizers, I'll have steamed oysters and she'll have sashimi sushi. Our main course will be the Atlantic bluefin tuna for me, and the lady will have the Peking duck, smothered in caviar. For dessert, the lady will have the Madeleine truffle and I'll have the Golden Plum Soufflé. Please bring us a bottle of Pinot Noir. That'll be all, thank you." The *maitre'd* left and we continued our conversation.

"How did you know I'd like sushi and caviar?" I asked, grinning.

"There's something edgy about you," he commented, and gave me a sly wink. "Yeah, so back to kids and family. To answer your question, no, I don't have anyone special in my life. I was involved with a young woman, maybe too young, and it didn't work out."

"How young is too young?" I asked and raised a skeptical eyebrow.

"She was legal." Anthony laughed. "I'm talking about mentally. She's 24, but her antics and childish behavior ruined the relationship. I had to let her go. I had no choice."

"Did you give her a chance? To grow?"

"I did what I could to make it work, but it didn't. Don't get me wrong, she's a beautiful, smart woman, but we started to grow apart."

"I'm not judging you, but I find that what people don't realize but making a relationship work is just that—work. Things don't just magically fix themselves. You have to put as much care, time and determination into them as I'm sure you put into your practice. If you want a wife and family, perhaps you should reevaluate your relationship with your baby-momma." I giggled, which made Anthony giggle, taking the sting off of what was sounding like a scolding session.

"I want you to be my baby-momma," he said and pulled me in close for a passionate kiss. His soft lips lulled me in and I didn't want to let go. I pulled back first and glanced around the room.

He continued. "What about you? Staying married forever?"

I thought about how I should handle this question, or why he was even asking it. At this point I didn't see a need to deceive him. I'd already gotten what I wanted, and only wanted more if he was a willing participant in my adulterous affair.

"Till the end," I stated. Anthony shook his head as if he understood, but his next question caught me off guard.

"Don't you think situations such as these, — you know, affairs — could jeopardize that?"

See, this is why I can't be straight up with motherfuckers, I thought. *They always have to start judging. My first mistake was allowing the affair to go farther than the bedroom.*

"I didn't plan for this . . . you . . . but there's something about you that I couldn't just walk away from. It was like we had this connection, it felt kinetic, and it pulled me directly to you. As I told you before, I've never done something like this with anyone else, but meeting you and sleeping with you doesn't negate the fact that I'm married."

"If anyone understands, I do. Trust me," he replied.

After having a delicious meal, I thought about Ed. My hubby loves the steak here. I called the *maitre'd* back over and ordered him a full meal to go.

Anthony huffed, "Who are you ordering the steak for?"

"Me. Since you took the liberty of ordering for me I couldn't get what I wanted. I wanted the steak and that's what I'm going to have," I replied, dismissively.

When the check came I offered to pay it and Anthony looked at me as if he was insulted.

"Well do you want to go Dutch?" I asked, further infuriating the doctor.

"Listen, I'm a man and I asked you out. That means I pick up the tabs. If you haven't noticed I own a multi-million dollar practice," and whipped out his platinum American Express Card. "I can afford to drop two-hundred on dinner."

I relented and inwardly laughed at the ego-driven doctor who owned his "multi-million dollar practice."

Anthony walked me to my car and I gave him a luscious kiss. He knelt between my legs and began to let his hand slide between my thighs. He wanted me to follow him home, but then my husband called.

"Hey, baby." My voice was jovial, hiding the underlying deception that was transpiring. "I'm on my way home now...we had a great time...Yeah, well, you know Vanessa, always wanting to be praised...I'll see you in 30 minutes...love you, too." I hung up. "I got to go."

"No. Come home with me. Call him back and tell him that you're staying with your girlfriends."

"I can't. I have to go."

"Come on, don't go. Please," Anthony begged. "I want you. Let's drive away together."

"I can't. My husband is waiting." I abruptly closed my car door and damn near ran him over in an attempt to get out of the parking lot. I didn't care if my behavior didn't sit well with Anthony. If I say I have to go then it is what it is.

My phone rang.

"Yes."

"What was that all about?" Anthony was pissed.

"Huh?"

"You could have killed me rushing off like that."

"I think you're being a bit melodramatic don't you think?"

"No I don't think!" He was still yelling in my ear like a crazy person. "I asked you to stay."

Calmly, I replied, "And I said no."

"Listen, I'm a busy man and if I take the time to take you out to an expensive restaurant the night shouldn't end with you running off to be with another man."

"The other man is my husband and he will always come first! This isn't a seduction playing out here. You don't have to woo me in order to fuck me. I thought that was understood. I could give less than a fuck about eating at five-star restaurants nor am I impressed. Did I not offer to pay the bill? Perhaps that would have taken away a little of your hostility."

He laughed, manically. "One thing I hate is a wannabe. I know that you don't work and sit home watching soap operas all day and that your little hubby maintains the household with his little Verizon job. But you're disillusioned with your fake brooch, fake diamond bracelet, fake earrings, and fake diva personality. My money is long Mrs. Lane and I was doing you and your hubby a favor by not embarrassing you at dinner tonight by allowing you to pick up the check. What your husband makes in a year, I make in two weeks!"

I chuckled at the rude, self-centered man with his reckless mouth. He was pissed. Obviously he wasn't used to women rushing off to leave him. I guess they were always begging to stay. The good thing is that Anika didn't tell him my whole situation. He must have only gotten bits and pieces. From what I could tell he thought that I was broke. Funny. In fact, hilarious. If he only knew....

While he was screaming, I calmly pressed END on my phone and then shut it off. I didn't tolerate such nonsense. Especially from a histress. Didn't he know his place?

Eleven

Anthony Cross

THERE WERE EIGHT MESSAGES LEFT ON MY HOME answering machine—all from women—but not one from Gracie. Last night when I heard a dial tone I wanted to give her the benefit of my doubt and think that maybe my cellular service had dropped my call. When I called back—numerous times—only to go to voicemail, I knew she'd hung up on me. In short, I felt very disrespected. Usually, I have been blessed with the knack to totally erase something or someone from my life and I expected that with her it would be the same way, but I missed her. I missed the disrespectful, rude, condescending, cheating bitch! And she was all those things. I mean she's cheating on her husband for Chris sakes. But why? Why did I miss her? Why did I want her so badly?

I couldn't understand how she could be so determined to rush home last night. Didn't she realize I was a man with pride, and I had swallowed it last night and practically begged her to stay with me? And that's something I didn't do. Something I never had to do.

It was just nearing 10 a.m. on a frigid Saturday morning and I was headed to my parent's house a few blocks from my residence. I put on a sweat suit and a NY Mets hat, and was off. A nagging feeling that I couldn't shake kept riding me. I didn't want to admit it, but I was annoyed that after I asked Gracie to stay, she'd left anyway. As if to say that her husband was more important. I mean, theoretically, she was only a fuck buddy. That was a given. But I was still Doctor Anthony Cross and there wasn't a woman walking this earth that I couldn't have. My terms. My time. My rules.

A cold, biting rain started to fall and I still had a few blocks left to go. Instead of hopping in a taxi, I decided to tough it out. When I got to the building, I was soaked. I ran up the twenty flights of steps, something I always did, and pounded on the door. My father opened it and greeted me with a warm, crooked smile.

"Hey, Pops," I said and gave him a firm handshake. My father didn't believe in a warm hug or tight embrace between men. "Where's Momma?"

"She's in her room with Shelby."

Shelby was my mother's nurse, and also my father's mistress, something he'd never admit. My mother had Alzheimer's disease and had been diagnosed three years ago. I still hadn't gotten up the courage to tell my friends. All they knew was my textbook answers: "My parents are great, my childhood was great, everything was great." I peered into the room and I could tell that Shelby was preparing to bathe my mother. I backed out of the room and went into my father's study. It was a fairly large room, with a huge, mahogany desk, four flat-screen televisions, all programmed on different channels: MSNBC, CNN, Bloomberg Television and NY 1 News. He had a custom floor-to-ceiling bookshelf that was littered with books, most of the books he and I read. That's how I would get to spend quality time with him as a child: I would sit in his office and read his book collection.

When I walked in, my father was pouring himself a stiff drink. Gin and tonic, no ice.

"Drink?"

"Pops, it's ten o'clock in the morning."

"Is it really? I had no idea…" he teased.

I smiled. "Sure, why not. You only live once."

As we sat there sipping on our strong drinks, my childhood flashed before me. "How's Mom doing? I mean, really?"

"Well, some days are good; other days are not so good. Shelby takes really good care of her, though."

"About Shelby—"

"What about her?" he asked, defensively.

"Do you really think that having your mistress look after your wife is a good idea? You don't know what she's doing to Mom while you're at work! She could be pinching her, slapping her, starving her, or — even worse — plotting to kill her."

As I said the obvious, my voice began to rise.

"Did I ever tell you that I was having an affair with Shelby?" My father asked.

"No."

"When you turned eighteen, what did I tell you about marriage?"

"C'mon, Pops, we've been down this road a million times."

"I told you not to do it until you were at least forty years old and had slept through almost everything walking."

"Yes, yes, I know."

"I married you're mother when I was twenty years old and wet behind the ears. We both said that we were in it for life, and I meant that. I meant that until I was working late one night and met Rita. Over the years there would be many Ritas, but I never allowed any of them to cloud my judgment. I've said all of that to say that I would never, ever, put your mother in harm's way or disrespect her by having my mistress be her caretaker. Your mother has given me her whole life and she is—always has been—the love of my life. And it pains me that the moment I realized that all of my womanizing ways could have destroyed us, and I had finally gotten my cheating ways out of my system, she got sick. I think I'm being punished. These are supposed to be our best years, and I have to live them without her. I'm not thinking about any other woman other than your mother. I'm tired. I don't have the energy."

Sitting there listening to my father helped me better understand myself. We both sat around, showing my mother old pictures from our family album but, of course, she didn't remember anything. The time at my parents' house was always uplifting because I always felt loved. When I got back to my apartment, I realized Gracie still hadn't called. Then I felt silly. Why couldn't I call her? We had a little situation but it shouldn't be anything that I couldn't get over. We were adults and it wasn't like I wanted her to be my wife. She just fulfilled something that at the moment was void. Besides, by next week I'll probably already be bored with her.

She picked up on the second ring, "Hey, Gracie...how are you?"

"I'm doing well. What a nice surprise," she replied. She seemed a little distracted and I heard a lot of noise in the background. I wondered if her husband was close by.

"Is now a good time?"

"Well, yes and no. I'm at work and I can talk until my supervisor comes through the door."

"I didn't know you worked."

"Obviously."

"About the other night—"

"Don't mention it."

"Well, I was thinking about getting tickets to a jazz boat ride that docks at Chelsea Pier, and I wanted to know if you wanted to go?"

"Sounds cool. When?"

"Tonight? Around six?"

"Can't. I'm working all evening. I'm helping to throw a party and I'm so excited about it. Do you want me to see if I could get away tonight and come by your place for an hour or so? How's your stamina...been eating your Wheaties?"

This was truly only a sex thing for her. I changed the subject. "Where do you work?"

"On Long Island."

"Where?"

"Like, the address?"

"Yes."

"Why?"

"Because I asked."

"I'll text it to you. I've got to go."

Five minutes later, I got the text with Gracie's work address and was headed back out the door. I took a taxi to Bloomingdale's on 59th Street and went shopping for my new lady. After perusing a plethora of high-end designers, I finally settled on an amazing Badgley Mischka backless dress and then headed to the shoe department. I wanted to purchase her a pair of black stiletto Prada shoes that went perfect with the dress, but the sales associate said that they were cut small. She also warned me against buying Chanel for my mystery girl "friend". She said that I would be safe with Gucci or Ferragamo but I settled on a great pair of Marc Jacob strappy heels, but I couldn't stop there. There was a matching clutch purse.

I didn't purchase anything for myself and felt satisfied leaving with a bag full of things for Gracie. When I got back home, I left the package with my doorman to send FedEx overnight priority to arrive on Monday. I left Gracie's work address and a small note: WEAR THIS NEXT SATURDAY...OR WEAR NOTHING. A.C. I planned to take Gracie on the jazz cruise next week and I couldn't wait to see how her curves would fill out in that dress.

Twelve

My worst nightmare

IN A PITCH-BLACK LIVING ROOM SAT A VERY ANGRY man. His expansive home on the Upper Eastside in the city seemed to be swallowing him. In a moment, he thought he'd snap and lose it. His once-attentive wife had begun to ignore his needs, and was coming home at odd hours of the day and night without solid excuses. He realized that these were signs of an affair. The mere thought made him recoil.

On this particular evening, Ed sat in the dark in his favorite chair, drinking his favorite wine. He wanted answers. Deep down he knew he'd believe whatever explanation she'd give, just as long as she looked into his eyes when she spoke. But the mere thought that she wouldn't look into his eyes had him feeling insecure.

One hour after Gracie was due home from work, she walked into the dimly-lit living room. She squinted through the darkness and steadied her eyes on the chaos. The once-tidy home was in disarray. Clothes were casually thrown across the sofa. A basket of clean laundry sat off to the side near the laundry room, instead of being ironed, folded and put away. Dirty glasses rested on top of the mantle. Even Ed had to admit his sister was a slob. Perhaps he was one as well, but he wouldn't know because Gracie usually kept their home immaculate with the assistance of their house-keeper, Elana, who came twice a week.

As soon as Gracie clicked on the light, she flipped.

"I volunteer my services all day almost each day and I have to come home to this?" Gracie yelled.

"Where have you been?" Ed prodded.

"Where is she? Tamara?" Gracie asked, ignoring Ed's question.

"She went to the movies."

"Movies? With what money? Oh, yeah, she has plenty of money because she's mooching off our stupid asses. Or shall I say my stupid ass!" She glared at her husband.

"I don't want to discuss Tamara," he replied in a low, throaty whisper. "Where have you been?"

It was at that moment that Gracie realized something was up. Something was wrong. Her husband's short, two-stranded twists needed a shape-up. His eyes looked withdrawn and puffy and he was sporting, to her dismay, a five o'clock shadow that needed to be shaved. Ed needed to be groomed because he looked a hot mess, as if he'd aged ten years.

"I was working, something your sister doesn't know about," she said, challenging Ed to dismiss her again.

"Didn't I just say I didn't want to discuss my sister!" he roared, and Gracie thought that the mantle mirror shook.

"Who are you yelling at?!" Gracie barked back. Not waiting for a response, she screamed, "Get the groceries from the lobby! And fuck you, while you're at it."

Realizing that he'd just made a fool out of himself, Ed hopped up and quickly dashed downstairs to the front desk and gathered up the groceries and brought them inside. Gracie immediately began making dinner. He stood back and took a look at his beautiful wife. She was gorgeous, could have any man she wanted, kept a clean home, always cooked his dinner and snacks no matter how late or early he asked to be fed, and she always made love to him, and made love very well. But most importantly, to his knowledge she'd been faithful for their entire marriage, as was he. They both seemed to have old-fashioned values, and that was what had him so stressed. He knew that if he ever found out that Gracie was cheating on him, he'd divorce her without any regrets. He hoped that he hadn't been taking her granted....

As Gracie diced red, yellow, and green peppers like a professional chef, Ed walked up behind her, embraced her around her now-tiny waist-line, and nuzzled her neck.

"I'm sorry, baby, for raising my voice."

"You should be, and it better not happen again." Gracie puckered up her lips and gave him a quick kiss. "Why are you so uptight? Did you have a bad day at work?" As she spoke, she tossed the peppers into the waiting frying pan and began to sauté them in olive oil. She was making stir-fry shrimps and brown rice. It was quick, healthy, and easy to cook.

"No, I didn't. Work is great but I need to ask you something." Ed waited until his wife turned around to face him. She knew what he was about to say before he'd said it. "Why are you keeping inconsistent hours lately?"

"What are you talking about?" Her face and voice appeared to be clueless of his implication.

"Lately you've been coming home at dawn from a night of partying, and hours late after work. I've been going to voicemail on your cell phone more than normal, and you don't want to make love." Ed couldn't disguise his hurt and insecurities.

Gracie ruminated about how she'd answer his line of questioning. "Are you suggesting I'm having an affair?"

"Are you?" he asked, blatantly.

"Ed, I love you."

"Are you having an affair, Gracie?" He stood stone still, staring directly into her eyes. She returned his stare.

"No," she said in an unwavering voice. She continued to cook. "I would never—could never—jeopardize our marriage. We took vows...and I love you more than I love life. How could you think such a thing?"

Ed waited for a long moment before he shut off the stove.

"What are you doing?" she asked.

He didn't reply. He began to passionately kiss her lips and walked her to the sofa.

He sat on the sofa and positioned Gracie between his legs. Gently he reached up and removed her shirt. It glided down her shoulders and cascaded to the floor. The spaghetti straps on her bra were the next to go. As his strong, masculine hands slid her clothing to the floor, Gracie watched Ed's glistening eyes as he looked past her breasts, then lingered on her flat stomach, and finally on her perfect, pedicured feet. Her flaming red, hooker toenail polish was turning him on. He knew he'd married a freak but up until recently he figured she was *only* his freak.

Ed put both hands on her hips and guided her to lie down on the sofa. Neither one of them knew or cared when Tamara would come barging in. Ed had to satisfy his uncertainty that his wife might have been with someone else. Gracie just wanted to be satisfied.

Ed entered her with slow, strong strokes. When his dick pressed against the opening of her pussy, he applied a controlled pressure. When her pussy resisted, he pushed harder until the head burst through. He teased her for a minute, just rocking his tip in and out. As her pussy walls opened wider, he sunk deeper inside her welcoming cave. Ed's strong pelvis rocked back and forth, keeping a steady rhythm. As he gently made love to her, he whispered sweet words in her ear.

"Is it good?" he asked.

"It's perfect," she said, her voice barely a whisper.

His broad shoulders, firm pecs, and ripe nipples covered her small waist and flat stomach. Tenderly he pulled out of her, separated her legs, and began kissing and sucking her inner thighs in circular motions, slowly moving toward her nether lips. When he took the tip of his finger and parted her lips, he applied pressure, and his fingers brushed her clitoris in a steady, firm motion. Inadvertently she gripped his shoulders tightly, trying to stop herself from shuddering.

Ed's eyes met Gracie's, and he held her eyes for a long moment. Careful not to linger in that hot spot for too long, he moved up to kiss her arms, fingers, and the nape of her neck before making his way to her breasts. As soon as the intensity was overbearing, he pulled back, but only for a moment. She slid her tongue inside his mouth, and they both began to grope each other passionately.

Still keeping a slow pace, Ed dug his hands deep inside Gracie's long hair. He sucked and licked her nipples until they looked like two copper nickels. She moaned as his strong hands groped her body. As he began to nibble passionately on her neck, she squealed with delight.

As the moment intensified, she wrapped her legs around Ed's waist, and they both gripped each other tightly.

"I'm getting ready to cum," he murmured. "Ahhhhh, I'm cumming."

"Me, too," Gracie crooned.

As Ed came, he whispered in her ear, "I love you, Gracie. Don't ever leave me...I love you...."

Ed and Gracie lay lovingly on their sofa, languishing after making love for hours in the comfort of their home, when they heard Tamara arrive. They both heard the keys jangling and Ed called out to his sister.

"Tamara, don't come in yet!"

They both tried to jump up and get dressed but Tamara, who wasn't fond of being told what to do, forged on and encountered a sight she never thought she'd see—her brother's big dick staring her in her face.

"Oh, my gosh!" she shrieked in horror. "What are you doing?"

"I told you not to come in!" Ed shouted.

"How rude," she continued, "and disgusting! I nap on that couch."

Tamara was appalled. She felt that they should have at least had the common courtesy not to fuck on the sofa, the same sofa that she lay on to watch her soap operas or take a quick catnap during the day. Now she'd forever remember Gracie's coochie juices and her brother's dangling dick.

Gracie stood stark naked, hands on hips—partly because she was angry, but mainly because she wanted to flaunt her new shape—and started in on Tamara.

"Don't you dare stand in my motherfucking house, talking about rude and disgusting, when your funky, non-showering, disrespectful, free-loading ass is living on our dime. Now if my husband wants to fuck me on the ceiling or on top of the television while you watch *Girlfriends*, so be it! And if you judge us again, you're gone!"

Tamara stood with her lips twisted up and her eyes tossed in the sky, totally ignoring Gracie's tantrum. Ed, who was trying his best to cover his manhood, attempted to put his pants on when Gracie snatched them away.

"Let's go and have dinner, honey!" Gracie demanded.

Gracie led Ed into their dining room and sat her husband down butt naked at the table, lit a few candles, and served him like a king. She refused to allow Tamara the satisfaction of ruining their makeup sex.

Some time after dawn Gracie heard the phone ring, but refused to answer it. She knew it had to be earlier than seven in the morning because her alarm hadn't gone off yet. Ed picked up.

"Yes, hello?" Ed asked in a gruff whisper. "Hello?"

When the caller hung up without replying, Ed couldn't go back to sleep.

"Wrong number?" Gracie asked, still half asleep.

"I guess. They didn't say anything. They just listened."

That news woke up both of them. Neither said anything further about the call, but both had separate thoughts. Gracie thought the call could have come from her brother, and Ed's insecurities resurfaced, making him believe the caller was Gracie's lover.

Finally, Ed had to hop in the shower and begin preparing for work. It was shortly after six in the morning. As the shower water rained on Ed, Gracie took the opportunity to dial George's house. He picked up on the first ring.

"George, did you just call here?" She grumbled with a deep morning voice.

"Gal, you better take that base out of your voice. I'm still your father and will go upside your head if need be."

Gracie could not believe his audacity.

"What do you want?" she snapped. Not waiting for a response, she said, "What did I tell you about calling here at odd hours? You're only to call after seven when Ed's left for work."

"How are you gettin' along with that fella?"

"How am I getting along with Ed? He's my husband!" Gracie replied, perplexed at her father's odd question.

"You gonna do him like you did that other fella?"

"Goodbye—"

"I suggest you not hang up on me if you know what's good for you—" George began a lung-rattling cough trying to catch his breath.

Gracie's mind raced quickly, trying to ingest the not-so-subtle threat. "What are you saying?"

"I'm saying that you owe me for my years of silence. You out there living in the lap of luxury, just as your mother did, and left us here to rot."

"I didn't leave! I was thrown out! How dare you twist this around!"

Gracie's voice was a strained whisper.

"No matter. These are my rules. You better listen closely, because I won't repeat myself. Too old. Either you get me the $20,000 I need to keep my house in one week, or you're going to get a knock at your door, and I promise you won't like who's on the other side."

"Are you crazy—" *Click.*

The line went dead. Gracie cradled the receiver in her arms and began trembling. If anyone had warned Gracie that her behavior years ago would ultimately cost her more than she could ever dream, she would've told that person to kiss her plump ass. Being young and living on the edge had caused a downward spiral, which ultimately culminated in a path of destruction for Gracie.

Gracie couldn't shake that memory, no matter how hard she tried. All she could do was cry and hope that she'd think of a solution to ultimately free her from her past. She dialed George back and took his bank's routing and account numbers. She told him that she wasn't making any promises but she'd do the best she could to get him the money. He, in return, told her to kiss his ass!

Thirteen

Anthony Cross

THE DOORBELL RANG, BUT I WAS HAVING A HARD TIME distinguishing reality from fantasy. I was in a deep sleep. I'd dozed off on the sofa waiting for Gracie to arrive. She was hours late. As I jumped up, I groggily made my way to the door and stubbed my toe against the coffee table.

"Ooowwww," I yelped and did a one-legged hop to the door. I flung open the door and there she stood—gorgeous, sexy, and juicy. "How did you get up here without being announced?" I asked.

"I have my ways," she replied with her hands placed cockily on her hips.

"*Mu-ah!*" I kissed her on her lips and led her inside. "You look sensational."

Gracie wore her hair pulled tightly into a neat bun; a two-piece, form-fitting skirt suit; and black heels. I had to admit, she certainly dressed her age. She never showed up in low-rise jeans, coochie cutting shorts, hooker shoes, or trampy dresses. She always looked and dressed like a lady, but in the bedroom it was a different story.

"Something smells good," she commented.

"Yes, I had my housekeeper prepare us a rack of lamb. You do eat lamb, correct?"

"Yes, I love lamb. That's Ed's favorite dish. He makes a delicious smothered lamb and won't tell anybody his secret ingredients. Not even me and I'm his wife...can you imagine that?"

Was she serious? So casually talking about her husband...I ignored her comment.

"Good. I'm glad you love lamb. Let me take a quick shower and then we'll have dinner. Make yourself at home. *Mi casa es su casa*," I joked. "I also took the liberty of renting *The Bourne Identity*. Did you see that?"

"No, no, but I don't know if I'll have time to watch the whole movie."

Immediately I grew annoyed. She was always rushing home. Her thirty-minute to one-hour stays with me were becoming infuriating. Surely she could think of a way to spend more time with me. I took another glance at Gracie and suddenly the gorgeous, sexy, and juicy figure didn't look so hot.

"I'll be out in ten minutes," I remarked, dryly.

In the shower, I contemplated my situation with a married woman. I was used to women being at my beck and call, vying for quality time with me, praying that I'd invite them to stay for dinner and a movie, and hoping that I didn't throw them out after sex. But this lady only came over to get fucked and wanted nothing more. As I lathered up my tight, fit body, I realized that I didn't need the drama. I had had enough of Mrs. Lane. I wasn't sure I even wanted her to stay for dinner.

Still lathered up, I could hear her on her cell phone.

"Baby, I love you," she said in a hushed manner. My stomach twisted up in disgust. Or was it jealousy?

Sneakily I stepped out the shower and allowed the water to continue to run, so she wouldn't be wise that I was trying to catch her. I listened intently to their little love call when I heard faint footsteps traveling across my parquet floors, only they weren't walking toward me.

"I got to go," I heard her call out.

Did I hear her correctly?

"What?" I asked. No answer.

Still lathered up, I grabbed a towel and stepped out into my living room in time to see her bolting out the front door with her cell phone clasped tightly to her ear. And then *boom*! My front door slammed.

With my towel wrapped around my waist and water dripping on my living room floor, I did a slight jog and flung open my front door. I caught a glimpse of her just as she entered the elevator.

"Where are you going?!" I yelled after her. No response. She never bothered to stop.

In a panic I ran to my room, threw on a jogging suit, and ran down the eleven flights of steps to the front lobby. I was breathing rapidly and had broken out into a sweat. As I pushed through the front door, the cold, winter air froze my body, only I didn't feel it. I was hyped off pure adrenaline. I stood outside in the blistering cold, heart beating, half dressed, and confused. I looked up and down the block, but I saw nothing. I stood there for a few minutes until I saw her Honda hybrid make a right turn onto my block, and then another right at the light. The last thing I saw were Gracie's brake lights.

"Gracie!" I called out like a maniac, but she didn't hear me. She continued on her mission. I ran back into the building.

"Is everything all right, Mr. Cross?" the overnight security guard asked. I didn't even acknowledge him.

I ran back upstairs and began to call Gracie incessantly on her cell phone. The first twenty or so times, the phone just rang. Then my calls began going straight to voicemail. I panicked. What was going on?

"Gracie, you have me worried. Is everything all right? Why did you leave so abruptly? Please, please call me when you get this." I left that and many other messages on her phone. Then waited. She never called.

Day number three and I still hadn't heard from Gracie. For some unknown reason, this situation had me stressed. My usual upbeat mood around the office had turned dark, and I began almost stalking Anika, waiting for her by the ladies' room, beating her to work, walking her to the elevator, all in an attempt to elicit information about Gracie.

"Where's your old-timer friend?"

"Again?"

"What do you mean?"

"Here you go again. What's this about?" Anika asked perceptively.

"I'm just worried about you, that's all. And I don't think you should be hanging around someone who's so much older than you."

"Nah, Gracie's cool. She's not like that. Like, she's not a bad influence. In fact, she's positive. Sort of like a mentor."

Just that little bit of information had me open. Gracie was so private that I couldn't get a bit of insight about her or her personal life. I pressed on.

"How so?" I asked.

"Well, when I came to New York, I didn't know anyone. I got mixed up with the wrong crowd and began smoking weed and drinking cocktails at all the hotspots. I was underage, but that didn't stop me from getting into all the clubs. I was going nowhere fast. Gracie told me, in a blunt manner, that I needed to get my shit together because me — and only me — was responsible for my future. I slowed down my partying and stopped using drugs altogether, enrolled in college, and started interviewing for jobs."

"What about her husband?"

"Ed? What about him?"

I needed to weigh my words carefully and make it seem that my only and main concern for bringing up Gracie was Anika.

"Is he a mentor to you as well?" I asked.

"No. I don't spend much time around him. He's awkward."

"Awkward? How so?"

"I dunno…like he's really quiet when I'm around. When he tries to join in our conversation I usually shut him down because he's so corny."

"Is that so?" My voice could hardly contain my excitement. It felt good to hear her trash Gracie's husband.

"Yeah, like you and him would never get along. You and me—we're just alike. You got a lot of style, you know how to dress, you're a corporate thug and that's what's up. Ed, on the other hand is a straight nerd."

"What does she see in him?"

"What the fuck do you see in her?!" Anika screamed, startling me.

"Huh?"

"Don't think I'm stupid. You won't stop asking about her!"

"She's my patient," I replied, calmly.

"I was hoping that the rumors that are circulating around here about you and her having sex inside the examination room wasn't true—"

"What? What rumor?"

"Samantha said she smelled sex!"

"Smelled sex?" My mind raced back to Gracie's sweet coochie. How I sucked and licked her juicy clit inside my examination room with the door slightly ajar and my nosey ass RN trying to catch us.

"Ant, please tell me that you're not sleeping with my friend." Her eyes pleaded for me to not break her heart. I wanted to confide in Anika in order to get more information about Gracie. Anika was like my sister and she was messing everything up. I decided to tell her what I knew she wanted to hear.

"I am not sleeping with your friend. I wouldn't ever cross that line with any of my patients. I'll speak with Samantha about spreading false rumors. Truthfully, I was asking about her to get to know you better. You don't have any family here and her and I are the closest thing."

"Really? You care about me..."

"You know I don't *really* give a fuck about you...but I had you going right," I replied, jokingly.

At this point, Anika had made it to her desk and was ready to hop on her cell phone and begin her morning chatter. It was barely eight o'clock. When she reached for her cell and gave me an "excuse-me" look, I had one last question I needed answered.

"Who are you calling?"

"My suga-daddy!"

"Don't be on that phone all day, because I will fire your ass!" I playfully threatened.

"Kick rocks!" she replied and gave me the finger.

Inside my office, I did my best to push Gracie to the back of my mind. From the way Anika described her situation, she was the happily married little wife, and all was good. So why was I stressing over another man's wife? Good question. Answer—I wasn't. I decided to call Dakota.

"Hey, baby girl."

"Hey, I've missed you." She stated the obvious. I'd been giving her the cold shoulder for weeks.

"I miss you, too. I've been so busy lately, but I want to see you tonight. Do you want to come over? I'll cook something and we can stay in."

"That would be nice," she squealed and then continued. "I got a surprise for you."

Was that a sexy, seductive tone I detected?

"Really? I'm usually the one giving out surprises. Give me a hint."

"No. Then it won't be a surprise."

"Just a hint," I said again, this time in a demanding tone.

"Okay. It's something I think you'll enjoy. I want to show my love for you, and also prove that I'm not the prude you think I am. I can be a freak."

Where did *that* come from? Immediately I thought she'd come over and do a striptease, which I was less than enthused about. Why did all women ultimately strive to strip for their man, as if that was the end all and be all? I mean, it was nice, but stripping had its place, preferably in a dark, crowded strip club. But if she wanted to do it, I would pretend to enjoy it.

"A freak, huh? I'll be the judge of that," I said, challenging her to come hard with her statement.

I just wasn't feeling Dakota. No matter how much I tried to get into her, I just couldn't. She was the quintessential good girl, but she just didn't do it for me. I couldn't see myself settling down with her and living happily-ever-after. I knew she was young, ambitious, intelligent, had a good family background, great morals, no kids (thanks to me), a college degree, and was pursuing her master's. She also had a nice body and nice face, but she was as dull and boring as a calculus book.

As promised, I had my housekeeper prepare a nice dinner, we talked, and then she wanted to make love. I truly wasn't in the mood, which was a first for me.

"Something's different," she whined.

"What do you mean?"

"You're not acting the same lately."

"What are you talking about?"

"At first, I thought the change in your behavior was because of my unexpected pregnancy."

"Unexpected? Well, what do you expect to happen when you have sex without any contraceptives?"

"Don't blame only me. You had a hand in my pregnancy as well."

"That's up for debate," I dryly remarked, intentionally being cruel.

"Are you saying that you doubt that you were the father?"

"I'm saying that's always a possibility. Mommy's baby, daddy's maybe."

"Anthony, how could you be so cruel?" she yelled, face flushed, lips quivering. "You know it's been only you!"

Why did I even go there? Why take cheap shots when I wasn't interested in arguing, or even being around Dakota tonight, for that matter? I was taking my frustrations about Gracie out on her, and that wasn't the right thing to do.

"Listen, you're right. I know that the baby was mine. I apologize for insulting you."

She began to calm down.

"I wouldn't cheat on you, ever."

"I know, baby."

"Is it serious?"

"Is what serious?" I asked, perplexed.

"Your new woman."

"You tell me, since you seem to know so much."

"Don't do that," she replied, shaking her head from side to side. "Don't play mind games. Just respect me enough to answer the question."

"You're being paranoid."

"Answer the question, Anthony! You owe me that much. I've given you four years of my life. I deserve a truthful answer."

"Look, you're crazy! There isn't anybody else."

For the moment Dakota seemed to let the topic go. We decided to play a game of Spades and as I was whipping her ass at the card game, she started in again just as I took her Jack of Spades with my Queen.

"Look, we're not married," she started off slowly, "and I understand that you're only a man and that you have needs. If you're seeing another woman or other women, then we can change the terms of our relationship and keep it open."

The selfish part of me took over.

"I'd kill you before I let you make love to another man!"

"Not me, silly. I could never let someone else touch me. I'm in love with you, and that's just not who I am. But what I'm trying to tell you is that if you trust me, confide in me, I'll understand. It may even bring us closer."

Maybe I'd taken one too many sips of the Patrón. Maybe her soft voice was enough to convince me my next move was the right one. Whatever the motive, I fell for her game.

We stopped playing for the moment.

"You asked for the truth, so that's just what I'm going to give you. I do have a few lady friends. I'm an unmarried, successful man, and I like to do me. I'm not ready to be married, nor am I ready to settle down and be faithful. But I promise you that if you ride this out with me, let me get all of being a bachelor out of my system, you're the one I'm going to marry. I want you to be Mrs. Cross."

Everything I'd said was true, up until the part about her being Mrs. Cross. I basically told her what she wanted to hear, or did I? I could see her holding back the hurt from her eyes, but she was doing a lousy job.

"Is there one or many?" she asked, but I thought I had already answered that. I decided to fall back a little. I didn't want to scare her into thinking I was some player, so I went with a safe answer.

"Really, there's just one other." Big mistake. I should have seen her angle.

"Do you love her?!" she shouted.

"Lower your voice. Did you not hear anything I just said?"

"What is it that you like about her?"

"Truthfully?"

"No, please lie," she sarcastically answered. Her spunk kind of turned me on.

"Well, for one thing, she knows how to treat her man."

"Go ahead. Explain yourself."

"She's uninhibited in the bedroom and allows me to explore all crevices of her body."

"So she lets you have anal sex with her?"

"All open crevices," I repeated. She'd have to decipher my words on her own.

"What else?" she asked. "Hold on for one second."

She reached inside her pocketbook, pulled out a pad and pen and began jotting down notes. I wasn't surprised. The ever studious, boring Dakota, at her best.

"She doesn't crowd me. I'm not getting a phone call five times a day at work and then again late at night to make sure nobody's here with me. She's secure in her skin and doesn't have low self-esteem." I was speaking of Gracie. "She doesn't need me to validate her. I don't have to shower her with compliments every moment, nor hold her hand in public if a hot woman is walking past. If my eyes roam, she doesn't trip."

"If she's so great, why do you want me? Why not marry her?"

"I met you first."

"No, seriously," she probed. Was she getting cocky? "Is she ugly? Is that it? Some ugly, fat bitch!"

"More beautiful than I could describe. Gorgeous face, nice boobs—nice, big, real boobs," I repeated. "A shape like a Coca-Cola bottle, and a great personality."

Gushing over Gracie only made me want her more. As I spoke, I wondered what had possessed me to say those things. Did I really feel that way about her? I barely knew her. And she was another man's wife. I watched, amused that Dakota was really taking notes. Then I began telling her what I didn't like about her. I was being selfish, cruel, mean, the whole gamut, but in my defense she was asking the questions and backing it up with how she could handle what I was dishing out.

After our meaningful conversation, Dakota became sullen and despondent. She sat on the sofa with her lips poked out like a little child. I excused myself, went into my room for privacy, and called Gracie for the umpteenth time, again going straight to voicemail. I must have drifted into a peaceful sleep because I woke up to Dakota sucking my dick.

"Whoa, whoa, be easy," I said as her teeth grazed my dick. When she did it again, I pulled her up.

"What's wrong with you? You're going too hard," I scolded. I didn't even notice that she'd been crying.

"I want to do it from behind," she claimed, almost in desperation.

"You do not," I replied in annoyance.

"Y-y-yes, I do," she stammered and it was at that moment I realized she was crying. She was like a wounded puppy—sad and pitiful. For the moment, I felt really low.

I reached for a condom and made love to Dakota, only I was thinking about Gracie. Exhausted and mentally drained, I didn't even persist when she crawled under my arm to cuddle. I was too tired to object. Moments later, the phone rang. I looked over at my caller ID and my heart began to palpitate. It was her, my baby.

Although I wanted to kick Dakota out and beg Gracie to come over, I knew that I couldn't. She'd disrespected me, and I refused to jump when she called. I had to play it cool.

"Hello," I said with a less-than-enthusiastic tone.

"Hey, baby," she purred and her voice was smooth as silk. "I'm sorry—"

"Listen, I can't talk right now."

"Then why did you pick up?" she asked, and I felt my blood pressure go up. How dare she talk slick!

"Look, I gotta go!" I said and slammed down the phone. Dakota pretended not to sense anything. I pushed her off me, turned my back to her, and dozed off into a complicated sleep.

The next morning started off superbly. After perusing the *New York Times* financial section, confirming that my stock was doing well, I dropped down and did one hundred pushups. Feeling rejuvenated, I asked Dakota to make breakfast. She was back to her old self. She made me breakfast and cleaned up the kitchen, then left for work.

I thought about how the consequences of my actions were simply surface wounds. Nothing I'd said or done was enough to put me or my lifestyle in jeopardy. I was living like a rock star. I had a plethora of beautiful women, all vying for my love and affection. Even a beautiful, married woman couldn't get enough of me. My heart had never been hurt in all my years of dating women. Again, I had gotten away with not only the insinuation that I was cheating, but actually telling Dakota that I was and could fuck around, and she'd just have to sit and bear it. And she would, as long as she thought that at the bottom of the ninth inning, she would be the last one standing at the altar with me. The routine was maniacal. I still couldn't get over how she sat there taking notes, listening to me pontificate about how good another woman looked, and how great another woman was in bed. I had all the women hooked on Dr. Cross. And even though Gracie was complicated, vague, elusive and combative—she was supposed to be. She was married and she'd never had an affair before. I was her first and that had to be confusing, wanting to be with someone other than your spouse. Her call last night, even though improper, let me know that she wanted me. And I wanted her. And that's the end of the story.

It didn't surprise me that when I fell back and stopped calling—she'd start. And that's exactly what she did. I was in my office, drinking an afternoon energy drink, when she called my private line. This line went straight to my office and bypassed Anika. When I saw her number on the caller ID, a sly grin emerged.

"Hello," I barked. My voice needed to reflect the anger I felt the past week, without any contact. The rude way she bolted from my apartment, and her blatant disrespect.

"Hey, baby," she sang.

"Don't 'hey baby' me. Where the fuck have you been? Why haven't you called? Better yet, why haven't you answered any of my calls?"

"I did call. Remember? Somebody couldn't talk."

"Don't be audacious. I'm not in the mood."

There was a long pause, and then, "Anthony, I can't keep going through this. I'm getting yelled at by you and then yelled at by Ed. I'm being pulled in two different directions and I'm losing my mind. I want to be with you because I care about you, but it seems as though I'm only pushing you away. I don't know what to do."

"All you had to do was pick up the phone. That's it. And give me an explanation of why you had to leave so quickly."

"Why? You don't know?"

"My thoughts are pure conjecture. I want you to tell me."

"Are you sure you want to know? Because once I tell you, there's no going back and I feel you might judge me." Her voice was soft and fragile. I wanted to pull her through the phone and cradle her in my arms. I had no idea what she was going to say, but I wanted her to say something. Give me anything of her, about who she is, about her past, present and future. Her silence, her need to protect her privacy, was like dangling cheese in front of a mouse. It made me chase her.

"Gracie, I'm not sure who you think I am, but I'm just a regular dude. I wouldn't judge you. It's obvious that you don't know how I feel about you."

"I know you care about me," she replied, and then exhaled. "But I won't allow myself to think that you could feel anymore than that. Ed used to feel the same way about me and then I cooked his dinner for longer than he liked and he displayed his anger with a closed fist to my right jaw. He showed me what it was to cry."

"He hits you?" I asked, incredulously. My Gracie was married to a woman beater. My stomach felt sick. I wanted to rip his fucking head off. Now everything fell into place. Always rushing off, in a panic. I thought it was because she loved him, but the underlying truth was because she didn't want to get that ass whipping he was laying on her. To think that she was risking her safety for me only made my feelings deepen. I wanted to protect her.

"I've been able to placate him for the most part, but we've got to be more discreet. When I say I have to go, please let me or else I'll have to suffer the consequences. And I'd do it…for you…but I'd rather not. Please, Anthony, work with me. I don't want to lose you."

"Then don't! You don't have to stay with him. Divorce him, and be with me."

"Anthony, it's complicated. Too complicated to discuss with you, now, at this moment."

"Gracie, he has you brainwashed. You're a victim of domestic violence and your fear is keeping you stagnated. No man should ever put his hands on a woman. Ever. Under any circumstance. I don't know how long this has been going on, but you've got to get out."

"See, you're judging me. I knew this would happen. I should have never—"

"Okay, I'm sorry baby. We don't have to discuss this if you don't want to but I want you to know that I'm here for you. Whatever you need don't hesitate to ask. If you are afraid to leave because of money—I got you."

"No, I don't need money. I have money."

"Oh, well, good, then you got *me*," I joked and we both laughed. It felt good to break the ice and also to put a smile on her face.

The subject shifted.

"I really want to see you," she stated, coyly.

"I miss you, too. Did I ever tell you about the dream I had with you down on all fours and I was eating you out from the back?"

"Did I cum…"

"Of course you did. And I ate it all up."

"I can't wait to kiss your luscious lips…" she purred.

"I rather give you kisses on your fat pussy."

Gracie and I hung up and I sat in silence for long moments. Thinking. Something inside of me wanted to step in and rescue her, like a childhood fairy tale. Her knight in shining armor. But I knew that life was more complex than that and it would be up to Gracie to get out of her situation. I only hoped that it would be sooner than later but frankly, I didn't know how long I could contain my anger, which had risen and settled in my chest. I knew that if I ever saw her with as much as a hair out of place, I'd probably risk my livelihood and freedom to break his woman-beating ass into pieces.

Fourteen

Gracie Lane

I SAT CURLED UP UNDER ED'S ARM ON OUR COUCH, listening to our neighbor, Gloria, cry her little heart out. Her husband, Jonathan, was a high-profile actor who'd gotten caught sleeping with their nanny. Their faces were splattered all over the local and national news and newspapers. She was humiliated.

"I can get past the affair," she sniffled, "but how can he say that he's in love with her? She's just a babyyyyyyy." She wailed so loud, a lung-rattled, sob that pierced my heart. All I thought about was Ed. What if Ed found out about my affair? How much pain would he be in?

"Gloria, I'm sure he's just confused at the moment. He loves you and his family. I'm sure he doesn't want to lose you. He probably—"

"He asked for a divorce yesterday. He said he wants to marry her." Her lips trembled and her fragile hands shook as she dabbed the corner of her eyes with her handkerchief. "What will I do? How can I start over? I'm 36 years old. Who'll want me…a divorcee with three small children? What will I do for money?"

She sounded so wounded and desperate. Ed intervened, "If he wants out you'll have to let him go. You're a beautiful woman and any man will be honored to have you but you must be strong for your children. I'm sure he'll take good care of you—"

"I signed a prenuptial agreement. He's worth three-hundred million and I walk away with the clothes on my back. I have nothing."

"Nothing my ass!" I piped in. "He'll have to give you 17 percent of his income to take care of your children. I know you're from Minneapolis but New York law is clear."

"They're not his..." her voice trailed off. "They're not his."

"Does he know?" My treacherous mind was racing.

"Oh, not like that," Gloria clarified. "We've raised them as our own but they're my sister's children. She and her husband died in a car accident up in Vermont when the oldest child was only four years old. My husband never legally adopted them."

The news was unsettling.

"I'm sure he would want the best. Perhaps you should sit and talk with him," Ed stated.

"Why do you think I'm here crying my eyes out? We've already discussed this in length. I have two weeks to get out, with the kids."

"That's fucked up!" I was outraged. "That piece of shit is going to trade you and his family in for the nanny?"

"Did I mention she's snow white?" Gloria remarked, dryly.

"What?" I roared. "Lionel fucking Ritchie! He's traded you in for a cracker-ass bitch!" I jumped to my feet and began walking in place.

"Gracie, calm down." Ed interjected. "Sometimes I don't know who you are when you have these outbursts."

My head swung around. "This isn't about me! Did you hear that her celebrity husband is leaving her destitute with three small children for the white nanny? Did you hear that part?"

"Yes, I did. But screaming and acting wild and obnoxious isn't going to get him to come back." Ed was calm. His legs were crossed and he was wearing his smoking robe and matching slippers with a $300 Cuban cigar dangling from his fingers. He sat there judging while luxuriating in a lifestyle I had afforded him. "She has to let him go while keeping her dignity. She signed the prenup. No one forced her hand."

We tag-teamed him.

"I signed it because I loved him! I didn't think the man I married would ever do me so dirty!" Gloria screamed.

"That's fucked up that you could sit there and take his side!" I bellowed. "She gave him the best years of her life!"

Ed conceded. "Ladies, please, I know I may sound harsh. He's completely wrong. My point was that a woman should never beg a man to stay. Let him go because he's going to go any way. Don't let him take your pride and dignity from you. If he's determined to leave don't stand in his way. Excuse me I'm going in the study to read."

I watched Ed scamper away and I rolled my eyes with disdain.

"Easy for him to say," I retorted. "If I left his sorry ass he'd be begging and pleading like there wasn't any tomorrow."

"I know that's right." Gloria attempted a faint smile.

"Now back to you. We gotta get girl power going and come up with a plan so that you don't leave empty handed."

"As I said I signed the prenup. I get nothing."

"I got that point at hello," I joked. "Now let's get passed the legal stuff. Do you have any money stashed away for rainy days that he doesn't know about?"

"He controlled all the money."

"So I guess it would be foolish for me to think that you two had a joint bank account."

"He gave me a monthly allowance to take care of all the household expenses and a little money to keep myself groomed."

"How much was that?"

"Each month he'd give me $10,000. Some months I had to stretch that."

"Cheap bastard! How much do you have in your checking account?"

"Less than $200. Yesterday, instead of a check he gave me divorce papers."

I shook my head, remembering when I was that stupid. On one hand her husband is a low-life piece of shit. That's granted. But this fool has lived with this asshole for 15 years. She should be sitting on a nest egg. How could she have lived under his thumb for so long and not outsmart him? Surely she had to realize there would be rainy days? And she wasn't the mother of any of his children. That alone was screaming divorce. I'd bet anything that Miss Doris Day was pregnant.

"I've been inside your apartment numerous times. All the expensive paintings, vases, and antiques. The certificates of authorities—are any in your name?"

She shook her head. I started to think she was going to be a lost cause.

"Jewelry. Please say that he doesn't have the crown jewels under lock and key."

Her eyes lit up.

"Well yes and no. We both have keys and are signers on the safety deposit boxes. And we also have a small, hidden safe in the apartment. We don't keep our priciest jewelry there but a couple of his expensive watches would be there. A few pairs of earrings of mine should be there."

"What about the safety deposit boxes? What's in there?"

"A host of things. Important papers, some cash, not much, and all of our jewelry."

"Important papers such as your prenuptial agreement." I was hopeful.

"No. He keeps his copy separate. Besides, his lawyer has the original."

"Okay, back to basics. You go right now and clear out any and all boxes including the one at the apartment. Can you do it without Jonathan suspecting anything?"

"He's in Belize supposedly reshooting a scene for a movie. That's why I have two weeks to get out. He said that if I leave quietly and not linger around he'll give me $50,000 startup money."

I was seething. That wasn't even 1% of the fortune he'd amassed.

"Call that motherfucker and tell him that black women don't leave any room quietly!"

We both laughed.

"Okay, first things first: Go and get all of that jewelry and whatever else he has in those boxes and bring everything here for safekeeping. I'm going to have my jeweler, Orlando, come over and hopefully he'll take all your pieces. How much do you think it's all worth, retail value?"

She tossed her eyes up in the sky as in deep thought. "I have all the appraisal records for everything. I would say close to ten million dollars over the years."

"Technically, you should only lose 20 percent of the initial cost but you'll take a bigger hit than that unloading everything at once. You can probably get 60 percent of the original purchase. Make sure you bring your appraisal papers."

Her face beamed.

"What a great plan. But couldn't I get a better deal if I go to our jeweler?"

Damn, she was a knucklehead.

"If you went to your jewelry and tried to sell back you and Jonathan's jewelry what do you think he'd do? He'd call your husband and your plan would be foiled. You have to do things on the low."

"Right, right...cool. I'm on my way now. I should be back in less than two hours." She reached up and embraced me. "Gracie, I can't thank you enough. You're like the sister I never had."

Her words touched me.

"Are you camera shy?"

"Camera shy?"

"Yes, because I hardly think six million is going to be enough for you and your three kids. Especially since you've grown accustomed to a certain lifestyle. I think we could milk another million with an on-air interview. Let's start a bidding war for your story. Barbara Walters exclusive or an US Weekly magazine spread. The press will go bananas over your version of *The Nanny Scandal*. Rich housewives everywhere, beware! Not to mention a tell-all book. I'm sure Jonathan has a few skeletons in his closet. Let them out to the highest bidder!"

She left with promises to return shortly. I was about to join Ed in the study but opted to go upstairs and luxuriate in a long bubble bath and enjoy my alone time. As I soaked I thought about my life and how I had reinvented myself but was I really living? Everything I did was on a cautionary level. I was hiding from my past. Hiding from my family. Hiding from my husband. I'd told so many lies over the years and used manipulation that I didn't know who I was. Who am I? Am I George's child? Gracie Lane? A wealthy widow? An adulterer? Or am I all the above?

I'm a woman who drives a hybrid during the day in order to keep her coworkers in the dark about the millions I have in the bank while I do my volunteer work to help sooth a guilty conscience. A woman who wears a faux brooch mixed with a million dollars worth of jewelry. A woman who loves getting fucked by strangers in dirty hallways while her attentive husband waits patiently for her to arrive. And most recently I'm a woman who has just told her histress that her non-violent husband beats her. What's wrong with me?

I loved my husband. I did. And I loved my new life. But I loved having my fun as well. I'm selfish and I want my cake and yes, I would love to eat it without having to explain the who's, what's, and why's. I wanted Anthony—the freak but not at the cost of losing Ed. But where was he going? Would he truly leave as he stated he would do if he were in Gloria's shoes? Or was that just tough talk? It's always easier when you're on the outside looking in to pass judgment.

I realized that life isn't always black and white and if I wanted all my needs fulfilled then I'd have to play the manipulation game and I'd have to play well. I was up against two-strong willed men and the last thing I wanted was to have to let anyone go. Not now…not when the fun just got started.

Fifteen

Anthony Cross

THE NIGHT WAS CLEAR AND CALM DESPITE THE SNOW storm two days ago. Gracie and I found ourselves cuddled up in a cozy bar in TriBeCa. We both felt terrific, despite any anxieties either one of us had previously about where our relationship was going or what we were both getting into. Gracie was gracious and charming this night, and she had a certain glow about her. I could swear I felt positive energy exuding from her pores. She was radiant as she drove up to *Lucas Michellini Restaurant & Bar* in a chauffer driven Mercedes Maybach. She stepped out in a full length mink coat and expensive alligator purse dangling from her arm. I was shell shocked.

"D-d-d-did someone hit lotto?" I stammered.

She smiled her dimpled smile. "I'll explain later. Let's go inside."

"Yes, you've got some explaining to do." I concurred.

Once seated, she took off her expensive frock and she was laden with huge, water-clear diamonds, sparkling and obviously real. My words came flooding back and I felt humiliated and like a fool for assuming that she'd previous wore replicas. These were definitely real.

"So, what happened to your hybrid?"

"I still have it."

"And the Mercedes..."

"Listen, I know you know my husband works for Verizon but you were being a bit presumptuous thinking you're the only one with seven or more decimal points in their bank account."

Sexy, smart *and* wealthy? Christmas was coming early this year. I listened intently trying not to show any expression on my face. Although, I was completely taken off guard.

"So your husband is really rich and Anika lied when she said he works for Verizon?"

"We have money and that's the bottom line."

"Why is everything always vague? You can't ever give a direct answer and it's annoying."

"So be annoyed. But get over it quickly. Preferably within the next couple of minutes so that we can enjoy our evening together."

"Why are you telling me now?"

"Why not?"

She was being indirect and combative like a ten year old child. I decided to fall back and see where this would take us. I'll let her play her little word and mind games—for the moment.

"What do you want from me?" I asked. "Why are you here?"

"You're gentle and tough, all wrapped up in one," Gracie commented as we sipped on the finest house wine. "You're intelligent and savvy, and I like spending time with you. All I want is some of your free time."

"You've been getting a lot of my free time. And I enjoy spending time with you as well."

I kissed her lips.

"We don't do anything except eat and fuck." She laughed, and I felt intoxicated by her presence. I wanted to give her a bear hug and take her home with me, for good. She didn't have to say it but her husband was the money man and that's why she allowed him to beat her. She's working some low-end job and he probably treats her like shit. I didn't have Maybach money at the moment but I was on my way. My five-year plan was going to afford me all the amenities that Ed had given Gracie.

I ordered the second round.

"Are you trying to get me drunk?"

"Why would I want to do that?" I laughed. "I've already had my way with you."

"You've had *some* ways, not all ways. All in due time," she replied, coyly, and my dick got hard. I pulled her hand to it so she could feel my bulge.

Gracie leaned in and we began a long, passionate kiss as we groped each other like two school kids. Just the mere fact that I was having my way with another man's wife, was an unexpected turn on for me. When her cell phone rung she gave me a stern look, put her index finger to her lips signaling me to be quiet and then picked up.

"Hey baby." Gracie's voice was jovial. "Yes, I've left your plate in the microwave…oh, for real? Yes, I totally understand…why he would say something like that…no, I'm glad that you didn't…yes, I love you too…bye."

When she closed her phone she gave me an apologetic look. I hated to admit it but I felt cheap. How many nights would I have to be quiet while she talked to her husband on the phone? Better yet, how many nights would she still have a husband?

"That was Ed…he's so funny. He said that his boss almost pushed his buttons to the point that he wanted to give him a karate chop." She laughed, hysterically.

I was deadpan silent. I mean, was I supposed to laugh? It wasn't even funny.

After our second round, she let her guard down a little. She was very flirtatious with me, as well as with the waiters. Soon our smooching subsided and I got serious, again.

"Tell me about your husband," I said. "More than what you've already told me. You've told me about his bad side, but I want to know about his better qualities. Why did you fall in love with him? Because he doesn't deserve you."

Gracie swallowed hard and then put her drink down on the table. I was looking her directly in the eye, challenging her credibility.

"When I met Ed, I felt lost. My life was spiraling into several different directions all leading to nowhere. His love and stability was what kept me focused."

At that time I didn't know that had I looked deeper into Gracie's eyes, I would have seen her love and devotion for her husband.

"And how do you feel now," I asked as I poured her the third drink.

"Well, as I've always told you, he's a good man," she started slowly. "It wasn't always like this…you know…the fights and arguments. We just began to grow apart."

"Did you try to rekindle the past? Maybe go to marriage counseling?"

"Yes, we've tried and nothing works. He just doesn't understand me and I'm so tired of trying. Everyday I'm trying to make it work but he just doesn't care. Like when I'm with you…it's like you get me. You know when to fall back and give me my space so that I don't feel overwhelmed. You know how to touch me until my whole body is numb from orgasms. You do little romantic things that make me smile—"

"He's not romantic? C'mon, I can't believe that."

"Not romantic anymore! Anymore is the operative word here."

"So why not leave? If it's so bad and you're so unhappy why don't you just go? If I didn't know any better I'd think you were feeding me lines and you and hubby are happier than ever, planning your next wedding anniversary."

"If I were so happy why would I allowed you into my life for more than one night? Huh? Why…"

"Again, you can leave. I don't want to sound pushy but I dig you. And I can see myself really getting into you and letting my feelings take control but I don't because you're married. If you're truly unhappy and have plans to get a divorce, all I'm saying is that I'm here for you. I want you. I want you all to myself. I need a strong woman by my side."

She closed her eyes and shook her head vehemently.

"It's soooo, complicated."

"What? Tell me…," I said, raising my voice out of frustration.

"You were right, about me, back at your office."

"What? What did I say?"

"About me having a kid. We do. We have a 9 year old son." She looked down into her lap and everything made sense. A young child, an abusive husband, a fortune at stake.

"Jeez, the plot thickens."

"I'm sorry I didn't tell you sooner but I didn't know that we would go farther than the bedroom. That I'd think about you every night and all during the day. Your strong hands, and cute little face." She leaned in and kissed my cheek. "I want you so bad but I don't know what to do. My hands are tied."

"No, they're not! You're husband is a loser and I'm tired of women thinking that there aren't any great men out here. Shit, I'm one of them. Leave him and find me because I want you. I want you to want me."

"If I didn't want you I wouldn't be here."

"Not like that, Gracie. Don't you want not a good man but a great man in you and your son's life?"

"He really is a great person."

"A great person?" I spat. "How did that happen?"

"You know what I meant," she said, clarifying her last remark while pouring yet another glass of the tasty, expensive wine. "He used to be a great person. Isn't that a given? Why would I have married him? I told you already about what he puts me through. Lately we've been going through marital problems and he keeps pushing me away. I'm sure he'll get it together," she said, opting, again, for the avenue of disillusionment.

"You're still his little cheerleader after he's beaten your ass and given you the cold shoulder? I don't believe this."

"I'm no one's cheerleader but he's my husband and I need to handle my marriage on my terms. That's it. Can we change the subject and enjoy our time together?"

Ignoring her plea I asked, "Is there another woman involved?"

"Of course not! We've been married for ten years and he's always been faithful," she exclaimed.

"You really believe that, don't you?" I had a look of pure shock on my face about Gracie believing she was the only one in her marriage cheating.

"I don't just believe it, I know it!"

"Okay, okay, don't bite off my head. Tell me how he keeps pushing you away."

"Well, throughout our marriage, I'm always supporting him in all his endeavors, and now I'm really feeling that he doesn't reciprocate. He gets so caught up in his life, job, and political career that he neglects my needs."

"Sexual needs?"

"Among other things," she halfheartedly replied. "I just don't want to delve into it. I could sit here and name a laundry list of things that are wrong in my marriage."

"Let me ask you a question." My voice became stern and any sign of intoxication had quickly vanished. "Do you still have sex with him?"

Gracie emphatically denied the implication. "Not at all."

Relieved, I exhaled. "How long has it been?"

"Way before I ever met you."

"Is that why you're here with me? Because you're feeling neglected at home?"

"No. It's not like that at all. When I saw you for the first time, I was captivated."

"Pah-leeze, you wanted to stab me."

Laughing, she said, "You sound like Anika with the 'pah-leeze.'"

"That girl is rubbing off on me with all her bad habits."

Suddenly our moods changed at the mere mention of Anika. An unspoken guilt loomed over both of our heads. We sat in silence for a few moments before Gracie spoke.

"What are you looking for?"

"What I've always been looking for . . . a woman like you."

"Anthony, I can't do this. I can't allow my feelings for you to escalate. I'm a married woman. You'll never respect me."

"Are you kidding me? Of course I respect you. I've looked in your eyes when you said that I'm the only one, that there's never been anyone else, and I believe that. Things happen and you can't question how or why. I'm feeling you, and that's all I care about. Gracie, can we just take one day at a time? I promise, I will never hurt you or make a promise I can't keep. Can you do me a favor, and trust me?"

"You're asking for a lot, and taking me out of my element."

"That makes me feel good."

"Why?"

"Because you're doing something for me you've never done. It makes me feel special."

"I feel guilty just being out having drinks with you. What if somebody saw us?"

"Stop worrying about what ifs and relish the moment. You only have one life and you have to do what's best for you. Remember I told you that..."

"Okay, I will."

"Last question about your marriage: Do you ever plan on leaving him or are you just saying that. Because either way I'll still be here but under different terms. If you just want it to be casual sex then I'm game. But if you see a door at the end of your tunnel and you're ready to walk through it and start a new beginning, then I'm game with that too. Don't lead me on and I won't lead you on. We're both adults."

"This is the God's honest truth. Next year my son goes to middle school. We're sending him off to Connecticut to a private boarding school. As soon as that happens I'm filing for an overdue divorce. I'll finally have my freedom."

When the check came she insisted on paying. This time I allowed her.

We sat there until Ed began calling.

"I have to get home," she said and I silenced her with a kiss.

Her lips were soft and plump, her mouth wet and experienced. She pulled back from the kiss as I got more aggressive, and she finally persuaded me to let her go home.

"I have to go...he'll be furious."

"Go to him. For now. But it won't always be like this. I won't be able to share you for much longer."

Sixteen

My Crush

IT WAS NEARLY 3 A.M.WHEN ANIKA WILLIAMS ROLLED
into her Park Slope, Brooklyn apartment after a night of partying in the
city. One of her close friends, Brandi, came stumbling in as well. They
were both drunk, drinking shots of straight Hennessey at club Roxy's in
Manhattan. Both girls were lucky to not be locked up in Central Booking.
As Anika drove Brandi's Toyota Camry over the Westside Highway toward Brooklyn, they encountered a police road block. There were several
police cars, parallel parked, and one police van to take away the perpetra-
tors. The flashing lights dazed Anika for a moment as her freedom passed
before her eyes. She remained stoic in the face of danger. Not only would
she fail the breathalyzer but Brandi had weed in her pocketbook. They
were five cars away when Anika told Brandi to pass her the weed.

"Huh? What are you talking about? You don't even smoke anymore."

"Just do it. No need for both of us to get busted. Look, I'm fucked up
right now and I'm going down. Do you want me to take you with me?"

"Nah, I don't but you my home girl and I don't want you sittin' in
Central Booking by yourself. That ain't cool. I'mma hold you down and
hold my own. Whatever happens, happens!"

Anika loved the Brooklyn "ride or die" mentality. Back home she'd
bet the ranch that any one of her friends in Burlington would have let her

go down by herself. Thankfully, she would never find out because one of the cars in the lineup decided to break the chain and bolt out of the line, full speed, down the highway. Every cop in the area jumped in their cars and on their radios and gave chase. Both girls exhaled.

Inside, Anika kicked off her boots and climbed disappointedly into her bed fully dressed. She lay across looking up into the ceiling while Brandi pulled a chair close to the window and lit up her weed.

"Open the window," Anika snapped. "I don't want to smell that shit."

"What the fuck do you think I'm sitting over here for? And what's the matter with you all of a sudden? You still shook about the cops?"

"No, I'm stressing over this kid."

"Who?" Brandi asked, and blew the smoke out the window.

"My boss."

"Your boss?! Doctor Cross?"

"Hell yeah."

"Y'all fucked?"

"No."

"Stop lying, bitch! I know you."

"I said no, for real for real. It's like he doesn't want to get to know me. All he does is sleep around with skeezers who only want him for his money."

"What's wrong with that?" Brandi laughed.

"It's not like that for me with Ant. I don't care about how much money he has. He makes me feel smart. We have fun together. And he's sexy...damn, I wish I was his girl."

"So tell him."

"Like he doesn't already know."

"Say's who? He's not a mind reader. I say go for yours..." Brandi inhaled her blunt, blew it out and then collapsed into the chair and stared off into space.

"Can I tell you something strange?"

"Please don't blow my high."

"Bitch, please. I don't know how to say this but I think Anthony and Gracie fucked."

"Old Gracie? Your friend?"

They both giggled.

"She's not old like that. But, yeah...what do you think I should do?"

"That's fucked up if she did fuck him when her ass is married. I don't know…if she did you can't fuck behind her. That's nasty."

"I know."

"So, scratch that. Me telling you to go for yours."

"But he said ain't nothing go down."

"Oh, you asked him?"

"Yeah, there was a rumor at work."

"Why didn't you say that in the beginning? If he said that he didn't hit it then believe him. You two are so cool he wouldn't lie to you."

"You think?"

"Hell, yeah."

Anika held onto the hope that she actually had a chance with Anthony and fell into a deep, peaceful, sleep.

Seventeen

Gracie Lane

THE STILLNESS OF MY HOME WAS SOMETHING I longed for. Ever since my sister-in-law moved in, my home had turned chaotic. Between Ed riding my ass every second of the day, and Tamara running up bills as if my first name was Trump and my last name was Rockefeller, a once very calm woman was turning into a nervous wreck. Not to mention, George's threat. If he did plan on going through with it, I had two days to wire $20,000 to him. I felt like my life had been plagued by defeat, and I refused to allow something as trivial as money to hinder my new life as I now knew it.

I sat in my kitchen at my granite island and contemplated dialing Chase Bank to do a wire transfer. My heart pounded and felt like it had risen to my throat as I contemplated my decision. If I wired the money I didn't want George to think that there was more where that came from. I didn't want to be extorted for the rest of my life. On the flip side, if I didn't give the money then as George would say, my ass was grass! I realized that I needed to pay the bounty George put over my head.

I decided to call my brother just to confirm if George's threat was real.

"Benjamin, what is George talking about?" I asked. I had planned to start off slow, but my brother jumped right to the point.

"He said that if you don't help him save his house, he's gonna put those people on you."

"What makes him think that I got that kind of money?"

"He don't care. All he cares about is himself."

I was enraged. I thought about how many times George neglected me and treated me like shit, only to cater to his boys, the same boys that left him destitute and on the verge of homelessness.

"All he thinks about is himself? This, from the son in whose mouth he put a silver spoon, and practically held your hand through life. He gave you everything, and you pissed it away!"

"He may have helped me out here and there, but I ain't the one who put him in this situation. Andre did. And he's long gone, and now I gotta put up with the bullshit."

"You got to put up with the bullshit, or do I have to put up with it? Look, Benjamin, I don't have any money. My husband and I are broke."

"Well, then, you gonna have a problem."

Like father, like son, I thought. My brother could give less than a fuck about me. He was probably the one who put it in the old man's head to go after me, by any means necessary.

"Can't you talk to him?" I pleaded.

"Nope. He stubborn," Benjamin exclaimed. "But if I were you, I wouldn't challenge him on this one. He's as serious as a terrorist and will execute his plan."

"You sound as if you're cosigning his trifling behavior."

"I'm just stating the facts and trying to help you. So, are you gonna pay?"

"Do I have a choice?"

"No."

"I'm thinking about borrowing the money from my husband's retirement fund and a little from our credit cards. That'll leave us in debt for years...but I guess I don't have a choice."

"Well maybe you could get an extra job or something or do some overtime to make ends meet."

"What a thoughtful suggestion," I stated, sarcastically.

"To make it easier on you, I can come down and pick up the money, if you'd like."

His slick maneuvering made my skin crawl.

"To make it easier on me, huh? You'd smoke up my husband's hard-earned money in a half day!"

"Listen, you better watch your mouth. I don't do drugs!"

"I'm going to say this once. Don't you ever call my motherfucking house again if you know what's good for you, because I'll have my husband come down there and personally whip your scrawny, crack-smoking ass!"

I slammed down the telephone in an attempt to release some portion of my anger. It didn't work.

I ended my conversation with my brother, more aggravated and annoyed than I initially was. My brother had put fear in my heart and I had to stop and pray before I totally lost control. I needed to breathe, make a decision, and then stand by that. My future depended on me being strong. I knew that my foundation was built on something as fragile and thin as a cracker, so I had to tread with caution.

Reluctantly, I called back the bank and did a direct wire transfer into George's bank account with the routing numbers he'd previously given me. I tried to convince myself that everything was going to be all right. But for the first time since my life-altering incident, I was afraid. After the money was transferred from my checking account, I felt somewhat relived.

With my feet propped up on several pillows, a cool rag resting on my forehead, and jazz music playing in the background, I tried to relax after a long, stressful day. When my phone rang, I contemplated not answering, but the number was private. Suddenly, I became curious.

"Yes, hello?" I breathed into the phone. I was exasperated.

"I'mma kill you, bitch," a woman yelled.

"Excuse me?" I asked. I sat up in bed, one hand holding my chest for support.

"Why can't you leave him alone?" the woman on the other end screamed like she was crazy.

"I think you got the wrong number."

"Listen, tramp, you called my man Anthony the other night, and I'm not going to tell you again that you better leave him alone!"

I weighed my options before settling on a response.

"He told me he had someone he was in love with, but I thought I'd give it a shot anyway. I don't want any trouble, and I won't call him again. But there isn't a need to threaten me. Nothing happened."

"If he told you he had someone, why didn't you back off?"

"Look," My tone was stern and unwavering, "I just said I wouldn't call again. So back the fuck off before I fuck your man!"

The woman took a moment to process the threat before hanging up in my ear.

Just when I thought my day couldn't get any worse, Ed came home.

These past few weeks all he wanted to do was make love. Although his lovemaking skills were superb, there wasn't anything like the new, juicy dick the good doctor gave. Ed, whose dick was much bigger than Anthony's, wasn't as experimental as the doctor. The first night me and Anthony fucked, he took charge and fucked the shit out of me. Ed, on the other hand, always wanted to make soft, sensual love. And that, after ten years of marriage, was dull.

"Hey, baby," he crooned all up in my face.

"Hey, Ed."

He sat at the edge of the bed and began massaging my feet.

"Elana cooked dinner. I've made a plate for you and put it in the microwave," I stated.

"You're not going to eat with me?"

"I'm not hungry."

As he continued to massage my feet, his hands began to crawl up my thigh until he reached my pussy. Immediately I swatted his hand away.

"Do you not see me lying here with a rag on my head? Isn't that a tell-tale sign that I have a fucking headache?" I roared.

"Watch your tone, Gracie."

Now his tone infuriated me. He always wanted to have the last word.

"No, you watch your motherfucking tone. This is my house," I said, throwing my weight around. "And I can speak in any tone I want!"

"Okay, okay, I see someone wants to be left alone," he replied, now a lot less assertive. "I'll be downstairs until you cool off."

I rolled my eyes. I'd just about had it with any and all bullshit. I sat here fuming about how I'd had just shelled out twenty-grand to save a man I despised and my gut told me he'd be back. Then I thought about that silly bitch calling my phone, and my husband whose insecurities were smothering me. As if all that wasn't bad enough, Tamara came home. I could hear her loud, cheery voice booming downstairs. Dishes clanked together as Tamara prepared herself a plate of food, a plate of free food.

Crash! Another dish hit the floor, and I hit the roof. I leaped to my feet and ran downstairs to confirm my suspicions. Just as I suspected, Tamara had broken another dish. As I looked on the floor at my expensive china, I could have sworn I detected a look of satisfaction plastered on Tamara's smug face. All along, my sixth sense told me that Tamara was deliberately sabotaging me and Ed. For some reason, today solidified any and all ill thoughts.

"Something funny?" I glared at Tamara.

"No," she replied dismissively and turned her back toward me.

"Since when did you become so clumsy?" I pursued.

"Excuse me?"

"You heard me. I've been to plenty of your apartments on many occasions, and I never recalled a time when you've broken any dishes, spilled so many drinks, had outbursts of hot flashes, leaving numerous windows gapping open, and the list goes on and on. But what I want to know is, if your new traits are only reserved for when you're living for free under my roof?"

"This is my brother's home, too" she sassily replied and cut her eyes at me in annoyance.

"Your brother's house, huh?" I had had enough. I grabbed Tamara by the back of her head and pushed her forward, tossing her into the kitchen chair and table. Tamara fell forward and began screaming for Ed. I pounced on her and began swinging heavy fists into her back before I was pulled off by my husband.

"Get the fuck out before I drag you out!" I yelled.

"I'm not going anywhere," Tamara challenged.

"You're getting the fuck out of here tonight! I promise you that!"

Tamara began to sob, trying to play on her brother's sympathy.

"Didn't I tell you to keep it down because Gracie was upstairs nursing a headache?" Ed asked.

"I said I was sorry. Look, I'll pay for the plate," she replied, trying to bargain for the roof over her head.

"Get. The. Fuck. Out. Bitch!" I said through clenched teeth, looking over at Ed and daring him to say otherwise. Tamara was also looking at Ed to intervene.

Ed knew when to throw in the towel. Sensing that our marriage had gone into left field out of nowhere, he didn't want to aggravate the situation. I had tolerated enough.

"Tamara, don't look for me to bail you out of this one. You did this to yourself. You've done nothing but disrespect our home and my wife, and we've had enough. You have got to go. Tonight."

"But where will I go?"

"Go to Aunt Linda's, or Cousin Maggie's."

"But I don't like them," she whined.

"Then don't stay long. You should have enough money saved by now to get your own place."

For the first time in her life, Tamara was being shut down by her brother. Quietly she went upstairs and packed her things, vowing to get me back one day in the very near future.

I told her to take a number....

Eighteen

Anthony Cross

"YOU THINK I'M STUPID? THAT'S YOUR NEW BITCH!"

Dakota leaped from the bed, naked, in a rage after I'd tried to discreetly make plans with Gracie for tomorrow. I thought she was asleep, but evidently she wasn't. Ever since I told her about this "new woman", Dakota's behavior had changed drastically. She was now acting crazy and deranged, and it was unnerving. The old Dakota wouldn't dare scream at me, use profanity, or act erratic.

"What are you talking about? That was Chris and I'm making plans to play pool later. You're just being paranoid."

"Don't lie to me, because I swear to God I will bitch slap you right here and right now!"

Did I just hear her correctly? My petite, five-foot-two-inch, good, innocent girl was going to resort to violence because she was so in love with her man? The thought turned me on. I was drawn to her immediately. I grabbed her roughly and began to kiss her lips passionately.

"Baby girl, I'm not seeing anyone," I murmured through each kiss. Dakota started to respond and I grew more excited. She started pulling at my pajamas aggressively, and I ripped them off just as quickly.

We fell onto the bed, groping each other like undersexed college kids. Our foreplay was rushed and intense. I wrapped my hands in her massive weave and pulled myself inside her tunnel with force. She was moist and warm as I eagerly mounted her. Dakota moaned in pleasure. She wrapped her legs tightly around my waist and we moved together. My tongue explored the inside of her ear, the nape of her neck, and then sucked each finger, savoring the taste like they were expensive delicacies.

As our passion increased, so did my stamina. I stroked harder and faster, sweat dripping down the small of my back.

"I want you to cum all over me," Dakota whispered. Not wanting to break my stride, I ignored her request. Dakota tightened her vaginal muscles, then pushed my shoulders back. I hoisted myself back on my legs and watched Dakota massage her ripe breasts. My penis was brick hard as I grabbed it and jerked off all over her chest. Cum squirted everywhere! The "new" Dakota squealed from enjoyment. As she rubbed the hot liquid all over her erect nipples, breasts, and stomach, she stared at me intently, enjoying the moment.

When did my baby become such a freak? I wondered. What other things didn't I know about Ms. Dakota? When she spread her legs open even wider, I knew she wanted more.

We engaged in lovemaking two more times that night, and I fell out of bed at a quarter after eight the next morning. I had to move my ass to make it into the office before nine. Dakota had forgotten about my call to Gracie while she was channeling all her attention into pleasuring me. I was glad, because I couldn't take another minute of arguing.

My affair with Gracie had begun to heat up. She was vivacious, caring, and secretive. But slowly, as time went by, she began to open up—just a little. She told me that she was originally from Philadelphia, and then her family moved to Burlington, New Jersey, hence the Jersey twang in her voice. She also told me that she had two brothers, and that was it. When I probed for more information about her parents, she shut down.

I don't know if it was a gift or a curse, but her time with me was always limited. Those stolen moments had me longing to hold her all night, but I wondered if I actually had that luxury whether I would have appreciated it, or if I would have clumped Gracie with the rest of the women I went through so quickly. For now, I decided not to analyze my relationship with Gracie, and just to continue to have a good time.

On this night, instead of my housekeeper preparing dinner, I decided to do it myself. I was a good cook, but rarely did it for anyone.

Gracie came in wearing a conservative, winter white dress with the matching shoes. Although, I didn't want to spend another evening in my apartment, Gracie refused to have a real date outdoors. I wanted to take her ice skating at Rockefeller Center but she said she was in the mood for a cozy dinner and a game, preferably, Backgammon. Her paranoia was the third person in our relationship.

Her tickling my back was indicative that she wanted to fuck. She'd only been inside my apartment for ten minutes and she was ready—I wasn't. I removed her hands from my body and put distance between us. I don't think she realized that she was more to me than a booty call. I wanted to get to know her.

"Are we going to play Backgammon?"

"Sure. That would be nice. Where is it? I'll get it," she said and hopped up. I pointed her toward the hallway closet and when she opened it she saw a basket full of clean laundry that I hadn't had time to put away. "What's this?"

"A headache," I laughed.

"There isn't a reason why you should live like this." She pulled the basket out and then reached up for the iron and then pulled out the ironing board. "As soon as the clothes come out of the dryer you should iron them and put them away. That way everything will always be neat and organized. And if you can't do it then ask one of your girlfriends to do it for you."

Gracie put up the iron in the living room and prepared herself to iron my clothes.

"You don't have to do that."

"I never said that I did."

"I'm not used to this...I mean, woman usually did nice things for me like cook; but never has anyone taken time out to iron my clothes."

"Anyone can whip up a dish. If you want to know if someone truly loves you see if she'll iron your clothes or clean up your bathroom."

Was she indirectly saying she loved me? I didn't want to play myself or challenge her at the moment. I watched as she ironed all my dress shirts, sheets, jeans and folded everything into neat piles.

"Get up and go put those away," Gracie ordered once all my jeans were ironed.

"Yes, Ma'am," I said and did a one-hand salute.

It took her almost an hour to iron all my clothes and we had a nice conversation really talking about nothing.

"What's your favorite song?" I asked.

"Umm, let's see…I have a lot. But my favorite song at the moment is *Father in You* by Mary J. Blige."

"Really? I don't think I've heard that one. Why do you like it?"

"It's just a song." She shrugged off my question. "Are you ready to play the game? I'll have to leave soon and go pick up my son and then go to the market."

"Couldn't Ed do that?" She gave me a smirk. "I'm just asking…"

We played Backgammon and of course I won. She was gracious about losing though and I couldn't help but have a little fun rubbing her face in my victory.

"I'm unstoppable!" I bragged.

"Wait until next time. Next time I'll win."

"Wishful thinking…You aren't hungry?"

"My appetite is shot," she explained. "I don't know why."

Concerned, I decided to probe. "What's going on? Is it home or work?"

She hesitated for a moment. "It's a little bit of both," she finally said.

I poured us both glasses of wine. We were sitting on my sofa in front of my huge plasma TV. I popped in a *Dave Chappelle Show* DVD but kept it on mute, since Gracie seemed as if she wanted to talk. She put her wine glass down and curled up on my lap. As her head lay in my lap, I began massaging her scalp and her eyes drifted closed.

"I've been going through so much these past couple of weeks," she said. "Ed won't allow me to do anything but go to work and come home. If I'm not home, he's calling my cell phone all day. He doesn't trust me."

"Why would he not trust you? I thought you said you'd never done anything like this before."

"That's why he doesn't trust me. If your wife has had the same routine for over a decade, and then all of a sudden things change, what would be your initial reaction?"

"I see what you're saying."

"You don't understand, Anthony. His family has done nothing but put strains on our marriage, and I can't take it anymore. Do you know that his sister and I had a full-on brawl the other night? I mean, I'm damn near 40 years old, and I'm out here tussling like a school kid in the yard."

"Who won?" I joked.

"Yo, son, you know I handled mines," she said in a gangsta-like voice. We both laughed, but I knew that wasn't enough to cheer her up.

"Is she still there?"

"No, she's gone, finally."

"So your husband has been on your back, and your sister-in-law has been making your life miserable. You've handled one situation, and I'm sure the other one will work out on its own."

"I know."

"Anything else?"

"A little trouble back home that I hope I straightened out once and for all."

"Is everyone all right?"

"They're fine," she replied in an attempt to end it there, but I took it one step further.

"Are you not close with your family? You never mention them, only Ed's relatives."

"Is it that obvious?"

"Not that obvious, but I'm quite perceptive."

"I had an estranged relationship with my family for years. I don't *hate* them, but there's no love there, if that makes any sense."

"I guess you have your reasons, but family is the most important thing to me. I can't even imagine being estranged from my parents."

"My situation is not for you to imagine."

"You're right," I said and realized that until I knew the whole story, it was wrong on my part to lay claim that I could never be on bad terms with my family. Obviously something deep had gone on, and in time she'd open up. "What are you doing on Saturday?" I asked, changing the subject.

"I'm not sure yet. Why?"

"I wanted to know if you wanted to come with me and meet my parents. My dad is cooking dinner and he asked did I have a special lady I wanted to bring."

Her face couldn't hide her shock.

"Ummm, how nice. What a sweet gesture...let me sort out my plans and get back with you."

"I figured you'd say that."

"How did you know what I'd say before you asked the question?"

"Nothing. Forget it. Listen, what about the holidays. What are your plans—Thanksgiving—Christmas."

"What about them?" She pretended to be clueless.

"How will we see each other? I don't want to spend the holidays alone and since things aren't working out for you at home I just figured you'd want to spend them with me. We could cook for Thanksgiving or go to my parents. On Christmas maybe exchange a few gifts...I don't know. I haven't put much thought into it."

"Obviously. Anthony I'm married. Must I keep reminding you of that fact?"

"I know that!" I snapped, and startled her. "And you're also someone who within the next year will be filing for a divorce. Why wait until next year to start our lives together. You could at least do the holidays with me. He gets you every other day thereafter." I was sulking like a child trying to get my way.

"Why are you always complaining? Why can't you just enjoy what we have? All I'm asking is that you be patient until I tell Ed I want a divorce."

"When?!"

"I don't know!"

"There isn't a need to travel at warp speed!"

"Well I'm not getting any younger."

"You'll always be younger than me," Gracie stated and rolled her eyes.

"You're being so selfish and cavalier regarding my feelings."

She thought for a moment. "What about my daughter?"

"What daughter?"

"I have a child, remember?" Gracie threw her hands up in surrender as if she'd been talking to a wall all this time.

"Clearly, I do. I remember you saying that you had a son!"

"What, are you crazy?"

"I know what I'd heard! You just said earlier that you had to leave early to pick up your son!"

"Why would I say I had a son when I don't!"

"That's what I'm asking you!"

We were in a shouting match and neither one of us wanted to back down.

"Okay, maybe I said son...Perhaps I was being guarded with my daughter's identity but you're acting as if I intentally lied to you and I resent that."

She began gathering up her coat and I panicked.

"Look, I'm sorry if I came across that way. It took me by surprise when you said daughter when I already had in my mind how it would be to meet your son. I apologize for making you feel slighted or disrespected. It's the holiday season and I'm under a little stress with bills and the office. Please, don't go," I said and gently took her coat from her arms and tossed it back over the couch.

Gracie began to relax.

"Can you do me a favor," she asked.

"I don't see why you think I should," I said, smiling.

"Can we not talk about me and my situation? I just want to enjoy you and our time together. We have so little time together…"

I nodded my head and smiled, slightly.

"What's this about bills and the office? Why didn't you tell me? You're always asking about me and my life and I'm so selfish that I hardly ever ask about you."

"It's nothing really too pressing. I'm just trying to pay off my student loans while maintaining my practice and lifestyle."

"You're having money trouble?"

"I mean not like that. I'm not getting kicked out on my ass or anything. It's just that in March it'll make two-years my practice has been opened and the first two years of any business are always tough. I do have a slew of patients but my overhead is crazy. Not to mention that my mortgage on this apartment is obscene and I still owe over two-hundred grand in student loans."

Any other woman would have never heard this information. I'm Dr. Anthony Cross, New York's most eligible bachelor. For some reason I felt comfortable with Gracie and wanted to just be who I really am and not put on any fronts.

"How much exactly do you owe?"

I tossed my head in the sky trying to remember the amount on my last statement. "I think its $240,000. Why?"

"I'll pay half."

"Excuse me?"

"You heard me." When she smiled I knew she wasn't kidding.

"What…why…how?"

"Don't worry about all of that. Just know that I'll help you. I want to help you. I want you to know that I'm in this for just as long as you are and I'm sorry that my situation has put you through any stress. I'll go with you next Saturday to meet your parents. That is if you still want me to."

"Yes, of course I want you to come. But I can't take the money."

"Don't be silly."

"Gracie I'm serious. I'm a man and I can't take another man's money!

In five years I'm going to be straight."

"I know baby," she said and cupped my face, "I believe in you. You've accomplished more at your age than most. You make me so proud of you."

I blushed.

"And you won't be taking my husband's money. The money...it's mine to give."

I was floored. Gracie had more sides to her than an octagon. She was so mysterious, secretive yet so vibrant. Just as much as she drove me crazy; she intrigued me. Of course her response opened the flood gates for more questioning.

"You're worth enough money that you could write me out a check for over one-hundred thousand dollars without speaking to your financial advisor?"

"Seems so."

"How? Your parents are wealthy? Was your money inherited?"

"Anthony, please not now...I don't have too much time here and I want to enjoy you. Maybe, take a little stress off the both of us."

I knew what she needed.

I walked slowly to my bedroom, with Gracie right on my heels. She stood back and let me undress her. I unbuttoned her shirt and let it cascade to the floor. Next I unzipped her skirt and she stepped out of it. There she stood with her hands covering her breasts, as sexy as any man could ever want a woman to be. She seemed bashful, yet alluring, and I could tell she was playing a role.

My large dick bulged through my jeans, and I hadn't even touched her. Her sexual prowess was intoxicating. She sashayed over and stood on her tiptoes to kiss me. I leaned over and met her lips, and we began to kiss passionately. Her soft tongue expertly maneuvered inside my mouth and left me wanting to have sex all night. I pulled her in closer, pressed my pelvis up against her pussy, and began to rock while I gently cupped both breasts and playfully licked her areolas. She moaned her pleasure, leaned her head back, and seemed to get lost in the moment. I picked her up, walked over to my bed, and gently laid her down. As she lay looking up at me, I began to undress.

I looked her directly in her eyes. They were talking nasty to me. Layer by layer, I took off each piece of my clothing and tossed it to the ground. When I was completely naked, my ripe dick stood at attention. I stuck my finger in her pussy and felt her wetness. I grabbed her pedicured feet and began to lovingly suck each toe. I knew she could tell this was going to be a lovemaking session, because I was sure the intensity of the moment showed on my face.

My warm, moist tongue sucked each toe as she lay back and enjoyed the moment. I took my time as I made my way to her inner thigh and then to her clitoris. Expertly I performed cunnilingus in a controlled manner. Twenty minutes later, I was still eating her delicious pussy. Her smell had me hooked. I could stay down there forever. She rocked her hips in a sensual method, and had to literally bite down on her hand to keep from screaming out. As her legs trembled, it turned me on. She was making little love sounds, as if she was enjoying it just as much as I was.

When the feeling got too intense, she reached down and gripped my silk sheets as strong waves of pleasure came pouring out of her like a waterfall. I pleasured her most sensitive area, then traced her erogenous zones with my tongue. Her body was hot and moist as I tantalized and tickled her most sensitive areas, making her feel a host of new sensations.

Finally I grabbed a condom and positioned myself to enter her.

"I'm just going to give you a little bit," I whispered in her ear. "I promise."

She lay passively as I applied pressure. I felt as if I was dominating her body as my pleasure intensified. She wrapped her legs around my waist, our limbs entwined, and we began to make love. Each deep stroke opened her resisting walls. I gritted my teeth as I broke through.

I prolonged my climax because I wanted her to have multiple orgasms, and I was still maneuvering her through erotic positions. We made love until we didn't have any bodily juices left to excrete. Soon Gracie told me she had to go home.

"You hungry yet?" I asked.

"No. But I'll take a plate home with me."

"You sure?"

"Yes. I want to taste your cooking."

"That's why I made it, so you can see that I can throw down in the kitchen. You were supposed to eat it here with me."

"I know, baby. Thank you . . . next time. In fact, next I'll cook for you. I'll bring the groceries and cook you something I'm sure you'd like. Would you like that?"

"Yes, I would."

I walked Gracie to the kitchen so she could make herself a plate of food, only she didn't make just one plate. Immediately pangs of jealousy shot through my body.

"Who's the second plate for?"

"Oh, I'm sorry. Am I taking too much? Did you want leftovers?"

"No, it's not that, but you're not going to eat both plates, are you? I would hope that you're not disrespecting me and taking a plate home to eat with your husband." My insecurities were back.

"Come on now, that's not fair. I could never do such a thing. I was thinking about my little girl. Is that all right?"

"Of course it is," I said, relieved and feeling dumb. "Not a problem. I just hope you like it."

As she fixed her plates, I began asking more questions.

"How did you and Ed meet?"

"It was a long time ago," she said, and then stared up at the ceiling, looking aloof. "I was in love with the idea of being in love."

"Was he your first love? The first man you really fell in love with. Not puppy love. The real thing?"

"Who remembers?"

"You don't remember what he had to do to get you to walk down the aisle?"

"He sold me a dream, and I fell for it," she replied sourly.

"If you had to do it all over again, would you?"

"I don't know. I've been so confused lately."

"So what type of men do you go after? What do you like other than handsome, successful men like me? Is your husband a good-looking guy, by a woman's standard?"

Jeez, do I sound insecure? Am I prying too much? I wondered.

"How does my husband look? Is that your question?"

"Well, not like that. I'm trying to get to know you better. His looks are inconsequential."

"I guess I'm attracted to more sexy than good looking, but there has to be a mixture of both."

"Do all your men look alike, have similar characteristics?"

"All my men? What are you suggesting?"

"No, not like that. I'm just saying—"

"What?" she challenged and I could tell I'd annoyed her.

"I'm wondering if someone saw me, whether they'd say I was your type."

"Fuck what other people would say. This is about you and me."

"You're right . . ." I replied, letting my words trail off. It was time to end that conversation before I dug an even deeper grave of embarrassment.

"Baby, I gotta go." She planted a nice, wet kiss on my lips. "Thank you for the food. And before I forget," she reached inside her purse and pulled out her checkbook.

"Gracie, please, this isn't necessary." My plea was weak at best.

She kept writing.

"I'll leave the top blank. One-hundred and twenty-thousand. That should do it. I'll see you next week, Saturday?"

I slapped her on her ass.

"Don't play. You better get your ass back over here way before then."

"Anthony," she looked over her shoulder, "I'm trying. Can you see that...I am trying...to make it work. Please just work with me."

"I know baby, I will."

I stared at Gracie's check for hours. What type of woman drops a hundred grand on someone she just met? What do I mean to her? Where is this relationship going? And if Ed isn't the bread winner why isn't she divorcing his ass? Maybe he'll stand to take a lot of her money and it wasn't only about her daughter. Gracie confiding in me had only left me more confused.

Nineteen

Gracie Lane

I WAS RUNNING APPROXIMATELY FIFTEEN MINUTES late after leaving Anthony's house. I had made up an imaginary volunteer job at New York Presbyterian Hospital to garner more time away from home, but I should have been home by now. And on the dot, Ed began calling.

"I'll be home in a few minutes," I said, slightly aggravated by his stalker-like ways. "I'm about to get off the highway as we speak."

"Okay, honey. Look, we should take it easy tonight. Elana had to leave early and left a note on the refrigerator that she wasn't able to prepare dinner. How about I order us Chinese takeout or pizza? Would you like that?"

"Ummm, I got us something already. I'll see you soon. Love you."

"Love you, too."

The cold winter air inside the unheated underground garage froze my cheeks before I entered the elevator and made it up to our house. Ed made a comment when I went to give him a kiss.

"You're frozen."

"I know, baby. Just from that short distance, too. It seems as though the temperature dropped from earlier this morning."

"It did," Ed said as he helped me take off my coat and noticed the bag of food in my hand. "Where did you get this?" he asked.

"Anika stopped by and bought us a couple of plates. Wasn't that nice?" Ed grunted. "Maybe we should test it for poison."

Ed didn't like Anika. He couldn't understand why she was always hanging around me. He hated that she came over and borrowed money, wore my clothes, ate up all our food, and washed and dried all her clothes as if we owned and operated a laundry service. The nerve when his sister, Tamara, did the same thing.

Ed set the table as I took off my clothes and came back downstairs in my pajamas for dinner.

"This looks great," he commented as he took a look at the T-bone steak, mixed vegetables, and sweet potato. "Since when does Anika cook like this?"

"You'd know if you allowed yourself to get to know her better."

He flicked a fork full of vegetables at me and we both laughed at his silliness.

I thought about how great of a catch Anthony was. He was successful, he could fuck, he cooked, he was handsome, he had brains, and the list went on. But he wasn't Ed.

Later that night, before we went to bed, Ed stepped out the shower, naked, and asked, "Babe, am I getting fat?"

I laughed. "You mean those love handles?"

"You see them too, right? No matter how hard I work on them in the gym, they just won't go away."

"Edward Lane, what is wrong with you?" I asked. "You have a perfect body."

He stood there for a moment, dripping wet, staring at me. Then he cracked a small smile.

"You still think I got a perfect body?"

"Did you hear me complaining?"

"Well, no, but I just wanted to be sure. I don't want you leaving me for no body-building jock."

I cocked my head back and laughed.

"We're gonna be old and gray, swaying on rocking chairs, before you'll get rid of me."

"'Til the end?" Ed asked and kissed me full on my lips.

"'Til the end, baby. I wouldn't have it any other way."

T.G.I.F. was all I could keep repeating in my head. Tomorrow I'd promised to meet with Anthony and his parents although that really wasn't my scene. Luckily I had my fingers crossed when I committed. I sat back and thought about how George had never even called to bid me a thank you for the $20,000 I'd dumped into his account to save his sorry ass. George and his gang of sons were the most fallible, stubborn men I'd ever met, and I was sure that if God didn't grant me immunity for my sins, then I'd meet them in Hell.

Today I was working a double shift and wouldn't get off until eleven PM. I didn't come in all week but the supervisor called and said they were short staffed and asked did I mind. It was just nearing 3:00 P.M. and I still had another whole shift left before I could go home and relax for the weekend. I had a facial and massage scheduled on Lexington Avenue this Sunday afternoon, and I was looking forward to that. A day of pampering myself was always enjoyable.

At this hour, my job was bursting with noise. All of the consumers — the name the workers used for the mentally challenged residents — were back from school, and all of my coworkers were busy finishing up their duties for the day. Skipper, my Brad Pitt look-alike coworker had arrived to work earlier than normal. He wasn't due to come in until the 4:00 P.M. shift. When he saw me, he grabbed me by my hands and hustled me into one of the empty rooms.

"Sexy, I need you," he said and began groping on my hips and ass. My adrenaline began pumping at the prospect of getting caught.

So this explains his early arrival, I thought. I had been having an affair at work with Skipper for over a year. Although he was a white boy, he packed a nice package. We'd have hot, sneaky sex in the most peculiar places around our job, from out back near the woods, to the basement where they stored the food, to the laundry room. None of our coworkers had ever caught on to our affair.

Keeping a fuck buddy at work was the smartest thing I could have ever done. Ed was none the wiser to my liaison. I had always made it home on time, and the affair with Skipper never spilled over into the outside world. It was strictly confined to our workplace.

Just as I began to slide up my skirt to give him access, Jessica yelled for me to come into the foyer.

"Gracie, could you come here for a moment?"

"Okay," I yelled out, "In a moment."

"Skipper, stay and wait until I come back. Keep it hot for me, baby."

I did a slight trot down the steps to where Jessica stood with her hands perched on her hips.

"Come with me inside my office," Jessica directed.

I walked behind my supervisor, and when I entered the office, Jessica closed the door to give us privacy.

"Did you ever get that situation straightened out with your social security card?" Jessica asked.

"No, no, but most likely it has to do with my wallet being stolen. I have a fraud alert filed with all the credit bureaus. This must have to do with my identity being stolen."

"Well I don't know how or what you're going to do to straighten this out, but the IRS called today. They said that you and another person named Gracie Ferguson are filing their taxes under the same social security number. Here's a number that they want you to contact them at."

My heart dropped into the pit of my stomach after hearing that bit of news.

"Human Resources called back," Jessica continued, "and we're going to have to lay you off until you get this situation straightened out. At this point, you don't exist."

"What?! Jessica, no! This is my life. This is what keeps me from going insane," I pleaded.

"You're not even getting paid for this. Why are you so upset?"

"I'm benefiting in my own way. Look, it's personal. You obviously wouldn't understand."

Jessica stared at me awkwardly. "This wasn't my decision. Do you think I want to be short staffed? Today will be your last day until we get a letter from the IRS clearing you as the authentic Gracie. Vanessa has agreed to cover your second shift. You can't work the second shift tonight."

I sat there, shell-shocked. Why was everything crumbling around me? What did they know? Were those people getting closer? Is it over for me? I realized that I was being paranoid. If they were coming there wouldn't be any warnings.

"Okay, I'll get this whole matter straightened out, and hopefully I'll be back to work next week," I replied with false bravado.

I hoped Jessica couldn't see the fear in my eyes as I slowly got up from my chair. Never taking the time to tell Skipper that I was leaving, I just grabbed my keys and coat, and bolted out the doors without looking back.

On the ride home from Long Island, I felt sick. The IRS and Human Resources were both after me. Things were moving too quickly. I had to think of a way to slow down everything. I knew I had until Monday morning to think of something before I called the government. I decided not to tell Ed about the layoff. I'd just look for another fulfilling volunteer job and use the excuse that I no longer wanted to travel the distance to Long Island.

Instead, I called Anthony on his private line at work and told him that I'd been laid off. He couldn't understand why I was upset when it was "only" volunteer work.

"Because I'm giving back to the community..."

"Oh, I see. Well, I'm sorry about your situation. Anything I can do to help just let me know. In fact, if you'd like to put in a few hours around here we could certainly use the help."

I thought about it for a moment.

"That's a really nice offer but it's not the same. I was putting in ten hours days helping adults who couldn't bathe or feed themselves. I helped them get dressed in the mornings and fed them dinner at night. They needed me. They depended on me and it made me feel as if I mattered and was making a difference in someone's life. Working for a plastic surgeon whose patients were vain, snobby whores—"

"Weren't you just in here a couple months back?"

"Exactly. Your patients are vain, snobby whores!"

We both laughed.

"I understand. I'll call around and see if anyone in a more "worthy" practice is looking for someone as caring as you. Just note that I'm only calling female practitioners!"

I didn't tell Anthony the true story only that due to office politics, they were phasing out their volunteer department. He was so sympathetic that he told me to go to his place, and he'd call security in his building so I could get in and relax until he arrived. As I drove there, I poured out my little heart. He gave me all of his attention, telling Anika to hold his calls. I sobbed like a baby as I told him my fears. I couldn't understand why it was so easy to talk to Anthony. Maybe it was his smooth voice, or maybe it was that I didn't care if he judged me. Although I didn't tell him anything incriminating because I trusted no one, I did tell him bits and pieces of my past, and it was somewhat cathartic.

"They're looking for me..." I cried.

"Who baby? Who's looking for you?"

"These crazy people...they hate me...they hate me..."

"Are you in danger? Huh? Is someone trying to harm you?"

"It wasn't my fault...If I could take it back I would...but I can't..."

"Baby, what do you want me to do? Tell me how I can make it better." His voice was shaky as I detected panic in his voice. I got my composure together.

"No, I'll be all right. I'll explain when I see you. I love you," I said out of habit when I'm in a crisis. I didn't know what made me say it but it was too late to take it back. I didn't mean it and I hoped Anthony realized I'd only said it under duress and because I was feeling vulnerable. He never voiced his feelings and I was happy.

I was inside Anthony's apartment for less than half an hour before there was a knock on the door. Hesitant to open it because I wasn't expecting anyone, nor did I live there, all types of thoughts went through my mind when I heard the head of security, Bruce, call out to me. I recognized his voice and opened the door. The aroma hit me first—a variety of smells, from food to flowers. Several delivery men and women came hustling into the apartment. Anthony had sent a huge flower arrangement of lilies,

long-stemmed roses, violets, and orchids with a card that said: SORRY BUT I
HAVE TO WORK LATE. I LOVE YOU, TOO. A.C.

So much for thinking that he didn't catch the *love you* thing. He also
sent a gourmet dish of steamed lobster, vegetables, and a tossed salad.
Finally, there was a masseuse equipped with her own massage table and
oils. For the next hour I was treated like a queen, and my stress was dis-
solved for the moment.

After a brief nap in Anthony's apartment, I had to leave. I'd only come
to get a quickie. I called Anthony at work to thank him, but he was in
surgery, so I left him a thank-you message on his cell phone. Before leaving I wrote out a note, sprayed it with my perfume, and signed it with a
kiss.

On my way home, I ignored a call from Vanessa who was undoubtedly
being nosy, and called Anika instead.

"Hey, girl," I said.

"What's up?"

"Don't say anything, but I lost my job today."

"What? How can a volunteer lose her job? Those motherfuckers
weren't paying you. Pah-leeze I wish someone would try to fire my ass
when technically I'm not really hired. I'd tell them to shove—"

"Anika!" I had to stop her because she would have gone on for hours
making threats.

"What happened?"

"Please, just let me vent."

"Oh, my bad. Why they let you go?"

"My past. Need I say more?"

"Are those peoples close?"

"No, it's not anything like that. There's a mishap with my social security number and I was flagged."

She exhaled. "Damn, Gracie, what's Ed gonna say?"

"You know I can't tell him."

"I know. Well, if there's anything I can do, let me know. You know I
got your back."

"Yes, I know," I replied. "Listen, I'm on my way home. I'll call you
tonight."

"Gracie—"

"Yes?"

"I know this is a bad time and all with you losing your job. But as I said they weren't paying you anyway. But I wanted to know if I could borrow $2000 dollars to catch up on some credit card bills."

"Sure, that's not a problem. Do you want to come over and pick up a check?"

"Ummm, could you put it into my account as you did before?"

"Done. And you don't have to borrow it. Consider it an early holiday gift."

"Thanks Gracie."

I was minutes away from home, and reality began to sink in again.

I told Ed that I was going to the Metropolitan Museum of Art to have an interview in hopes of securing another volunteer job. Ed, who worked 40 hour weeks at Verizon, was just happy that I was using my free time productively. Unbeknownst to him, I was using my free time to help facilitate my affair.

I arrived at Anthony's early enough to make breakfast. I scrambled us both an egg white omelet with peppers and mushrooms and then we climbed back into his bed for a quick fuck. When I went to take a shower before preparing to leave for his parent's home, I glanced in the mirror and noticed that Anthony had left a hickey in the middle of my back. *Kinky*, I thought. And I loved it. As I lathered my body, I replayed our sex session and wondered if Anthony could be more to me than just a fuck buddy. He'd begun to show signs of wanting more from me other than sex. We spoke on the phone, having long, meaningful conversations. He loved to do romantic things for me, and kept making references to me leaving my husband. No, Anthony had definitely moved from fuck buddy to histress. *And what was a histress?* I thought. It was a long-term, secondary relationship. He was the opposite of a mistress. Yes, he was my histress.

Fully dressed, I met Anthony at his dining room table, where he was drinking a mid-afternoon coffee. He'd poured me a cup.

I blurted, "Can we talk?"

Anthony looked up with fear in his eyes.

"Sure, what's up?"

I grabbed my coffee cup and began to sip the rich, hot liquid. "I know I'm not an open book and I'm sure that can be tiresome. But I've put up a wall around myself for legitimate reasons."

"Of course you have. But I also know that I have to earn your trust, and I hope that I've done that."

I shook my head yes. "I've been awful to you…" My eyes began to well up with tears.

"Shhh, baby, what's wrong. Why the tears?"

I spewed, "I'm so confused lately. I don't know what I'm doing anymore. I don't want to hurt Ed because he's a good man. And I don't want to hurt you, either. I know that I'm in a precarious situation and everything won't end amicably." I was sobbing uncontrollably.

Anthony raced over and grabbed me into a tight embrace. His strong arms felt comforting as I clutched his forearms.

"You know it's over, don't you. With your husband and marriage and you're afraid. You're afraid that you may trade in your husband for me and that I may turn out to be your worst fear. Is that it? Is that why you've been so emotional lately?"

"I want to leave him. I want to leave him now but I just don't know how. We both said we were in it forever but my forever has turned out to be ten years. What kind of wife am I?"

When did I become such an actress? My lips were trembling and for a split second I actually believed my words. Truth be told, I was scared shitless about my situation. When I walked out my apartment building today I was looking over my shoulders. A man came up to me in a trench coat and asked did I have a light for his cigarette and I thought my world as I've known it for two decades was about to come to an end. And then, finally, I thought about Ed. I loved him more than I could ever express and I didn't want him getting caught up in my past. I even considered packing up and fleeing. Leaving everything and everyone behind. I'd done it once and I was sure that I could do it again so why was I still here? The heat was definitely around the corner…

"Gracie, don't beat yourself up. You're human with feelings and emotions and values. Don't be this martyr for married women. People get divorced everyday. I'm sure your daughter will understand and your husband will get over it. Let me ask you a question…"

"Anything."

"Am I the reason you're getting a divorce?"

"Truthfully?"

"Please."

"No."

"No?"

"No."

I don't know if my response was what Anthony wanted to hear because he didn't probe any further. The awkward moment was tempered by his home phone ringing.

"Yes, hello…hey Dad…is she all right? Okay, no problem…we'll reschedule…tell Mom I love her."

Anthony hung up and turned to me.

"Is everything okay?"

"Yes. That was my father. My mother isn't feeling well today so he thought it best to cancel our plans. I really wanted them to meet you."

"They'll be other times."

"So, what are we going to do today? Any suggestions? And please don't say that we should get back in bed!"

"Okay, you didn't have to say it like that. As if that's all we do," I said, giggling. "Hey I got an idea. Why don't we go to the shooting range and let off some steam."

"Shooting range?"

"It'll be fun."

"I've never handled a gun before."

"Stop being a pussy. You're only shooting at targets. We can go to the shooting range in Bayridge, Brooklyn. You in?"

"Yes, I'm in. Sounds like a plan."

"I'll need to borrow one of your shirts. This shirt is too dressy," I said, looking down at my silk blouse that I'd planned on wearing to his parents.

Anthony drove us to the firing range and we stopped along the way and got frozen smoothies from Baskin & Robbins. I hated to admit it but I was having a superb time really doing nothing more than hanging out.

When we arrived we both showed our licenses and were told that we could pick out our guns. I chose a 9mm glock and Anthony chose what I considered to be a more personal gun—the revolver. I paid for us to both have four rounds of cartridges and we were given our eye and ear protective gear and after we holstered our guns, we proceeded to our target areas. At Bay Ridge Gun Club only paper targets at 25 ft distances were allowed. But in other shooting ranges, such as Upstate New York, Mexico and a few other areas have outdoor ranges where the targets are more interesting such as bottles, cans, or scarecrows.

I took aim at my target and began to shoot. I must admit I was a little rusty. I hadn't been at a range in over two years. Once I pulled the trigger, my heart began palpitating. I can't quite explain the adrenaline rush or sense of satisfaction I got but I would almost compare it to the anticipation you get when slowly climbing a rollercoaster track and then the drop your stomach feels when you plunge down. It was euphoric.

Anthony went through his four rounds quickly and didn't want to re-up his cartridges.

"What's the matter?"

"I don't like this."

"You don't? Why not? I'm having fun."

"It's not stimulating. This isn't my idea of a fun day with my girl. You and I aren't having any contact and my mind isn't doing much but focusing on a stupid piece of paper and trying to see how close I can land a few bullets. I can't believe you like this sport."

"No big deal. This just isn't for you. I'm sorry I wasted your time. I was being selfish."

"Any time I get to spend with you isn't wasted. And believe me I'm most grateful. But I'd preferred to do something like I suggested before like ice skating in Rockefeller Center. We can hold hands. We can fall together...you know, couple stuff."

Anthony was really trying to make this work. On impulse I said, "Hey, I got a better idea. Why don't we go away? Let me plan a trip for just the two of us. We'll go right after the New Year. Would you like that?"

"Hell, yeah, I'd like that."

"So that's what it is then...."

Twenty

Anthony Cross

"YOU'VE GOT TO BE KIDDING ME, MAN," I SAID INTO the phone to Chris. He had just gotten a check in the mail with his return on his initial investment.

"This guy was a pure genius," he bragged. "A financial guru who could triple my net worth in two years, if I played my cards right."

"I hate you right now!" I could have kicked myself for not getting in on that investment. Although I was doing all right for myself with the help of Gracie and a few new customers this month, it would have felt great to have earned a return on an investment. My common sense told me that before I invested anything, I still needed to check out Gabriel.

"Haters never win," he replied in his normal soft voice. "Would you believe he has something else in the pipeline. A bigger deal. Same margin for return."

"He wants me to get in on this one?" I asked, skeptically.

"You can't get in on this one."

"Not even with the lowest investment? The twenty-grand?"

"Nope. He's got all the investors needed. If he and I weren't cool, I wouldn't have gotten in either."

"So why are you calling me bragging and shit." I was pissed. Although

I really didn't want in at this moment, I was upset that I wasn't afforded the opportunity. And it seemed that Chris only called to gloat.

"I'm not fucking bragging. I'm calling my man to share my good news thinking that he would be happy for a brother. But, again, it's always only about you!" Click.

Chris hung up in my ear. I shrugged it off. He was too emotional.

Two hours later he called me back.

"Gabriel has invited us down to his art gallery on some top secret shit. You down or what?"

"I was on my way out to the gym. Why does he want me to come along and what's this about?"

"Again, I just said it's some top secret shit. Either you're in or out. No one's going to beg you. He said he's sending his car and driver to pick us up."

"Okay, sounds like a plan. I'll be ready in an hour."

Gabriel's chauffer-driven Bentley arrived, and again I had to admit that Gabriel impressed me. Sitting in the backseat and smoking on a cigar was Chris. I openly smiled as I got in.

"Hey, man, I didn't know you smoked cigars."

"No, you didn't know I could *afford* cigars…the good shit," he replied, and I detected tension.

"So did Gabriel tell you why he wanted me to come?"

"You're only invited because of me. Don't think that he's really checking for you like that. You are here on the strength of me!"

"Gabriel is your man. If you're taking my relationship with your friend personally, don't. It's purely business, and you need to get over any and all hang-ups you may have."

I needed to set Chris straight. He was acting as if I owed him something.

"C'mon, you my man, and Gabriel is my man," Chris said, now pretending as if he wasn't just giving me attitude. "I don't have anything but love for both you guys, and I want all of us to get that money. I'm only going today to purchase some art from him. He bought a few pieces from

Christie's two years ago, and sold them at a sixty percent profit."

"Really?"

"Yes, really. This time next year, my bank account will look like yours."

"You wish," I said and punched him in his arm. "So this is about art?"

"Yes. He has some good pieces and thought you'd be interested."

Only I wasn't. He should have said this before he dragged me out the house. I decided to keep quiet. There wasn't anything I could do now.

In the middle of our male bonding, my phone rang and it was Dakota. I wasn't in the mood for her at the moment but I knew if I didn't pick up, she'd call and leave a million messages.

"Hey, baby," she said after I picked up.

"Hey, Dee. I have to be in surgery in ten minutes. I'll call you as soon as I'm done."

"Promise?"

"Without my fingers crossed?" I joked. "Never."

"Okay, love you."

"Okay."

"Say it," she whined. "Say you love me."

I really needed to cut her loose so she could find someone that was deserving of her, because I truly felt little to nothing for her. Everything she did and said irked my nerves. She could barely hold my attention for more than a few moments, and those moments usually involved sex.

"Goodbye, Dee." *Click.*

We pulled up in front of an upscale art gallery on Long Island. It was huge and took up most of the block. Gabriel's black Maserati was parked in his RESERVED spot. I started to seriously feel poor compared to this guy's wealth. I started to wrestle with the idea of investing a small portion of money. Gracie had paid a chunk of my debt but I didn't want to start mooching off of her as I'm sure her husband was. If I invested my money wisely perhaps I could repay her even though she said the money was a gift. I think I'd feel better with myself as a man if I were able to give Gracie back her money.

Maybe I would invest a conservative amount of money if I wanted to play with the big boys.

Several people were in the gallery, admiring the art. I crept up behind a woman who was staring intently at something that looked very abstract. She was an ordinary looking white woman with a black girl's shape. That StairMaster was every white girl's dream. Finally they, too, had a butt and thighs.

"What do you think about the painting?" I asked her out of curiosity.

"Which one?"

"Ahhh, this one." I pointed to a picture of a house and grass.

"It's a post-impressionist piece—*Restaurant de la Sirene at Asnieres* by Vincent Van Gogh."

"Van Gogh, huh? Personally, I prefer Monet," I lied and then switched the subject so as not to make it too obvious that I was a novice art observer. "My friend Gabriel owns this place."

For once, I used another man's credentials to impress a lady, instead of my own.

"I've seen him around here, but I've never been afforded the opportunity to meet him. Do you think you could introduce me to him? I'd love to discuss art with him."

I looked at this small-framed, assertive woman going for hers. She looked to be around 25 years old and was possibly looking for a husband, but not just any husband: a successful husband. I admired her for knowing how to play the game. You want to meet successful men, then go to the right places. I told Anika that all the time. She always ran out to the nightclubs thinking she was going to find something worth marrying there. All that was there were a bunch of wannabe rappers, wannabe record producers, wannabe drug hustlers, and wannabe single men who were married.

"I'll see what I can do," I responded as Chris called me into the back to have our business meeting.

Gabriel had a huge office. There were several paintings on canvases and propped up against the walls. He was sitting behind a massive mahogany desk with an oversized leather chair. His Breitling watch glistened, peeking out from the sleeve of his cufflinked shirt.

I shook his hand.

"Man, thank you for inviting me here today. This place is really impressive."

"Don't mention it. I'm glad you could come down."

"I want to hear about these paintings," Chris said, taking the focus off me and putting it on himself.

"I'm going to auction off three paintings from my collection at Sotheby's and Christie's next week. I bought them for a handsome price a couple years ago and will sell them for a nicer price. I'm willing to sell them to you for my asking price, minus the fee that the auction houses will take. So it's a win-win for everyone."

"Well, how much are they worth, and how much do they cost?"

Gabriel tossed Chris a book with Post-It notes marking three pages. Chris flipped through the pages and saw the three paintings with descriptions. Then Gabriel walked us over to three paintings.

"This one will go on the market for $250,000," Gabriel said, pointing to the first painting. "This one for $285,000, and finally the last one will go for $320,000."

"Are you sure these will sell for those prices?" Chris asked.

"No."

"No?"

"Correct. It's an auction. They will sell much higher, to the highest bidder. Those prices are what I'll take from you, but I could potentially sell for much more."

"So why would you make this direct sell and not try to get the maximum amount?" I asked. I was curious. It seemed risky.

As Gabriel educated us on the art world, he turned over paintings and showed us their certificates of authenticity. I gained a new respect for something I knew virtually nothing about. Art was like fine wine. You purchased it, held it, let it marinate, and then sold it at a profit. Easy. Some paintings you had to hold longer than others, but all were worth the investment in the end. During the time you held the painting, you placed it on your wall and discussed it at dinner parties.

By the time Gabriel was done talking, I had bought *View From The Artist's Window at Eragny* by Camille Pissarro for $280,000. I almost had to pry it out of Chris's hands. He didn't even have all the liquid to purchase it, but he didn't want me to have it, which only made me want it more.

When the deal was done I knew I'd fucked up. I used all of the money

Gracie had given me and also most of my liquid I had in the bank. Although I felt there was a light at the end of my tunnel with the potential profit I'd make at an auction, I hoped I hadn't made a grave mistake. This deal seemed less risky than the investment deal Gabriel had spoken about prior to today. These paintings were authentic and Gabriel had the certificate of authenticity to prove he was the rightful owner and Christie's had a picture of each painting which was exactly what I was staring at.

After the art deals were done, Gabriel went into detail about his next business adventure. He explained that he owned 1.2 million shares of Microsoft stock that he had accumulated over two decades, and that he was now optioning those shares at $85.00 per share. Chris quickly told him that he was in for 5000 shares. Where the hell was Chris getting all the liquid to keep investing? I decided to intervene on behalf of my friend as a precautionary measure.

"Chris, why don't you have Gabriel send over the prospectus and have your lawyer review the documents before you proceeded?"

Instantly, I realized that I ruffled a few feathers.

"I assure you that I have nothing to hide," Gabriel remarked dryly.

"Ant, I know how to handle mines. You just worry about yours. I got this. I've been doing deals with Gabriel before you came around."

"So be it," I said, relenting.

"So be it."

In the car, I called my baby.

"Gracie, I miss you!"

Twenty-One

Secrets

CHRISTOPHER WILKENS WANTED MONEY SO BADLY that he thought he could almost do the unthinkable to get it. No one knew this but right before he'd met Gabriel he actually thought about robbing a bank. He had the plan down to the last minute detail along with his alibi. He hated the fact that he owned a co-op in Brooklyn and Anthony owned a condominium on the Upper Eastside. That he had to bail out criminals and Anthony had a distinguished career as a plastic surgeon. Most importantly he hated that it was hard to get women because they all thought he was gay and living on the down low.

"What's going on with your friend, Anthony?" Gabriel asked.

The two men were in Gabriel's plush home in the Hamptons out on Long Island. The two men drove up for the weekend at Gabriel's request. He wanted to show Chris the location for a new hotel that he was going to build once he got together all the investors.

"What do you mean?"

"I thought you said that he had a lot of money."

"He does."

"And he doesn't want to invest any of it?"

"Didn't I say that I didn't want you letting him in on any deals until

I've made a good chunk of money?"

"Why? I thought he was your friend."

"He is but you wouldn't understand our friendship. Ever since I've known him I've always had to stand in his shadow. He grew up in a two parent home; my dad was a deadbeat who never came around. I had to study twice as hard in school to get Cs; he got As without even breaking a sweat. Then to add insult to injury he announced when we were in high school that he was going to medical school!"

"And?"

"Don't you hear me? He never wanted to be a doctor. That was my dream! He'd said he was going to be a lawyer so he wouldn't be a cliché and follow in his dad's footsteps. I wanted to follow in his dad's footsteps. I wanted his dad to be my dad!"

Gabriel looked at the pathetic man who he figured had hit a low point in his life. Or maybe he'd gone and totally lost his mind from all the drugs he was doing. Gabriel had provided the grade-A quality of pure, uncut cocaine that Chris was sucking down like a Hoover vacuum cleaner.

"You can't be serious."

"But I—" sniff, sniff, "am serious. I fucking can't—" sniff, sniff, sniff, "stand him."

"I understand," Gabriel empathized. "And you said that Kevin and Lance wouldn't have any money to invest. Is that right?"

"Those two are freeloaders. They definitely don't have any investment money. Kevin is living off his wife and Lance ain't shit!" He summed up his two friends in two sentences.

"So are you ready for this big deal I got going? I told you that I wouldn't let just anyone in on this but I want you to be able to compete with Anthony. I want you to be able to throw your weight around and make him live in your shadow for once."

"That's what the fuck I'm talking about!"

Gabriel walked slowly over to Chris and put his hands on his shoulders and began to massage. "Just relax and take it easy..."

Chris swatted him away and continued to do his line of the expensive powdery white substance. Gabriel was unrelenting. He watched as Chris fell into his own zone and collapsed back into the plush sofa, eyes closed, while surfing on his own high. He began tapping his feet and snapping his fingers while singing a song Gabriel didn't know. Slowly, Gabriel touched his face. Groggily, Chris' eyes opened lazily. He wasn't sure if he'd really felt the touch or if he was imagining it. As Chris' eyes opened to their full potential they were shocked to see Gabriel's paper-thin lips approaching at warp speed ready to plant a wet kiss on his lips. Chris went nuts.

"What the fuck are you doing man?!"

"I thought you and I were cool?"

"We are but not like that! I'm not fucking gay!"

"Okay, okay, calm down. It's not a big deal."

"If you ever pull that fag shit again, I will fucking kill you!" Chris reached into his oversized jeans and pulled out a large gun and flashed it in front of Gabriel to prove he meant business. As a licensed bail bonds-man, Chris had a gun permit and wouldn't hesitate to use it; on anyone. "I'm no queer alright. I'm just a regular black man trying to get that paper and you're going to help me! Do I make myself clear?"

"Crystal."

Twenty-Two

Gracie Lane

ED WAS BEGINNING TO BECOME A PAIN IN MY ASS, I thought. Every day and night, he was screaming about something or another. "You're not spending enough time at home," or "You don't do anything with me." Well, how was I supposed to want to do anything with him, when he was complaining all the time? His nagging was running me out of the house. Some nights I planned on going home, but then I thought about Ed's constant bickering and detoured right to doctor good dick's house.

I didn't understand Ed's problem. I micro-managed our housekeeper and kept a clean house, did the laundry and most times went food shopping, made love to him when he wanted to make love, and still he wasn't satisfied. He wasn't approachable anymore, so I kept my distance.

This was the first time I had an affair with someone and took the chance of staying out the entire night. But I wasn't sloppy about the situation. I told Ed ahead of time that I was going to drive with Anika to her hometown, and that we'd be staying overnight. He hit the roof, and said he didn't give a damn about Anika or her hometown, and that I'd better bring my ass home!

I refused. When I awoke the next morning at Anthony's, I was scared to death. But then I convinced myself that Ed really didn't know anything. He only *suspected* something, and that was a huge difference. I wished that he would just relax and let all this blow over. If he allowed me to get whatever fantasies I had in my system out, then we could live the rest of our lives together monogamously. Sometimes I just wanted to leave for a while, and tell Ed to wait for me, I'd soon come back.

When I went home the next day, Ed was seething. I tried explaining that we had gotten drunk and neither one of us were able to drive back impaired. Ed was belligerent as his voice rose to levels I'd never heard before. He was irate. Had I looked deeper into his eyes I would have saw he was masking his pain. I realized that my husband could very well think I was fucking around all day. But could he prove it? For all I knew he was running up in some chick half my age.

"Ed, you're going to have to trust me. If I say that I'm out with friends then that's what it is."

"Who are you?"

"What?"

"I don't even know you anymore! You're not the woman I married ten years ago. You've changed…"

"I've changed? I've changed," I asked, perplexedly. "You're the one who's gotten all insecure on me! You used to walk around here with a swagger now all you do is nag and complain like a little bitch!"

"Fuck you!" he bellowed and I was temporarily dazed. I can't recall ever hearing him curse at me. Ever. I was insulted.

"No, motherfuck you! You piece of shit. Get the fuck out my house," I roared.

"I'm not going anywhere! You want me out—put me out!" I guess he got his swagger back.

"Since you won't leave—I will."

The next day I went home and tried again. To me, it was like training a dog. I walked through the door and Ed was silent and solemn. I thought he was trying to make me feel guilty or something, but instead he gave me an ultimatum.

"If you ever disrespect me, our marriage, or this household again by staying out the entire night, I will divorce you. There won't be any discussion, no mediation, no marriage counseling—just an old fashioned, no-nonsense divorce."

From that moment, I put things back in the proper perspective and began acting the doting wife once again. Ed didn't have to ask for a cold beer, because I'd already placed one in his hand. He didn't have to wonder about dinner, because it was prepared, hot, and waiting when he arrived home. His threat was exactly what I needed. It took me a couple weeks to sneak off to see Anthony again, and now *he* was furious.

"You can't just walk out of our relationship without provocation," he screamed. "Where have you been? I've been going crazy!"

"I went home and after spending those two nights with you, Ed started yelling. He even threatened divorce."

I took off my jacket and slipped off my shoes.

"You sound as if you're surprised. What did you think he'd do? Perhaps run you a hot bath to wash my scent off of you. Maybe, purchase you a douche to wash my semen out of you!"

Anthony was being facetious.

"Is that really necessary?"

"When you come in here talking crazy it is."

I exhaled. "I really hadn't thought ahead that far. I didn't know how Ed would react because I felt that knowing and suspecting were two different things. And I was so consumed in my own pleasure that I never stopped to think about Ed's pain."

"Whoa, let's not make this into a *'poor Ed'* story. What about me? And my pain?"

"I'm doing the best I can," I exclaimed. Anthony stared at me intently.

"Do you love me?" he asked.

"Of course I do," I said without hesitation.

"Well I love you, too. I'm in love with you and I know that you're not in love with your husband. I can tell by the way you touch me and make love to me. It started out as just sex for the both of us, but we both know that it's way beyond that now. I want you to leave him. Leave him and marry me."

Anthony's words were so sincere that I got lost in the moment.

He continued. "We could be a power couple!"

I hated when people said that. Ignoring his last remark I began telling him what he wanted to hear.

"I do want a divorce, but I don't know how to tell him. I can not hurt Ed. I just can't." My eyes began to well up. "But I don't want to lose you."

"You won't lose me, baby," he soothed. "But Ed has got to go."

Twenty-Three

Anthony Cross

CHRIS AND I TOOK A CAB OVER TO THE WAVERLY INN to grab something to eat. I was in love with their banana shakes and chicken pot pie. And every now and then, you could get a glimpse of a celebrity. On those nights, it was tough getting into the semi-private restaurant.

Once we got to the restaurant, we laughed together and caught up on each other's lives. The prospect of new money entering our hands had us both giddy. I was stoked about the painting I'd purchased, Gracie's impending divorce and my practice and Chris was excited about his investments, and new outlook on life.

Chris really looked better lately. The tell-tale signs of a coke user weren't as apparent. The bags of stress around his eyes from work and gambling were gone. He looked like a new man on the verge of owning the world. I confided in him about my feelings for Gracie. I spoke of her with a great deal of respect and adulation and Chris gave it to me raw.

"How could you respect a woman who would leave her husband for you?" His dark eyebrows furled together forming one line and made me feel a little uneasy. "You're always falling fast for a pretty woman, but that never lasts. Pretty women are your Achilles' heel, but then you dump them and move on to the next. What's so different about Gracie?"

"She's everything I've always looked for. She doesn't like drama. She has a nonchalant attitude that I admire. She's funny, strong, and whenever she hears some of the problems other women put me through, she says she'd never behave like that."

"That's easy for her to say, because she's not your wife. At the moment, she's another man's headache. Do you know how stressed her husband must be right now? I can't even imagine all the shit you got her doing up in your place. Imagine if she were married to you. You could never trust her. A ho don't change her stripes for no one! Don't let her innocent demeanor fool you. You're too smart for that."

"It's not an act. I know acts. Dakota—act! The girl from the gym—act! Gracie is the real thing. She jeopardizes so much just to be with me and that should never be taken for granted. She's not even having sex with her husband and before you say it I know for a fact that she's not lying."

"Did you get smacked with the "dumb" stick because you sound dumb as hell right now? I know her husband is dicking that down. There's no way she's laying next to him 24/7 and not be hitting that. From what you tell me she's a superstar…"

"That she is…" I retorted. Thoughts of my baby dancing in my head.

"And the way she throws it right back and takes dick from the back like no other is amazing but you don't—"

"Excuse me?"

"What?" Chris asked.

"How do you know how she throws it back or takes it from the back?"

"You told me."

"No…I never did."

"Shit, well then I got her mixed up with one of my jump offs."

"You wish you had someone like Gracie."

Chris shook his head.

"What?" I asked.

"She's playing you like how we play bitches and you can't see it. I bet I can run down her whole game because it's something that we've both done on the regular. I thought game recognized game!"

"I'm telling you I got this."

"Just tell me if I'm right," he urged.

"All right, proceed."

"Okay, I bet it started out with you both knowing it was going to be a one night stand—"

"I told you—"

"Let me finish and don't interrupt. You both knew what it was when you took her home to fuck. You knew that she was married and neither one of you thought that you'd want to take it farther but you didn't realize there'd be chemistry. Maybe you like how she slung her pussy and she must have liked, well, you know what I mean. There was chemistry…at this point she's loving the danger of the affair but she's smart enough not to play you too close. She wants to be just nice enough to you that you allow her to get dick when she wants it but not too nice whereas it looks like she wants more. So for awhile when she came over she'd make it clear it was only about sex. Maybe in the beginning she'd verbally display this. But as time went on she did it with her actions. Like she'd never stay much longer after sex. Cuddling was out of the question. Just hit it and break the fuck out.

"Then she realizes that it's no longer casual. You start putting demands on her because your ego is kicking in and your mind is playing trick on you. You start to think you really have feelings for this broad. Your girlie ways come out and you start saying shit like, 'fuck him stay here with me.' 'Leave that nigga.' 'You don't ever spend any time with me.' Your mind is asking you what does he have that you don't and you begin to make more demands on her so now she has to resort to plan B. She's getting a divorce. Let me guess—it's complicated. Am I right? She can't do it because of the kids?"

My face was stone as my gut twisted into knots. I wanted to punch Chris in his big, block head.

"Nah, it's not even like that." That was the most I could muster up.

"Well either she's used the kid or money excuse but I know she's used one of them."

"I just said it's not like that."

"Then why do you have that sour expression on your face?"

I looked at Chris and needed him to feel where I was at this moment in my life and how much I felt as though I'd grown, mentally.

"Listen, man. Remember when we were in college and all we wanted to fuck were the girls with the big asses?"

"Yeah, so?"

"And all we'd say was that when we got married, our wife needed to have long, soft hair because we didn't want any nappy-headed rug rats running around."

"Yeah, I still feel like that. You know I love me a Puerto Rican girl."

I shook my head.

"See, I've been taking an introspective look at who I am. How I really am and what type of man I want to be. I've realized that I'm too judgmental and childish. Life is too short to be judging a person about their past. I don't care who she fucked before me, what color her skin is, how long her hair is—all I care about is that she loves me and that I love her."

"I hear you, but a person's past is what defines their future."

"I don't buy that. Not anymore. Not after meeting Gracie."

Chris began gawking at me. "You're delusional."

"I don't know why I even bother to sway your opinion. You make me so mad I want to punch something."

"Boo hoo, alright. Cry me a river."

"Keep it up and I'mma whip your ass in here."

"I got goose bumps," Chris replied.

"You're too stubborn."

"Don't you realize that she isn't capable of giving you anymore than she's given her husband which is a bag of lies and deceit. Why would you want that for yourself? You're a smart and successful man. Why are you belittling yourself and willing to take someone who's beneath you?"

"She won't do me like she's done her husband. Gracie would never cheat on me. Look at me…I'm a great catch. He's probably some dweeb who can't fuck."

Chris shook his head. "And to think I used to look up to you. Cheating doesn't have to do with who looks better or who has a bigger dick. Cheating has to do with character or lack thereof. Gracie is a person of low-moral character and incapable of commitment. Bottom line. Come to think of it it sounds as if I just described you. Maybe you two are made for each other."

"Fuck you."

"What's the point? Like, why are we even discussing her?" Chris took a large bite of his turkey burger.

"We're discussing her because I brought her up. We're discussing her because she means a lot to me. Can't you see that I'm different? I've changed?"

He huffed, "Changed? The weather outside just changed. You're still the same Anthony I've known almost all my life. New York's most eligible bachelor. And you're such a hypocrite. You're still dicking down that young chick, and how many others? So stop preaching to the choir, because I know Anthony Cross. The *real* Anthony Cross."

Chris' words had me stunned. Was I a hypocrite talking all this love, when the woman I'm saying I love is married and any night of the week I'm washing different pussy juices off my dick?

I needed to clean out my closet and figure out what was really good.

I changed the mood. "Gracie's a slightly used sistah, with a recently refurbished body, she keeps her coochie cleaned...how could any man give that up?"

"Don't. Don't give it up...lease it...don't buy it."

We sat around the Waverly Inn for another hour when a few women that we'd met this past summer at a Keyshia Cole concert came strolling in. I could tell that they had spotted us and were easing over to our table. Normally, I would have stayed and fucked around, but not that night. That night I was going home. Alone.

Twenty-Four

Gracie Lane

THE NIGHT AIR WAS BRISK AS I WALKED THROUGH THE underground garage leading to my home. It was almost eleven o'clock. I hadn't spoken with Ed since I had left the house that morning, pretending to go to work. I was back to my same tricks. I did give him a call during his lunchtime, but he'd skipped lunch and was out in the field working on mainframes. I thought I'd call him later, but it slipped my mind.

Anthony and I had made love five times that night. He was a real beast, matching my stamina thrust for thrust. I thought a lot about loving two men, though. It was a conflicting thought. But my love for Ed had pulled me out of Anthony's bed to return home. I missed my husband.

Anthony had given me a long, succulent kiss goodbye that was still lingering on my lips. Once I told him that I was ready for a divorce, he began helping me to be careful about our affair. He was such a gentleman and didn't want the divorce to get ugly due to our affair. He was also an idiot for thinking that I would leave my marriage, my husband of ten years for a fling. It didn't surprise me though. My actions were saying that we had something. That combined with his massive ego, and we were damn near engaged in his mind.

I've been thinking that I may have to put Anthony on a time out because he's getting beside himself. Or maybe I should use another angle and tell him that divorce isn't an option at the moment. Last week I was in Anthony's apartment, on the phone with Ed, and as I began to tell Ed I loved him, Anthony decided to answer his home phone and have a full-on conversation as if I wasn't there or on the phone with my husband. Of course I had to tell Ed that I was over Anika's and the voice was her maintenance man. When I got off the phone he gave me the cold shoulder until I was forced to leave—without getting any dick. He actually had an attitude. His lips were poked out, he had this distant look in his eyes and when I reached for him he pulled away.

The ride home was slow. I had deliberately driven the speed limit. I needed the time alone to clear my head. I said a silent prayer before I put my key in the lock, asking God to please let Ed be asleep, so I could just crawl into bed and hold him all night.

God was definitely on vacation because the moment I walked through the door I heard this, "I was about to have the police post an all points bulletin for your whereabouts. Did you forget where you lived?"

"Ed, please don't start. I've been with A—"

"I know you were with Anika. Only I called Anika and she hasn't seen you all day."

"I wasn't with Anika. I was with Van—"

"Vanessa? Try again."

"You tell me where the fuck I was!" I screamed.

"Typical. Go ahead and scream and act crazy because once again you're busted."

"Busted? What have I gotten busted doing? Staying out and getting fresh air instead of being stuck in the house all day? Busted, having a life outside of you? What have I gotten busted doing because it sure ain't having an affair. Please show me some evidence of that."

The calm Ed was back. I guess he was going through phases.

"Good night, Gracie. I'll see you in the morning."

When I finally went upstairs a couple hours later, Ed was in the bed and all the lights were out. I quickly slid off my clothes and climbed into bed. When I wrapped my arms around Ed's back, he turned around to face me. I didn't say a word. Nor did I want to fight anymore. I just stared into his eyes. They were consumed with hurt and pain. He touched my face gently, and then brought my lips to his. We started to kiss, and it was an *I-want-to-make-love* kiss. I backed off slowly, but he reached for my pussy and, again, I gently pushed him away. I hadn't taken a shower before I left Anthony's, because Ed would smell the soap on me, and that would have been another argument. And I could literally feel Anthony's juices getting ready to ooze out of me. Yes, we'd began having sex without any condoms. Although I knew it was foolish—not because of any potential pregnancies—my tubes were tied. But because I was married and this was sooo disrespectful. Both Anthony and I took regular H.I.V. tests but again, I knew better.

Usually when I pushed Ed away, he'd turn over angrily, but he'd leave me alone. But tonight he came back a little more aggressively. How long had it been since I'd made love to my husband? I was becoming careless. What was I going to do? I couldn't sleep with him right now, with Anthony's juices still inside of me.

Ed slid underneath the covers to try to persuade me with some head. I gently pulled his head back up.

"Not tonight…I'm tired," I said, and tried to get up to go and sleep in the guestroom.

His next movements were swift. Ed grabbed me roughly by my shoulders and pushed me back onto the bed. As I lay on my back, shocked, he positioned himself on top of me.

"Get the fuck off me!"

"You can't fuck your husband anymore? Huh?"

I tried to squirm out of the position, but his strong arms had me pinned down. He started to aggressively kiss my lips, face and neck. He was a wounded man out of control. I tried to reach up and slap his face, but he grabbed both my hands and pinned them by my sides, with his thighs holding them in place. I wanted to kick the shit out of him, but my legs were also immovable. I knew where this was heading and I refused to let my husband do something I was sure he'd regret for the rest of his life which was rape his wife. I submitted, completely.

Ed had his way with me and then cried himself to sleep in my arms....

Ed was on me like a hawk. It was Christmas Eve and I'd promised Anthony that I would spend the day with him. It was a beautiful morning in the city as the first snowfall of the year began to fall. The news forecast said we were going to have a white Christmas. Ed and I both sat on our huge windowsill, sipping hot apple cider, watching last minute shoppers brave the winter weather. We listened to Patti LaBelle's latest Christmas CD. She had an amazing rendition of *Every Year, Every Christmas* that I fell in love with. At that moment, I knew that I wasn't going to make it over to Anthony's. I was having a relaxing, lazy day with my husband and I certainly didn't want to ruin our holiday by disappearing for a few hours. Ed would hit the roof. Besides, I loved spending the holiday's with Ed. He was my only family. I'd only agreed to be with Anthony on Christmas Eve because he went ballistic when I couldn't get away during Thanksgiving. The nerve of him. He knew that he was asking the impossible but his ego wanted to see if he could actually pull it off. He wanted to see if he could actually get me to disrespect my husband even more.

I realized that the year was flying by. We were already heading into 2008 and I was still up to no good. I had started the year off wrong. I'd already booked a South Pacific vacation on the Fiji islands for Anthony and I. A little getaway that I'd promised him we'd take. Ed doesn't know anything about it nor have I come up with a sensible lie to cover myself for three nights, four days. Sometimes I'm so stupid. When I'd made the obligation I felt that Anthony deserved it for tolerating so much from me and my situation.

We'd decided to have our old neighbor, Gloria, over for an early afternoon lunch. Ed had also invited Tamara but she declined. She was still furious with her brother for cosigning with me and tossing her out. I told Ed that she was grown and that eventually she'd get over it. After our lunch we planned on watching old movies and lying around in our pajamas. We'd bought *Wuthering Heights, Casablanca* and *What Ever Happened to Baby Jane?* All the old black and white classics.

Gloria beamed as she walked through the door. She was simply radiant. She had taken my advice and walked away with millions after she cashed in her jewels and landed a seven-figure advance on a tell-all book deal. She'd bought me a little gift; a journal. It was a keepsake for all the help and advice I'd given her. Gloria didn't stay long. She didn't want to run into her estranged husband. The divorce was being finalized next month.

As our evening died down we both looked out the window and the snow looked to have reached at least ten inches. We turned down our thermostat to 69 degrees, started a fire in our fireplace, and curled up on our sofa and began our movie marathon. It was so cozy as our feet touched and Ed ran his fingers through my hair. Earlier, I felt a little guilty for ignoring Anthony and not having the common courtesy to call him and tell him that I wouldn't be able to make it but I knew he'd have a fit and I didn't want to hear his mouth. I'd cut off my cell phone but that didn't stop him from calling my house phone. Yes, another stupid move on my part. He had the house digits. Ed had picked up and no one said anything. My first inkling was that it was George calling to harass me but when I called—no one answered. George and Benjamin were quickly ruled out. The only other culprit to consistently call here and hang up would be Anthony.

I'd just started to doze off when our intercom phone rang. I nudged Ed to get it but he was snoring like a big bear. Groggily, I went to answer.

"Yes, who's there?"

"Mrs. Lane, this is Albert."

"Hi, Albert. Is someone here for us?"

"We have a problem in the garage. Could you come down? It has to do with your car."

"I'm on my way."

Quickly, I threw my overcoat over my pajamas and scurried down to the parking garage where I met Albert. I took one look at my car and gasped.

"What happened?"

My beautiful Mercedes Maybach had been vandalized. Each tire had been slashed and someone took a sharp instrument and cut deeply into my car's exterior. All the windows were intact but they could have very well smashed those too. The car was totaled.

"We've pulled the surveillance cameras and they're working on finding out who did this. Don't worry Mrs. Lane. We're on it."

"Now you're on it? This should have never have happened. What are these cameras for?" I pointed up toward the ceiling where at least five cameras were installed. "You're supposed to be watching in the security booth to stop something like this from happening! I could have been killed!"

"You're right Ma'am and I take full responsibility. But it's a holiday and we're understaffed—which isn't an excuse. I'm very sorry Ma'am."

"Where's the tape?"

"Back in our office. Do you want to come with me to see if they found anything?"

We went back upstairs to the security room and they'd found the culprit. I watched a clear image of a Dr. Anthony Cross going berserk on my innocent car. After he banged it up he looked around to see if he'd been caught and then scampered off. I could not believe my eyes.

"Don't call the authorities or give them this tape. Please call and have a towing company get my car out of here before the morning at any cost. Have them take it to the parking garage around the corner and I'll handle everything after the holiday. I don't want my husband coming down and seeing my vehicle in this condition. If for any reason my orders aren't followed, jobs will be lost. Do I make myself clear?"

"Yes, Ma'am. I'll take care of it."

I decided not to mention my car to Anthony. It was the cost I had to pay to be the boss. He was a wounded puppy and needed to vent his hostilities on someone or something. Besides, it was only a car. His heart was worth more than that.

Twenty-Five

Anthony Cross

"EMMMMM, HMMMMM, DADDY...FUCK THIS PUSSY!"

I was making love to Gracie on my dining room table. I had her on her back with her legs spread-eagled. It had started to get really good when she said, "I want you to pee on me!"

My eyes flew open in horror, and not even two seconds later she slapped the shit out of me and said, "Do it!" I felt like a little bitch that wasn't up for the challenge.

I pulled out of her and I swear I didn't even have to pee, but the fear she'd just instilled in me got my juices going. I let out all I had and gave her a golden shower. As I watched my piss physically assault her delicate skin, she stuck her finger in her pussy and gave me a freak show. She thrust more fingers in her pussy and then put them into her mouth, and moaned and groaned as if it was the best experience in the world.

"Fuck me!" Gracie demanded.

Quickly I reentered her and my senses were heightened.

"Is this my pussy?" I asked as I banged her back out.

"Yours, baby . . . it's all yours." Then she started screaming. "Fuck me harder . . . fuck this juicy pussy harder . . . harder . . . harder!"

Those words were music to my ears. I pumped in and out with gusto. I loved when she spoke nasty to me. It turned me on, although I had to admit that she could be a little controlling at times. She flipped over and let me enter her from the back. The sensation was sooooo good. She had me babbling like a baby.

"Sweet Jesus!" I screamed as I came hard.

Exhausted and sex sweaty with an exaggerated case of the munchies, we somehow managed to make it to the bedroom, where we both collapsed face down on my king-sized bed. After I ordered Chinese takeout, I finally got the wind back in my lungs.

I was a satisfied man, and she was a satisfied woman. Or so I thought.

"You like making love to me more than your husband, don't you?" I asked. She just smiled and languorously stretched but said nothing. "Answer me."

"I thought it was more like a statement. You know how you make me feel in bed."

"That's not an answer to my question," I retorted. My voice was stern and demanding. The situation started to become uncomfortable.

"It's different," she stated honestly, and then continued. "When I make love to you, it's hard, exhilarating sex. There's always an element of surprise. When I'm with my husband, it's soft and loving. He treats me like I'm his baby who needs nurturing. He makes love to me like he *needs* me. Also, inside you two feel different. He's much bigger than you—thick and long. It feels as if his dick doesn't end when he's inside me. His dick grabs my pussy and doesn't let go. I feel each and every thrust. But his bigger dick doesn't allow me to do what I can do with you. It's just too much. When we make love, your dick allows me to explore different positions with ease."

Whatever pleasure I'd felt only moments earlier was gone. I was physically sickened by her answer. No man—I don't care how secure he is in his manhood—wants to hear about a man with a bigger dick fucking the shit out of the woman he was in love with. I didn't care if he was there first. Each time she mentioned his name, I didn't care if she was bashing him or praising him—I hated it. Immediately I got upset. The mere mention of Ed always triggered a negative reaction inside my body. I wanted to kick her ass out. But I couldn't. I was in love, and it was at that moment that my emotions were defined.

I turned on my side so I could see her, face to face. As I looked in her eyes, I didn't say anything for a long while.

"You're still having sex with your husband?" I finally asked.

"Well, I am married. That's what married people do."

"That's funny, because I can remember you saying that you two never fucked. That your sex life with your husband was done. Over."

"It is."

"Then what the fuck are you talking about?! 'You two feel different, he's bigger.' What type of shit is that to say to a person?" I said, mocking her voice. I was livid.

"Oh, grow up! Do you know what I got to go through in order to be here with you?"

"Cry me a river," I spat.

"Anthony, don't go getting insecure on me. I love making love to you. You two are just...different. There's no other way to say it. And you can't get mad because you asked the question."

"Insecure? Is that what you think this is about? I'm just trying to keep things in the right perspective. I'm the most sought-after bachelor in New York. I got dime pieces at my fingertips—educated, articulate, gorgeous women. I wanted to see where you were at because I didn't want to hurt your feelings if I started seeing other women."

"That's silly. Thank you for thinking about me, but how could I ask you to be exclusive when I'm married? That would be selfish, and I couldn't do that. I love you too much." That last line made me feel somewhat better—not totally, but a little bit. I also felt like she was running game.

Gracie got up to take a shower and I stayed in bed, relishing the moment. When the water came on I decided to call Dakota. I needed a distraction from Gracie. I was getting caught up and I needed to level the playing field.

Twenty-Six

Gracie Lane

THE REDDISH-YELLOW SUNRISE CAME BURSTING through my Venetian blinds, while the rays playfully kissed my face. I sat back on my bed, surrounded by massive pillows and a goose down comforter staring at the sun and loving the tranquility it brought me. It was amazing how a little thing like watching the sunrise could make you appreciate life. I dragged my body from my bed and walked over to the window. The house had that winter chill in the air. I stood there looking at the sun for nearly ten minutes before going downstairs to grab the *New York Post*. We had weekly delivery. I shuddered at the brisk, morning air and realized Ed had turned down the thermostat to an unreasonable 68 degrees when he knew I couldn't survive on less than 80. I hated to be cold and he knew it. He was being evil. I turned it back up and ran back upstairs in and hopped back in bed.

After me and Anthony's heart to heart, he put a little distance between us, but it was all good, because sneaking around took a lot out of me. Constantly keeping up with my lies and having enough energy to satisfy two virile men was draining. After a week or so, though, Anthony finally gave in and we had made plans to see each other later that afternoon.

I exhaled as I arrived at Anthony's apartment. I was bored. Although the sex was good, possibly the best sex I'd ever had, I was looking for more thrills. It started off as a fleeting thought, and emerged into a strong possibility.

"I want to mix it up a bit," I told Anthony.

"Mix it up? What do you mean?" he asked.

"It'll be something you'll like. Don't worry."

"Should I be worried?" he asked cautiously.

"Why do you take everything so seriously?" I asked, laughing at him mockingly.

"Babe, I'm just asking. What do you mean by mix it up?"

"I want another companion to join us."

Anthony wasn't shocked by my admission, but he seemed disappointed. Perhaps he couldn't understand what provoked this discussion. Immediately his manhood was in question.

"Am I not satisfying you?"

"Why would you ask that?"

"Why would you ask what you did?"

"Because that's what we do for each other. We make each other happy."

"I am happy, baby. I don't need another woman added to the equation to feel happier. You're all I need."

I walked over to Anthony and kissed his lips softly while I ran my fingers over his chest. "Awww, Anthony, that's so sweet. Can't you do this for me...peeeaassss," I said in a baby-like voice.

He kissed me again. "Oh, all right. Since you insist, I'll do it but I'm telling you that she better not be too sexy. You better be worried because there's a chance she might take your man."

I slapped him hard on his ass. "I'm not worried."

"You're not worried, huh?"

"Nope. But you should be."

"Why should I be worried? I said I didn't want another woman in our bed—that's all you."

I burst into laughter at his humor and then got serious. "Anthony, we're both adults, correct?"

Sensing that my mood had shifted, Anthony almost didn't want to answer me. He looked deep into my eyes and couldn't read me.

"Yes, we are, so spill it. What are you getting at?"

"Well you were being a bit presumptuous when you assumed I would want a woman in our bed. I was talking about a threesome—with a man— my choice."

The thought sickened Anthony. His mouth immediately stopped salivating and his throat dried up. He began clearing his throat.

"Did you think . . . you *really* thought I . . . wanted a woman to join us?"

"Why would I ever think that?" he sarcastically replied.

"Stop being a big baby," I clowned him. "I thought you said we were adults."

Anthony went berserk.

"You're going to cause me to have an ulcer! I feel like I've aged ten years. What female asks to have another man in the threesome? That's asinine! Wasn't that against protocol. Ethics? Morals? Code? Something...who's wearing the fucking pants here! Am I your bitch?"

"Calm down."

"Fuck that! There isn't any way that I'm going to allow another *naked* man in my bed. That's some real gay shit, and I'm not down. Not even for the big butt and pretty smile that you got!"

"What about for a blow job and a hundred thousand?"

"Are you kidding me!" he growled.

"Yes, but not about the threesome."

"Listen, listen, listen," he snapped, "Go take that fag shit to your husband! Don't you ever come up in my motherfucking house with your soft voice, trying to play me like a bitch. I like you, but I don't love you."

Anthony was lying. I knew he was in love with me. A blind man could see he was in love with me. He was only saying those harsh words to hurt me because he was hurting.

"Okay, so we don't love each other. Now back to the threesome. Can I count you in?"

"Get the fuck out!"

"For good?"

"You heard what I said."

"So it's over?" I pressed.

"Yes, it is!"

I shrugged and tried to give Anthony a parting kiss on his cheek, but he swatted me away.

"It's been real," I said and made my theatrical exit.

I spent all morning and most of the afternoon in my home library, plotting. I needed to do some research on legal matters but after six hours in my library, I finally realized that I'd have to have access to a law library. Determined not to have a pity party for myself, I decided to prepare something nice for my husband. I went to the market and ordered a couple red snappers, picked up a bottle of white wine, then stopped at Barney's New York and bought Ed a pair of gold cufflinks. I was planning a romantic dinner for Ed and wanted to have it prepared before he came in from work. Growing up in a house with three brothers, my cooking skills came with ease.

After dinner was prepared, I still had about thirty minutes before he came home, so I hopped in a warm shower and put on my Vera Wang's *Princess* perfume. Since I was doing this whole seduction thing, I put on my trampy scarlet-colored, silk teddy. I then lit twelve candles and put the wine in the fridge to chill. I flipped through our enormous CD collection and put on some Billie Holiday. I decided Billie would best represent the melancholy mood I was in.

As time passed, I realized Ed was an hour late. Perhaps he was working overtime. I never considered that possibility nor did he call. I called him on his cell phone but he didn't pick up, so I decided that the mood wasn't quite right. Quickly I dressed, hopped in my car, and went to the local neighborhood flower shop and bought a dozen, long-stemmed roses. When I returned home, I plucked the petals off a couple of roses and made a trail leading to the bedroom. I thought I'd wait for Ed, naked, in bed. I was feeling very horny since me and the doctor had broken up. He hadn't even bothered to call me to see how I was doing—I never called him, either.

Finally, after almost two hours of waiting, I walked downstairs toward the front of the house as the door opened and slammed.

"Is that you, Ed?" I asked. I was waiting for Ed to show his gratitude for my gestures by making love to me for hours upon hours.

"Who the fuck lives on 69th Street on the Upper Eastside?" he asked instead.

"What are you talking about? I don't know anyone who lives there."

"You are a liar, Gracie."

"Baby, please, not tonight," I said, "I do not know anyone who lives there. Who is supposed to live there?"

"I don't know. That's why I'm asking you! You got a ticket in the mail for your car with this Upper Eastside address."

"Darling, don't you know how much I really love you? If you did, you wouldn't do this. Not now, not today."

"Why are you ruining our marriage?"

"Look, I'm tired of this shit, Ed. Okay?" I exploded.

"You're tired of this shit? No, I'm tired of *your* shit!"

"Well, leave then. Yup, get the fuck out!" I had reached my breaking point. I was tired of Ed's paranoia.

"You want me to leave?" His voice was barely a whisper.

"You can do what you want. If you're so tired of my shit, as you put it, then leave!" My voice was stern and unwavering. I ran upstairs and began to frantically get dressed. I trolloped back downstairs.

"Where are you going?"

I didn't respond. I was fully dressed and heading out the front door before he could do anything. When he realized I was leaving him alone, he had the stupidest expression on his face. And that was how I left him standing there—dumbfounded.

I wanted to go to Anthony's house but realized that we had broken up. I detoured to the mall to do a little shopping when, to my amazement, Anthony called. I was shocked, but I really wasn't. I knew it would be just a matter of time before he swallowed his pride and called.

"Hello." I had the sweetest voice, syrupy and soft.

"Hey baby, don't hang up."

"Yes…"

"I need you and I love you and most importantly, I'm sorry. This is all my fault the—"

"You—"

"Let me finish. Please, I've been working on this for two weeks. The way I spoke to you was uncalled for. You're a lady and you deserve respect. My respect. If you give me another chance, I'll promise not to be such an ass."

"I've missed you."

"I've missed you, too. Gracie, I was so angry and I filled up with rage because something inside of me kept telling me that you wanted something casual. That I was only good for the moment, and that bothered me."

"You mean more to me than I could ever express. You're too good for me Anthony."

"You're the reason I wake up in the mornings."

"Awww, baby, I'm sooo glad you called…"

"Are you having a bad day?"

"More than you'll ever know."

"So fill me in."

"It's nothing…it's all right. Forget it."

"Why won't you let me know you?"

I thought about his statement and wondered if he really knew me, would he still love me? We decided to meet for coffee at a Starbucks near Broadway, and patched things up.

Ed had threatened me a few more times over the next couple of weeks, telling me that if I didn't get my act together, he'd divorce me. I used to believe his words, but now I knew that they were just that—words. He wasn't going anywhere.

This girl is driving me crazy, I said to myself a few days later. I had been trying to get my beauty rest, but Anika wouldn't quit calling.

"Hello?" I asked groggily.

"You home?" Anika asked.

"Yes, I'm sleep."

"I'm on my way over."

I was confused. I didn't invite Anika over, nor did I want her over. I was tired and annoyed.

The heavy banging on the door should have been indicative of Anika's mood, but my senses were dulled from just waking up.

I barely was able to click the locks open before Anika was pushing through the door.

"Did you do it?" Anika asked.

"What? Do what?"

"Sleep with Anthony!"

I looked around suspiciously, afraid that Ed was home.

"Ed?" I called out. No response.

"It's a Wednesday morning. He's at work," Anika concluded.

"Now, what were you saying?"

"Did you sleep with Anthony?"

"Yes."

"How could you?!"

"Because I wanted to. What do you mean, how could I?"

"You know how I feel about him!"

"Well, obviously he doesn't feel the same way about you."

"But you're my mother! You're not supposed to be this way!"

I hadn't heard that word in two decades and it sounded odd to my ears. From the day Anika was born, I hadn't raised her. I rarely saw my daughter and by the time Anika was three, I was already heading to New York.

Anika knew most of my murky past, but she didn't know everything. Four years ago I went looking for Anika—she was an easy find. I told her who I was and that I wanted to foster a relationship with her but under any circumstances could she ever tell anyone—not even Ricky, that I'd been in contact with her. I was amazed that Anika didn't harbor any resentment toward me. All she wanted to do was develop a relationship and get to know me better. When she said she wanted to follow me back to New York, I laid down my rules. No one could know that we were mother and daughter, especially Ed. Anika agreed to be my friend, and so it began— more lies in my web of deceit.

"Anika, we both know that I'm a lot of things, but 'mother' is not one of them. I love you, but I don't know you, and you don't know me, because if you did you wouldn't be here, in tears, asking questions."

"I hate you," Anika declared.

"Anika, come on now, don't do this. I'm doing the best I can."

Anika glared at me with contempt and hatred.

"I will never speak to you again. You're nothing to me. You no longer exist!"

"Anika, let's be reasonable. All this over a man?"

"If he's not worth my anger than he shouldn't have been worth your deception!"

I nodded and then acquiesced. She was absolutely right.

Anika pushed past me, bumping my shoulder as she made her speedy exit. I had no idea that Anika would take the news so hard. And how did she know? Did Anthony tell her? More importantly, did Anika tell Anthony that she was my daughter? I panicked as I called his office.

"Anthony, did you and Anika get into an argument this morning?!"

"An argument? No. She asked me numerous questions about you and then excused herself. She said she had to leave early to take care of something urgent. Why? What's up?"

"She just accused you and I of having an affair."

"How . . . how did she know?"

"She hasn't told me any details, but she's very upset. I'll straighten everything out and call you back."

"Perhaps I should call her."

"No. If she doesn't mention it, then you shouldn't. She may be embarrassed about her feelings for you."

"Okay, you're right. But I'm worried about her. She must be so disappointed."

"Yes, she is. I have to go."

"Are you all right?"

"I'll be fine."

I didn't know what to do. It was one bad situation after another. I couldn't take all the drama. I felt a knot rise in my chest as a troubling possibility began to emerge. *What if Anika went to the authorities and exposed me?* After drinking a cup of green tea I sat on my sofa, with my knees pulled closely into my breasts and just stared blankly off into the distance. I started to remember my past.

Ricky couldn't be anymore happier than he felt at that present moment. His first day on his new job as an armored-car driver had went off without any hitches. He proudly wore his gray and black Brinks uniform. He had his wife, Marie, iron and starch his shirt, and his new patent leather shoes were shining. He felt like a king. This new job was going to give him the steady income he needed to take care of his wife and hopefully get his baby girl back. They had to put her into foster care three years ago because they didn't have enough money to raise her properly.

He was eighteen and his wife, who was his girlfriend at the time, was only fifteen. He told anyone in listening distance at the hospital where Marie gave birth that one day he planned on getting his baby back, and he knew he would do just that. He figured that it would take him one year in his new position to save up enough money to prove to the court that he and his wife could provide for their child.

Originally he wasn't due home this day for another hour or so. But he was let go earlier than expected on his first day. His boss told him to go home and study his routes and defensive driving manual, and Ricky obliged, although he didn't need to study. He had practically committed every word in that manual to memory, but he figured his boss was only giving him good, sound advice. Ricky wanted to prove himself to so many people, especially all the naysayers who thought that he'd never amount to much.

The sounds coming from the back bedroom were familiar. Ricky had heard them on more occasions than he could count. He'd made those noises, moans, and groans, when he was making love to his wife. Only Ricky wasn't making love to his wife—some other man was. He pushed the flimsy door open and saw a large figure pumping his naked ass up and down. His wife's hands were bound to the bedpost, and he couldn't see her face. Panic and rage consumed his body.

"What the fuck is going on?" he yelled in a loud, maniacal voice.

"Ricky! Help me!" she screamed. "He's raping me!"

Shamefully relieved at the word rape, Ricky braced himself and proceeded to defend his defenseless wife.

Twenty-Seven

Anthony Cross

GRACIE WOULDN'T LET UP. I WAS LEARNING THAT SHE was the type of person that when she had something in her mind, she'd do what she had to do to see it through. She was constantly nagging me about her threesome. I knew it was every man's dream to have a threesome. By the time I'd reached seventeen, I'd had two. But now it was sort of like been there, done that. Truthfully, I was over that whole scene. What I couldn't get Gracie to understand was that it wasn't the "average" three-some. She wanted me to be in close proximity to another man's dick—the mere thought gave me the creeps. So why did I agree?

Mike, Chris, Lance, and I were sitting in my living room, playing high-stakes poker. Collectively we had close to $50,000 on the table, and I was losing my shirt. I couldn't concentrate.

Anika had never come back to work, and when I called her, the phone kept going to voicemail. Finally, Samantha came and told me that Anika had sent in her resignation letter. For a moment I thought she was taking it too far. You didn't mess with your livelihood over a man that was never yours. That young girl had bills to pay. And even if it wasn't Gracie, it would have never been Anika. No matter how much we kidded around with our sexual banter that was all it was to me — sex talk.

Then the more Anika sent me to voicemail, the more I got it. She was hurt. Maybe in her mind, our conversations were the prelude to something concrete. I decided to send her a bouquet of flowers with a note that said simply: I MISS YOU, KID. I hoped that my gesture, although small, was enough for her to come back and work for me. I needed her.

"Man, I don't want to share my bed," I protested to my boys as I took a swig of my Corona beer. It was my third one. I sort of bent the truth and told them that Gracie wanted a threesome. Naturally they assumed it involved another woman.

"Or is it that you don't want to share Gracie?" Mike asked.

"That too," I retorted.

"Man, are you kidding me? This woman is giving you pleasure on a platter. I wish I could double up. You're missing the whole scenario," Lance commented.

"Lance, I'm not married. I'm a bachelor. I can always double up, if that's what I want. I'm saying that's not what I want."

"This isn't the famous Dr. Anthony Cross that I grew up with," Chris said, shaking his head. "Man, you're going soft."

"Soft? Never that. I mean, I still do me. I still got the stable full, but Gracie stands out."

"How are you going to take her seriously? That chick is married. You gotta go with the flow. Any chick, shit, my *wife* can tell me she wants a threesome with another woman, and I'mma go with the flow. We're men. This is what we do!"

Mike had gotten himself all worked up with the fleeting thought that his wife would come to him and ask to bring in another woman.

"Are you kidding me?" Lance asked. "My wife be on my balls. I can't breathe around that motherfucker, let alone her offering me another woman. All Gracie wants to do is have sex—exciting, kinky, uninhibited fucking. Something you used to know about. Now you want to *make love*."

I could see that the joke was on me. Maybe they were right. I was taking the threesome situation too seriously. As long as he didn't brush up against me and as long as I knew that it would be meaningless to Gracie, I should be fine.

Gracie's got me under pressure, I thought. Who was she gonna get for this threesome? I didn't want her asking anyone she knew, but who wanted a strange, unknown dick inside their bed? The fucking thought was making me berserk! I thought that it would be a good idea to ask one of my home boys. At least I could trust them to not fall in love with my baby and not try to come for me in the bed. But then I realized that it could jeopardize our friendship. I didn't know if I would ever feel comfortable around them, knowing that they helped me make love to my baby. Anonymity was best.

A couple of days later, Gracie and I headed out for a night on the town. She could roam the night life with me because her husband was placed on the 12-8 A.M. shift at work. At Verizon, they were on rotation and it was his group's turn. Once inside the club, I saw a lot of men checking her out and I got nauseous.

"What's wrong?" she asked as her hands ran up and down my back.

"Every man in here is checking you out," I replied.

"You seem surprised that you're in here with the hottest lady in the place," she challenged.

I cracked a smile. "Am I? Because I thought that little cutie over there had you beat!"

Her dimpled smile was on full display. "Maybe next time she could join us but for tonight I want him."

She pointed to a light-skinned, pretty boy with triceps and biceps, curly hair, and a goatee.

"Why him?" I asked.

"Because he's not my type," Gracie said and I felt a little more at ease. He was on the dance floor with a nice-looking girl who was twirling her hips to Beyonce's *"Upgrade You."* I watched as his lady friend wound her hips in a figure eight, dropped down to the floor, and ground her way back up. She danced like she could fuck. I almost wanted to ask for a foursome.

I turned to Gracie and I could see she was turned on. Gracie reached down and grabbed my dick. It was brick hard—proof that I was turned on, too.

It was on. She stood up and walked hesitantly toward the couple and began dancing just as seductively, outdoing the obviously younger woman. The guy was absolutely amused at Gracie's antics and began showing her attention. He eased away from the younger girl and began grinding his dick into Gracie from behind. Deep pangs of jealousy shot through my body and I had to keep my composure.

I watched as Gracie whispered something into his ear and then they both looked at me. He gave a quick head nod and they both exited the dance floor. Gracie came up and whispered in my ear, "Let's go."

When I hesitated, she cheered, "You can do it, baby."

I glanced back over my shoulder at the woman I was having an affair with and smiled. She was anything but ordinary. We were in a night club and she looked as if she were going to church. But, oh boy, what she did behind closed doors would make the pastor in any church pray for her soul.

Gracie made introductions and I could have choked her quiet, but then realized that we never talked about the particulars.

"Anthony, this is Nico." Damn, I should have used an alias.

"Nice to meet you," I said, extending my hand.

Eagerly, grabbing my hand he replied, "I've seen you on *E News*. You're famous!"

"Somewhat."

"My name's Nico."

"So I've been told."

With that, we all left and headed to the W Hotel. There wasn't any way I was taking this groupie dude back to my place.

I had them wait in the taxi while I secured the room. When I came back to get them, I noticed that they were engaged in a conversation as if they'd known each other for years. Both seemed rather calm in light of what was about to happen. I think I was the only one on edge. They both slinked ahead of me into the hotel holding hands, a gesture that infuriated me for a short moment.

Inside the hotel room, Gracie took charge. She roughly pulled Nico's shirt and they began kissing. My stomach got sick as I stood there watching Gracie's hands grope his chest and moved down toward his ass. Gracie tugged at Nico's pants, and Nico helped to remove his clothes. I sat on top of the hotel's dresser and watched as each stripped off their clothing. I truly didn't want to join in.

Nico had velvety, light skin; a tight, athletic body; and a massively hairy chest. His six-pack abs were experiencing Gracie's well-skilled tongue. My eyes cut to Gracie. Her honey brown-colored skin glistened in the moonlight that illuminated the room. Her new body was that of a woman half her age. Her ample breasts were a feast for Nico, and he sucked on my baby's areolas, something that was turning me on.

"Come here, baby," I said, and Gracie came over to me.

Gracie and I started off kissing slowly, and Nico soon joined in. He began kissing Gracie's back and ears, and licked her earlobes. Gracie caressed my chest and massaged my dick, which had become erect. I could feel that Nico wanted to experience all I had to offer but I aggressively pushed his hands away, and he got the message. I pulled Gracie over to me.

"Sit on my face," I told her.

She climbed on top of my face and spread her legs wide. My long tongue slithered inside her pussy like a snake. She was now facing Nico. As she fucked my face, Nico fondled her and they continued to kiss passionately. When Nico leaned over and began to caress Gracie's breasts, Gracie didn't stop him.

As she was about to climax, I gently began to bite Gracie's clit just the way I knew she liked it. This drove her crazy. Her legs began trembling as I anticipated hot waves gushing through her body. She began grinding her hips methodically until she reached her peak.

"I'm getting ready to cum!" she yelled.

I gripped her hips and felt her body shutter. We all switched positions. I sat on the edge of the bed and Gracie got down on her knees and deep throated my dick as Nico wrapped up his dick and entered her from the back.

She moaned in pleasure mixed with pain, but she took his entire dick.

"How it feel?" Nico asked.

"Fuck me harder," she said in between licks of my dick.

After Gracie came for the second time, she was ready for my dick. I pushed Nico to the side and gently climbed on top of her. Gently, I eased my dick inside her deep cave.

"Your pussy is so tight," I crooned in her ear.

We started off slowly until our bodies were in sync. As my ass pumped in and out, she wrapped her legs tightly around my trim waist. Her fingernails gently dug into my muscular shoulders as I sunk deeper and deeper inside her. Her pussy was so wet it, began to sing a love song to me. Tiny tears escaped her eyes as she nibbled on my shoulder blade. Nico kept trying to get in, but we wouldn't let him. We both came with such intensity that we screamed out in ecstasy.

We lay there for long moments, breathing heavily and unable to speak. "I'm ready to go again!" she said finally.

This time we allowed Nico to join back in. After we all fucked again, we were exhausted. Gracie fell asleep wrapped tightly in my strong arms.

When I awoke a few hours later, Nico was gone. So was my Rolex watch and my wallet. I knew no good could have come from that situation.

Twenty-Eight

Gracie Lane

I HADN'T HAD A DRINK IN WEEKS, AND THE VERY FINE, single malt scotch, although it burned going down, had also opened up my pores and unclogged my cloudy head.

If it weren't for my newfound, thrilling sex life, I would be one very tense woman. I was turning forty in a couple of weeks, and noticed that I was at my sexual peak. If the wind blew too hard, I was horny. Despite all my issues — estrangement with Anika, looming blackmail, and losing my volunteer job — I was still trying to keep a positive outlook on my future.

My ruse that I still had a volunteer job was starting to affect me as well. That, coupled with Anthony and his constant requests that I leave my husband, was daunting.

As I walked through the door from my imaginary day at work, Ed handed me the phone.

"Who is it?" I asked.

"It's the service department at Honda. They said your car's due," Ed replied as he gave me the phone, leaving the room.

"What? I just had service," I said. "Hello?"

"We gotta talk."

"I thought I told you not to call me here again," I whispered into the phone.

"They were here and they're not playing. They're kicking in doors looking for you."

"What did you tell them? Why do they care about this old case?"

"His family won't let it go. They're screaming for justice."

"Justice? It was a mistake, a bad judgment call."

"That's neither here nor there. The old man said that you better be here in the morning, or else."

"I'm not ever—"

"He's dying."

"Don't start that bullshit again. Aren't you the one who said he'd outlive us all?"

"He's fucked up and he swore on his death bed that you're gonna pay for your shit!"

The next morning, I took another drive to George's house. I decided to sport a red wig and a ton of makeup in an attempt to disguise myself. Again I drove around to the back of the house, got the spare key, and entered.

No surprise to me that the house was still in disarray. What was the surprise was how George looked when I finally found him in his bed. He'd aged forty additional years in a matter of days. He looked at least 100 years old. His already frail-looking body had shriveled up, and his features were even more pronounced. His gaunt face was sunken in and his eyes bulged. His hair had grayed and looked wooly, like cotton.

"George," I gasped. "What has happened to you?"

"They lookin' for you," he whispered, struggling to talk. "They gonna get you soon. They hot on ya tail."

"Why do you take pleasure in my unhappiness? Why?" I screamed. "I never got one full hug, no kind words, nothing! All I ever wanted was for you to love me."

"It wasn't my place to love you. I had two boys to raise."

"WHAT ABOUT ME, YOU CRAZY BASTARD!" I yelled and began to beat my frustrated fist into his weary body. He was too weak to fight back. When I couldn't beat him anymore, I collapsed on his chest.

"You can hate me all you want, but I ain't the one who did you wrong. Your momma did you wrong when she messed up your birthright."

"What are you talking about? Stop talking in riddles."

"You not mine," he stated in a matter-of-fact tone. "You my brother's chile, only he didn't want you either. I told you, ya mother was a whore. She dipped out on me with my brother and had you. When I told her I ain't want you 'cause you not mine, she left. My brother didn't want to take you, either. He had a wife and kids, and you woulda ruined that for him. So I was stuck with you, and all you caused me was aggravation."

I stared down at George without emotion. And in that moment all the pieces to my life's puzzle had been answered—the neglect, the harsh treatment, the lack of love, everything. Always being the black sheep of the family, but not knowing why. How my aunt, my real father's wife, wouldn't allow me to come over and play with my cousins, and the list in my head went on and on.

"You're like a scab over my heart that keeps breaking open," I said. "I want to walk out of here and leave you for dead, but I'm better than you. I'm calling an ambulance."

"Chile, I'm a dead man talking. All that ambulance will do is leave someone with a bill. Look" —a lung-rattling cough made him pause, and then he composed himself—"go in that dresser drawer and hand me that stack of my important papers."

I pulled out a clear, plastic bag of old papers and brought them over to George.

"Benjamin has finally done it and killed me," he declared.

"What? You're not dead."

"Yet. But I'm about one day from it. I think he's been poisoning me for the insurance policy."

"What insurance policy?"

"I had one for over four decades. It used to be payable to Andre and Benjamin, but after Andre disappeared with my money, I changed it to be for Benjamin only, and made the mistake of tellin' him. Those drugs done got his mind and he was desperate. He pulled the money you put into the checking account and went through that in a few hours. He came in here and beat me senseless. I just recovered, but he broke my ribs."

George lifted up the covers and his shirt to reveal an awful sight. His bruised and broken ribs were protruding.

"Oh my gosh, George, how can you stand the pain?" I was aghast at my brother's cruelty.

"This pain is nothing compared to the pain I feel inside my heart for my boys and how they've betrayed me, and how I betrayed you. I'm sorry how I've treated you, but I'll only say it once. The hate and betrayal I felt inside my heart were dished out to you. Every time I saw your face, I saw the mixture of my brother and my wife. I'd imagine them in bed makin' love and it was slowly killing me. I thought that my boys could dull my pain. If they were successful and you weren't, I'd finally win the brotherly rivalry. It was foolish. I was foolish."

"George, Benjamin could never harm you."

George pulled out the $250,000 life insurance policy.

"I got two hundred and fifty thousand objections. But he's no longer my problem. He's yours."

"Mine? How's that?"

"After I got ill, I changed his name for yours. You're now my new beneficiary, and when Benjamin finds out, he'll sick those boys on you. You're not safe. You gotta take your family and go."

"But I don't want your money."

"Too bad. It's yours."

Again he began coughing incessantly and holding his stomach, trying to squash the pain.

"Why have you done this to me? You had to know what Benjamin would do when he found out about the policy. My life, as I know it, is at stake."

"Take the money and run. It should be enough to start you over with a new life."

I was frantic. A million thoughts ran through my head.

"You've ruined me and you don't even know if Benjamin has done anything to you! He's a crack head, not a murderer."

"He's a dumb criminal. And his drug use has made him dumber. Look in the kitchen, check the food, and I'll bet you'll find something incriminating down there."

I charged downstairs on a mission. It was quite hard trying to search the refrigerator for poisoned food. Everything was spoiled. Maybe Benjamin was feeding George spoiled food, and that was what got him sick. I searched for another fifteen minutes until I stumbled upon a bottle of thallium. It was a silvery substance in a clear bottle. I put the bottle to my nose and smelled it. Nothing.

Could he be using this? I wondered. I didn't have to wonder long. In the back of the refrigerator was a small bowl of what looked like ravioli, and on the very top was what appeared to be the thallium. He hadn't mixed it up yet. Perhaps he planned on feeding this to George later. I ran back upstairs to George. I was getting him out of here tonight while he was still alive.

Only he wasn't. When I pushed through the door to George's bedroom, George was still on his bed, eyes open, and papers tossed on the floor. Tears streamed down my cheeks as I picked up his paperwork, kissed his leathery forehead, and crept back to my car. There wasn't anything I could do. From my cell phone I called 911 and waited in the shadows of the night for the police, ambulance, and finally the coroner to show up. I waited hours, but my brother never came around.

On the drive home, I wrestled with whether I'd tell on my brother and if so, how? I couldn't just waltz into a police station, trying to give him up for murdering his father without sealing my own fate. Was I being selfish? What did I owe George? No matter what, he didn't deserve to be murdered slowly by his own son. I no longer felt safe in my own home. Danger was looming overhead, and it was only a matter of time before it showed up at my front door.

Twenty-Nine

Anthony Cross

TMI. TOO MUCH INFORMATION.

I was forced to listen to Elizabeth talk about a night of wild sex with a local firefighter she'd met when his wife came into her office to get her bunions removed.

"He was soooo good in bed," she squealed. "The best I've had in months. When he stuck his long tongue in my asshole—"

"Elizabeth, can we finish this conversation later? I have a Grafenberg-Spot enhancement in an hour and then I'm leaving early to do some last minute shopping for my trip."

"What trip?"

"My lady and I are going to Fiji. We're leaving tomorrow morning."

"How nice. Who's going to take care of your patients?"

"We'll I don't have any surgeries planned and Samantha can do any follow-ups."

"What's this about a Grafenberg-Spot enhancement? What's that about?"

"It's something I'm sure you don't need," I laughed. "But it's a simple procedure whereas with the patient's help we locate her G-Spot. I inject a small needle which makes her G-Spot hypersensitive therefore it's easier for her to have orgasms. The injection usually lasts around 3-6 months."

"Anything involving a better sex life I'm all for it."

"Elizabeth."

"Yes?"

"Get out."

"My pleasure."

After surgery, as planned, I left the office early with promises to bring everyone back souvenir's. I went to Bloomingdales men's department and bought me two pairs of Ralph Lauren Polo swimming trunks, a pair of RayBan shades and a pair of Gucci sneakers. I had already packed my other outfits and the only thing left for me to do was to go and get a shapeup.

Before I headed to my barber, I wanted to buy Gracie something nice. Something sentimental to give to her while we're on our trip. I went into David Yurman's jewelry store and perused a few gorgeous pieces. Flashbacks of the expensive pieces Gracie had wore on several dates came gushing back. How could I compete?

"May I help you, sir?" The friendly, middle-aged saleswoman asked.

"Yes, you may. I want to get something nice for my lady friend to show her how much I care about her. We're going away tomorrow to Fiji and I thought it would be a nice gesture."

"Do you have something in mind? Earrings, perhaps?"

"Well, she has a lot of expensive jewelry. Earrings, bracelets, necklaces...she has everything but nothing from me. If you get what I mean."

"Yes, I do. Come here and take a look at these charm bracelets," she began opening up one of the display cabinets. "Charm bracelets are nice for a few reasons. They're sentimental, dainty and rarely go unnoticed on any woman's wrist."

I took a look at the gorgeous white gold bracelet, dangling with diamond and ruby charms. It was absolutely stunning. I couldn't wait to see her face when she opened up the gift. I purchased the bracelet and then called Gracie. I hadn't heard from her all day. Her phone immediately went to voicemail and I left her a brief message. I'm sure she's doing last minute errands just like I am.

It was almost midnight and I still hadn't heard from Gracie and it didn't sit well with me. Surely, she's gotten all my messages. I reassured myself that everything was all right and that she'd be here at seven o'clock in the morning. Just as she said she would.

Thirty

Gracie Lane

IF I WASN'T A DESPERATE WOMAN, I MIGHT HAVE warned Anthony that there wasn't a need for him to pack for our trip. Not that it was canceled—he was canceled. I decided that my future was no longer crystal clear and that I needed to repair my marriage. If the boy's in blue came knocking loyalty to me would lie in my husband. Anthony was flighty at best and wouldn't hold up under the pressure of my past for more than a season. Ed and I took vows and he'd hold me down for a lifetime as long as I didn't give him a reason to walk away. I offered Ed my credit card to buy him a few things for our trip and of course he declined.

"Babe, you know I'm not taking your money," he sang in an upbeat mood. "How long have we been together and never once have I asked you for anything."

He was speaking truth. Ed has never taken my money for granted. He didn't require VIP treatment, high-end vehicles, lavish spending sprees. All my money could afford him. In fact, he was the one who kept me grounded. He told me when he asked to marry me that it wasn't about my money. That he truly loved me and that he'd pay his own way until death do us part. When my lawyer prepared the 60 page Prenuptial Agreement, his hand never wavered as he signed on the dotted line.

"What's a few hundred dollars amongst millions," I said, jokingly.

"Well since you put it that way—"

"Yeah, right."

We both laughed and felt jovial about our impending, impromptu trip. Ed thought it was a trip to celebrate our love. Truthfully, it was a trip to clear my head. I so desperately didn't want to deceive him but it wasn't in my nature not to. Not only did I lie about a few things — well more than a few things — if the shit hit the fan my husband could be in for the shock of his life.

Ed and I had to take a plane into Miami, where the ship was docked for departure. The ship was huge, bigger and more intimidating than I thought it would be. I was a little nervous about being surrounded by only water for hours at a time but I was use to facing my fears. We were going to the Bahamas, St. Thomas, and St. Martin. I contemplated on taking Ed to Fiji but when I called to change Anthony's name to Ed's, one week later they still had Anthony Cross as the second passenger. I couldn't take any chances that we'd get there and there would be a voucher with Anthony's name on it. Mix-up's such as those happened all the time. And with my luck, I decided not to take any chances.

We both slept for most of the three-hour plane ride in our first class, luxurious leather seats. When we awoke, we were in Miami. It was 2:30 P.M., and the sun was beaming brightly. We both looked out the window from the plane and huge grins covered our faces. I realized that we really only traveled twice a year—once for Ed's yearly family reunion—once for Ed's yearly accumulated vacation time from his job. My money allowed us to travel spontaneously but Ed was always reserved.

My heart was racing, and eagerness showed on both our faces. Soon we boarded the larger-than-life vessel, and were ushered off to our first-class cabin to unpack.

It was a beautifully decorated cabin with a small window and a large, marble bathroom. The ship had an outdoor and indoor pool, and the outside one was heated with a waterfall. There was also a swim-up bar, and all types of water sports. We didn't stay long in our room. I took a shower first and put on a sexy, two-piece Gucci bathing suit. Ed hopped in the shower after me, and then put on the Nike swimming trucks that he'd purchased.

Ed was amused with every aspect of our getaway vacation. I knew that was partly due to the strain I had put on our marriage. To Ed, the trip was a gesture on my behalf to say that I was sorry for any and everything I'd done over the past few months.

Our four-day, five-night trip flew by. Once we touched ground on each island we went horseback riding, explored a bat cave, and windsurfed. I was the doting wife and felt so alive during our escapade. I was happy that the trip had brought us closer together from all the nonsense that I'd put our marriage through. On the first night, Ed asked me again if I had anything to tell him. My response was that I loved him. He never brought the subject up again. When it was time to leave, we both were sullen. We discussed our time together and realized that we needed to get away more often to keep the spark in our marriage.

We arrived back on a Saturday evening, and Ed didn't have to go back to work until early Monday. Reality was kept at bay for the rest of the weekend. I didn't turn my cell phone back on until after Ed left for work on Monday, and I left for my imaginary volunteer job.

The first phone call that came through was from Anthony, and my heart dropped. One week prior, I could have cared less what Anthony thought about my taking off on vacation with Ed instead of him, but today I was concerned.

"Hello," I answered.

"Who did you go on the vacation with?" he asked. His voice was icy.

"My father," I lied, taking Anthony off guard.

"Your father? But you never talk about him."

"We were estranged. Hopefully my gesture will help mend our quarrels."

"Did it?" He was putty in my hands.

"No. We're no closer now than when I was a child," I replied, glumly, and tried to portray defeat in my voice.

"Don't you think you should have told me that I was no longer going?

I had blocked out my whole calendar for that week, canceled all surgeries and told my staff that I wouldn't be in. Don't you realize how much money I lost out on behind your being inconsiderate?"

"Yes, I'm sorry. I do apologize. Everything happened so suddenly…"

"I see…you needed to take your father…and to think I thought that you went with your husband."

"Why would I disrespect you like that?" I asked.

"That's what I've been trying to figure out."

"There's nothing to figure out, because it isn't true."

"Bitch, are you trying to play me!" Anthony roared. His anger rattled me through the phone.

"Did you just call me a bitch?"

"You heard what the fuck I said! I know you were on a cruise with your husband, because Anika told me!"

"How would Anika know when she isn't speaking to me!"

"She went looking for you and your doorman told her that you and your husband went on a cruise! Are you going to continue to lie to me or are you gonna give up now?"

"If you couldn't take the truth, then you shouldn't have gone looking for it!"

"This is what I get? After all I've done for you?"

"Well, what do you want to do? Do you want to end it?"

"Damn right, I'm ending it."

"Well, thank you for the courtesy call." *Click.*

Determined not to allow my conversation with Anthony to ruin my day, I decided to take a taxi into lower Manhattan and have lunch with my husband as a surprise. I was going to try really hard to stay faithful and repair our marriage. We had done some serious bonding on the trip, and I felt as if I needed him now more than ever. So much was leaning on my weary shoulders.

I knew that one day in the very near future, I would need to pick up and go. Whether Ed was going to run with me depended on the stability and love in our marriage.

I took one last look into the mirror, making sure I looked great. My new tan had given my already honey-colored skin a nice glow. I knew that Ed would be showing me off to his boss and coworkers, so I was determined to look my best. I wore a conservative, form-fitting, dark blue dress with matching pumps. My hair was loose with curls dangling seductively around my face. The weather report stated that it would be sunny and unusually warm today. That was a plus.

My lobby was buzzing with early-afternoon activities. Housekeepers, chauffeurs, tenants, and deliveries were being made.

"Mrs. Lane." I turned to see John. He sat at the front desk during the morning shift.

"Yes?"

"This delivery is for you." He pointed toward a dark-chocolate, 6 foot 3 inch, extremely handsome man. All my tension faded as he walked toward me.

"Mrs. Lane I have a package for you. If you could just sign here and I'll be on my way." His pearly white smile was endearing. He looked no older than Anika.

"Sign my name here on your pad?" I asked, playing dumb.

"Yes, Ma'am."

"Please, I'm no 'Ma'am'. Call me Gracie."

He just smiled.

"What's your name?" I pursued.

"Who me? My name's Michael."

"Nice. Michael how long have you been working for UPS?"

"For about 4 months. I'm working my way through college. I want to open up a chain of restaurants. I'm majoring in Business Administration."

"How nice…how old are you?"

"I'm 20."

Yikes…a little young…But I bet he could use a suga momma.

"I may have a few connections in that field. Why don't you give me your number and I'll see what I can do. Do you have a card?"

"No, Ma'am…I mean, Miss Gracie. But I have a cell phone."

I smiled at his innocence. I took Michael's number and stored it in my phone as "Michelle." I'd begun to get tired of Anthony. He was too clingy and temperamental. I needed a new distraction. Someone younger and easier to mold in to the man and relationship I wanted.

I trudged along as I stepped out of my building and maneuvered down the block. I listened intently as the traffic rumbled, horns honked, and tires drove over the dilapidated New York City streets. I was suddenly accosted by a deranged-looking woman.

"I told you, but you didn't listen!" the woman screamed.

My heart was pumping with fear. My eyes darted around for help. Ironically, the street became desolate within seconds. I looked out and made a brief eye contact with a passerby in a car. My eyes imploring for help. The young, dark chocolate woman had rage in her eyes.

"Are you talking to me—"

The punch was swift and accurate as it landed directly on my nose. The force temporarily blinded me. My breath emptied out my lungs. I stumbled back, fell into a parked car, and began to shield myself as best as I could until I was able to refocus. The litany of hard, angry punches dazed me as I cowered on the ground, screaming. Every nerve in my body went slack as my body grew numb. Soon I began fighting back with all my strength. I got back onto my feet and began matching each blow with a newfound strength. I was now fighting for my life. I reached up and gauged her face with my sharp fingernails leaving long whelps oozing with blood. We fell back onto a parked car and she began pounding my head into the car's hood. I heard a sickening thunk as I almost lost consciousness.

"I hate you," the angry woman kept yelling. "I hate you!"

The crazy woman then reached into her pocketbook and pulled out a four-inch kitchen knife, swinging it wildly. I instinctively grabbed the woman's wrist as we tussled for the knife. I bit the woman's wrist, and she screamed out in agony, dropping the knife. We both scuffled on the ground, scrambling for the deadly weapon. I got to the knife first, but the woman, who had more determination and strength, was able to pry it out of my hand. Just as the woman swung it in the air in an attempt to bring it down into my back, my doorman and a neighbor's friend, who happened to be a detective with the NYPD, came to my rescue. The detective grabbed the crazed woman, tossed her up against the car, and then forcefully tossed her to the ground.

"Don't move! You're under arrest!" He twisted the woman's arms behind her back and handcuffed her as she continued to squirm and scream. "Ma'am, are you all right?" he asked me.

The experienced detective had everything under control in a matter of seconds. He helped me to my feet, secured the scene, and called for backup.

I was in shock. I remained numb as I was led back to my home. My head felt as if I'd been hit with a bat, my knuckles as if they'd went through a cheese grater. My swollen eye was half closed, and a thin line of blood slid out from my nostril.

"Ma'am, my name is Detective Brown. Do you want me to call an ambulance, so someone can take a look at your injuries?"

I was seated on my living room couch while the big, burly detective hovered over me.

"No, sir. I'll be fine."

"What's your name, ma'am?" He took out his small notepad and began jotting down notes. My heart began beating rapidly.

"Gracie Lane."

"The lady taken into custody has refused to give us a statement. Can you tell us what happened?"

"I . . . I honestly don't know," I said and began massaging my temples. "One moment I was going to meet my husband for lunch, and the next I was being attacked."

"Do you know her? Was there a recent argument?"

"I've never seen her in my life."

"Really? Did she try to steal anything? Your pocketbook?"

"Nothing."

"Well, her identification says her name is Dakota Blair. Does her name ring a bell?"

"No, nothing."

"What did she say exactly?"

"She didn't say anything. She just began beating on me," I lied.

The detective's eyebrow rose.

"Are you married?"

"Yes. For ten years . . . happily," I added.

"Mrs. Lane, I really hate to imply this, but do you think this has anything to do with your husband? Could he be having an affair?"

"No."

The firmness in my voice indicated that I no longer wanted to discuss that theory.

"Okay, fine. I'll need your husband's telephone number, so that I can speak with him."

"You'll do no such thing. He wasn't here, so there isn't anything he could do to help you. Now if you would please leave, I would like to lie down for a while."

"I'll be in touch."

"Why?"

"We're locking up that female for your assault, and possibly attempted murder. The DA will need to speak with you."

"Good day, detective," I said dismissively.

"Good day, ma'am."

I knew that the incident had nothing to do with my husband, and everything to do with Anthony. How foolish was I to have called Anthony from my home phone without blocking my number? That would be the only way the woman would be able to find out where I lived. But how did she know how I looked? There were a thousand people who had access to this building. Had she come around, snooping? Perhaps gotten up to my floor? Negative…this building was Fort Knox with our security. Anthony would have to answer that question. I had gotten careless, and now the drama had landed on my doorstep. What if the woman came back? What if next time she succeeded in hurting me, perhaps even killing me? What if the woman told Ed about my affair? I knew I needed to contact Anthony and have him put his woman in check but for now, I needed time to think. Too much was at stake.

By the time Ed arrived home, I felt as if a bulldozer had run over my body. Every joint, muscle, vein, and bone in my body hurt. Damn, even my skin hurt. I'd opted not to tell Ed about the incident while he was still at work, because I didn't want him to worry. As soon as he pushed open the front door, I called out to him.

"Ed, don't worry, but I had an accident at work," I said.

"What kind of accident?" he asked as he took off his overcoat and hat.

"This type of accident." I appeared in the doorway and Ed's eyes grew wide with concern. He rushed to me.

"Baby, what did they do to you?"

"You know those wild consumers are always pumped up on that Ritalin we give them, making them angry, strong, and crazy."

"Which one of them did this to you? I'm going there tomorrow to kick some ass!"

"You can't do that. They're mentally challenged."

"I don't give a fuck! Look at you. Look at your beautiful face."

I stared at my husband and fell in love again. Although my body was beaten and bruised, I walked over and gave my husband a luscious kiss. We fell into bed and made love for hours. And although I knew that at that moment I felt safe and secure, I knew problems were just around the corner.

Thirty-One

Anthony Cross

I DID EVERYTHING IN MY POWER TO GET OVER GRACIE. I had a string of women in my bed, was on the straight Vodka diet, and partied with my boys almost every night, but I just couldn't shake that cavalier temptress. In the beginning of our affair, she pursed me aggressively. Almost every night she was in my bed making passionate love to me whenever she could get away from her husband. Soon things slowed down to a moderate pace and now, after the trip fiasco, she didn't call at all. I hated to admit it but I was fearful that our relationship could really be over. I'd called it off numerous times before but we always seemed to get back together.

I called her.

"Yes," she answered.

"Gracie, I need my shirt."

"What?"

"My shirt. I need it. You wore it out of here one day and I need it."

"Anthony, you can't be serious."

"Yes, I am serious, so if you could bring it by my apartment tonight, I'd really appreciate it."

"Listen, I'm not bringing any shirt tonight or in the future. I'm not coming anywhere near your residence!" she screamed. "Your crazy-ass girlfriend came to my home yesterday and tried to kill me with a knife!"

"What?" My heart began to beat. "Are you all right? Which girlfriend? What are you talking about?"

"You have that many?"

"No, no, I told you that I'm not with anyone."

"Well she's claiming you, and she tried to kill me. Her name is Dakota Blair."

The color drained from my face. *Dakota?* Sweet, innocent Dakota was trying to kill people? She could have been the mother of my child. The news had me stunned.

"Gracie, I truly apologize. She and I have been over for some time now. She can't take the rejection."

"Make her take it, because I cannot go through another ordeal of this magnitude. She's a few cards short of a full deck, and her anger is directed at me. Only me. So I'm begging — no, I'm insisting that you handle her."

"Where is she? Do you know?"

"Why do you care?" Her jealousy began to show.

"So I can help."

"She's in jail, Anthony."

"When can we meet, so that we can discuss this situation?" I knew it was a cheap ploy, but I was desperate.

"There's nothing further to discuss with me. You need to check your bitch!" I could feel her anger seeping through the phone.

"What about my shirt? I need that back," I snapped.

"Is it that serious? Your shirt? Because you're acting as if I stole something."

"Jeez, Gracie, I know this isn't the time, but I truly miss you. I need to see you."

"You're right. Now isn't the time." *Click.*

I called Chris a little later to vent my frustrations.

"Yeah, Gracie keeps calling my phone," I told him.

"You're not picking up, are you?"

"Nah. I keep letting her go to voicemail. I don't have anything to say to her. She's lucky I'm not that type of dude to go upside her head for the shit she pulled!"

"That was some bullshit she pulled. How she gonna take her husband on your trip? She played you like a little *bitch*," he stated and made my skin crawl.

"She's begging to make it up to me, but I'm not going for it, right?" I asked.

"Of course you're not going for it! Who does this woman think she is?"

"Whoever she thinks she is, I'm not that dude!"

"Man, you should change your number on her. You know how chicks get. She's nothing but a whore, and I would leave her where she stands. Give that back to her husband."

"All right, man, thanks."

"Anthony!"

"Yes?"

"You're slipping. No woman is worth your pride."

I thought about Chris's words and although each and every word was correct, I couldn't just write Gracie out of my life. How could she take her husband on our trip? How could she do that? There had to be an explanation. Maybe she took him out of guilt. Maybe she felt guilty about our affair. Maybe she felt guilty because she was in love with me. There could be so many reasons for her actions and until I sat her down and had a face to face, I couldn't just give up on us.

Thirty-Two

Gracie Lane

IN THE WEEKS AFTER GEORGE'S MURDER, I SAT ON PINS and needles. I didn't want to provoke my brother Benjamin by calling him and accusing him of murder. I had been careful not to leave any evidence that I'd been by the house. But my intuition told me that Benjamin would be calling as soon as he found out that he was no longer the beneficiary. I had taken all George's paperwork and anticipated that this would slow my brother down in connecting the dots. Sure enough, it took him about three weeks after George's death to call.

"Hey, sis." It was shortly after eight in the morning when I got the call.

"What do you want, Benjamin? Because if you or George is calling about more money, I don't have it!" I screamed into the phone, hoping to deflect any suspicions my brother might have.

"Nah, I'm not calling about any money. George is dead. I just thought you should know."

"What?" I mustered surprise. "When?"

"A couple weeks back."

"George died a couple weeks back and you're just now calling me? What if I wanted to pay my respects at his funeral?"

"Well, for one, we both know that you could never do that, because those people would snatch you up faster than you could put your car in park. And second, he ain't buried yet."

"You've got to be kidding me!" I bellowed. "Let me guess, you're calling me to pay for the expenses."

"Don't nobody need your money!"

"Well, then, bury your father!"

"They won't let me. The coroner has requested some big-shot forensic pathologist to run some tests on the old man. He still at the morgue."

Benjamin's ass was in deep shit, and I was relieved, for the moment. He was going down for murdering his father.

"Tests? What kinds of tests?" I probed.

"I don't know, and I don't care. They won't find anything."

"What are they looking for?"

"Didn't I just say that I didn't know? But I guess that response didn't register to your stupid ass!" he snapped. "You always were slow."

Benjamin had inherited his father's rude mouth, but I had long ago grown numb to their disrespect.

"Again, what is it that you want from me?"

"Do you remember the name of the insurance company that Momma had her policy under?"

"Why would I remember that? I didn't receive any of the payout."

"I just thought that you would. I'm trying to find Daddy's insurance policy papers and they seem to be missing. If I knew the company, I could call them up. I swear, I think the old man burned all his paperwork, just to spite me. But I'm going to get the last laugh."

I was disturbed by the phone call. What kind of family had I been born into? Was I just as cuckoo and remorseless as my siblings? The one positive aspect that I had been able to glean from the conversation was that my brother had no clue I was the beneficiary of the policy. So he had no reason to turn me in to the police just yet. I already knew that George hadn't been buried yet, because I had called trying to get the death certificate to submit to the insurance company in hopes that I could get my name off as the beneficiary and restore Benjamin's but legally I couldn't do it. They said that once the coroner states the manner of death and releases the death certificate, it was my decision to do whatever I wanted to do with the payout. Of course I wasn't accepting one penny of that blood money.

Hours later, after ignoring several telephone calls from Detective Brown, and the front desk, a heavy knock landed on my front door. As I stood there trying to decide whether I'd answer, the heavy knock turned into a thunderous boom. I rushed to the door and flung it open.

"Yes?"

"Sorry to disturb you—" It was Detective Brown.

"No you're not! I've already told you that I don't want to press charges. It's over."

"Ma'am, this woman could have killed you, and we'd rather not have someone like that out on our city streets."

"Listen, Detective, please come in."

I led the detective into my enormous, stylish living room. He sat down on the couch and I sat directly across from him on my husband's recliner. Looking directly into his eyes, I began my story, hoping he'd understand my plight and stop harassing me.

"Detective, I've been happily married for ten years, as I stated previously. A couple of months ago, I met a man and had a brief affair. I was lonely and feeling slightly neglected. I'm not offering that as an excuse. I'm simply stating the facts." I suddenly dropped my eyes into my lap and began twirling my fingers. "We both thought it wise to end the affair so when I was attacked, I had no clue why. If my husband ever found out that I'd been unfaithful, he would divorce me. I'm asking that you please make this go away."

Detective Brown shrugged and shook his head.

"Sorry, I can't do that. This is my case, and I plan on seeing it through to the end, whatever that end may be."

I let the detective out, not feeling any better about what my future might hold. I decided to lie down and try to get some sleep.

"You've made a horrible mess of things," George declared. "Now that Ricky's locked up, possibly facing a death sentence for killing that fella, what you gonna do? 'Cause you not gonna come back up in here to live."

"I don't know. It wasn't supposed to happen like this. Why-y-y-y?"

"You make me sick to my stomach. You done ruined two good lives! And what about your chile? What that baby gonna do now?"

"I can't think about that now. What about me? My baby will be all right. Some good family will adopt her, and she'll have a better childhood than I did!"

I awoke from a frightful sleep. The dreams were back. My past was back.

Thirty-Three

Anthony Cross

EVER SINCE DAKOTA WAS ARRESTED AND THEN BAILED out by her parents for assaulting Gracie, she'd been out of control, a total lunatic. So it wasn't a shock when Dakota showed up at my office, unannounced. As I sat at my desk, totally consumed in paperwork, I looked up and there she stood. She was still wearing the same clothing from the previous night; her hair was tossed about; and her eyes were puffy, as if she'd been crying.

"What are you doing here?" I asked. It took all my strength not to totally lose it.

"You didn't say you loved me." She had the strangest look in her dark eyes, as if she was permanently out to lunch.

"What are you talking about?"

"This morning, when you left, you didn't say you loved me."

At that moment I realized that I'd made yet another mistake. Still down over Gracie, I called Dakota to come over, and had sex with her, trying to see if I could recapture something from the past—a feeling, something, anything to feel nostalgic about when we first met. Of course, no sparks flew. My feelings for her were dead and buried.

"Dakota, listen. We need to talk, but unfortunately now is not the time. I'll swing by your place after work. Is that good?"

"It's over, isn't it?" she asked and looked aloof. For some reason, I couldn't bring myself to be straight up. I wanted to tap dance around the topic.

"I'm working more than usual. I just think that we should cool it for a while. It wouldn't be fair to you."

"Stop it, Anthony, and be a man for once. Tell me the truth. I need closure."

Her plea forced my hand to be straightforward. "I'm not in love with you anymore."

"I love you with all my soul," she began and collapsed into an empty chair. "But it wasn't enough. I wasn't enough. What is it that you wanted from me?"

Her eyes pleaded for me to say something that would make our breakup seem logical in her mind.

"Baby, I'm just not ready for the type of commitment you're looking for."

"I've sacrificed my life for you, and risked my freedom!"

"I had nothing to do with your choices. I thought you were better than that. Your actions were deplorable."

During my heated discussion with Dakota, I heard a loud commotion coming from my waiting area. I jumped to my feet and ran to the door, just as it was pushed back into me. I fell back and immediately regained my composure. Several police officers came bustling in and littered my office. My heart started to palpitate for Dakota. What had she done now?

"Dr. Anthony Cross?" one police officer asked.

"Yes?"

"Turn around and place your hands behind your back. You're under arrest for illegally selling and distributing pornography. You have the right to remain silent. Anything you say can and will be used against you . . ."

I was stunned. I couldn't speak. I assumed the position in a daze. I could see Dakota's mouth moving, all my staff running to my defense, news cameras being thrust in my face.

Am I really under arrest? I wondered. *Are they leading me out of my high-end office into the back of a seedy police car?* Things like this didn't happen to guys like me. Finally realization sunk in as I was being stuffed into the back of the police vehicle.

"Call my lawyer," I belted out and Samantha, my RN, nodded her head rapidly. At that moment, I missed Anika more than ever. She would have handled the situation and did what was in my best interests.

One thought entered my mind as I was carted off. *Who the hell called the news?*

My ordeal ended just as it had begun—ambiguously. I had no idea how or why I was being charged with selling and distributing pornography. The police told me very little once I invoked my rights and requested my attorney. I was shipped to Central Booking, where I was processed and had to await a judge to set bail. The cell was disgusting and quite intimidating. I stood up for most of the seventeen hours I was there with wild thoughts going through my head.

Yes, I have a vast video collection of women I've taped without their knowledge. That is fucked up, I know. But I never, ever thought about selling those tapes. And since I didn't do it, who did? I wondered. I was determined to find out.

I called Anika from the holding pen, collect, half expecting her to deny my charges but she didn't.

"Hello."

"You have a collect call from "Anthony" an inmate at a correctional facility. If you would like to accept the charges, please press 1. If you'd like to deny charges, please press 2," the automated system stated.

I was put through.

"I heard what happened," she began, her voice depicted concern and bewilderment. "What's going on?"

"I have no idea," I stated, honestly.

"Did you do it?"

"Of course not!"

"I'm just asking. I'm not your number one fan anymore."

"I know I've hurt you but you're a good friend and I need all my friends right now."

"What can I do?"

"I need you to call Gracie and tell her what's happened—"

"This is about Gracie? You're actually calling me so that I can call that bitch—"

"Anika, please, this isn't about you right now. Did you forget I'm in jail? And Gracie's been through a lot lately. Dakota went over to her house and beat her up and tried to stab her with a knife—"

"Tell me when the fuck I'm supposed to care! She just ditched your trip together and went on a cruise with Ed. Don't you get it? She doesn't love you! She's in capable of love. She doesn't love me and I'm...I'm her best friend! You know what? I don't even care anymore. You're just stupid!"

"You do care. You care about me and you care about Gracie because that's who you are. Under your tough exterior lies a soft heart. I know you—"

"Know this!" Were her last words before she hung up the phone in my ear. I called all my boys but none of them were home. Kevin's wife picked up sounding concerned and said that she would get the message to Kevin to show up in court and moreover to have funds available just in case the DA asked for a bail.

I expected Dakota to be sitting in the front row of the courtroom, crying her eyes out while waiting for me to be arraigned; but to my surprise, she wasn't anywhere around. I looked out into the audience and saw no one there—not one friend, staff member, lady friend—no one. It was five o'clock in the morning, but was that really an excuse? My fucking life was on the line.

Jeez, this is the treatment I get when I'm in a fucking crisis, I thought.

They brought ten of us into the courtroom at one time to appear before the judge. Samantha did get in touch with my lawyer, Vallerie Mallore, and she was there, looking great I might add—if you were into white women. Her long legs, blue eyes, and svelte figure were a welcome sight after my ordeal. She got right to the point.

"I wasn't able to get a lot of information, but it appears that someone has been selling and distributing pornographic tapes with titles such as *Doctor Good Dick and Nurse Betty,*" Valerie whispered to me. "They show you and several women engaging in different sex acts. Most of these women have been contacted and although they're furious with you for taping them without their consent, only one thus far has agreed to testify against you—a Ms. Dakota Blair. I pulled her name and she has a criminal record. She may want to plea bargain with the DA, giving her testimony in your trial for leniency in her case."

Again, sweet Dakota had rocked my world. I now knew that I never knew her at all.

There wasn't anything I could do at that moment but concentrate on getting out. Valerie requested that I be let go on my own recognizance. The judge declined and set bail at $50,000. As I was being led to the back of the courtroom, I heard a familiar voice.

"Anthony," she called.

My head spun around, only to see Gracie. She had come for me. My heart filled with so much emotion that I almost cried. My eyes spoke what I couldn't. Valerie noticed her and went to speak to her. As they were engaged in conversation, I saw my father and Anika come through. Anika had swallowed her pride and held me down. Although, I was overjoyed to see my father, I didn't want the stress of my situation on him. He had a lot on his shoulders to deal with concerning my mother. That's why I didn't call my parents. And who was watching my mother? My Pop's eyes were filled with concern and as soon as we'd made eye contact, he called my name. "Anthony!"

"Quiet in the courtroom, sir!" The judge hit his gavel and several court officers went to tell him to either take a seat or leave the courtroom. I gave him a smile and a head nod to let him know that I was all right. With my Pops and my girl by my side, I could take on the world.

Three hours later, Gracie posted my bond and I walked out of my holding cell and was on my way back home in a taxi, with her by my side.

Thirty-Four

Anthony Cross

AFTER THE PORNOGRAPHY SCANDAL I FELT LIKE A bad boy, like I had a little more flavor than the average plastic surgeon. Not only that, but my already blossoming practice had suddenly almost tripled with patients. There were so many freaky women, all vying for "Doctor Good Dick." You couldn't plan better PR. I was now busier than ever. I had hired a private investigator to find out who copied each tape from my house and then sold them on the Internet.

My relationship — or lack thereof — with Dakota was officially over, and my relationship with Gracie had resumed. We still had to be very discreet, but more and more I wanted to marry her. I wholeheartedly wanted her to leave her husband for me. She wasn't happy there—she wanted me. I knew it and she knew it.

"Dr. Cross, your ten o'clock consultation is in examination room two," Samantha told me.

"Thank you. I'll be ready in five minutes."

I finished my third cup of coffee and headed with Samantha to examination room two. There stood a fairly good-looking man with funny-looking twists in his hair. He was slightly taller than me, so he probably stood at 6 foot 4.

"Dr. Cross, this is Edward Lane."

My face showed no emotion when I heard the last name. Could this be Mr. Lane, Gracie's husband? If so, why was he here? Did he know? Was I in danger? Then my fear subsided. He didn't look intimidating. He looked like a pussy. I could take him down if he tried any bullshit.

"Dr. Cross, you operated on my wife, Gracie."

Bingo! I was right.

"Yes. How may I help you today?" I asked in an agitated tone.

"Well, you did a great job on my wife, and I wanted to surprise her and get liposuction on my stubborn belly fat."

Was he serious? I gave him another look. His funny hair-twist, lanky body, and uncoordinated clothing were a far cry from what I expected Mr. Lane to represent. His wife was worth millions and he looked like a poor man walking. I couldn't see one characteristic that would remotely convince me he was Gracie's type. I couldn't understand what she saw in him. My observation of her husband had plucked my nerves. If he wasn't the money man, and he couldn't hold a candle to me, then why was she holding on to her marriage? He looked like a loser.

"If you could open up your examination robe, I can begin your consultation...."

One week later, Mr. Lane was under anesthesia and at my mercy. I could have ended it for him right there if I wanted to, and no one would have been the wiser. Ha! That was all bullshit. If I tried anything, they'd have my ass in jail—no bail.

I couldn't resist taking a peak at his Johnson after Gracie had done all that bragging about how big her husband was. Inwardly, I was hoping she was lying. But to my dismay, she wasn't. Her husband was huge. Talk about a swift kick to my gut.

I actually did a superb job on this guy, despite how I felt about his wife. My ego kicked in and wouldn't allow me to do a botched surgery. Anyway, I felt that he was getting his fat sucked out because he was feeling my presence in his marriage. He was struggling to hold on to a wife that no longer loved him. She had one foot out the door, and the other walking over my threshold when we got married.

I visited Mr. Lane in the recovery room and gave him his filled prescription. He was in minimal pain, and coherent, but his speech was a bit slurred.

"Mr. Lane," I said softly, "I've filled your prescription, and in an hour you're free to go. Can you hear me?" He nodded.

"Than-n-nk, you," he struggled to say. I pushed a small, brown paper bag in his hand with two bottles of meds and their instructions. He had to come back in five days for his follow up.

I chuckled at my devious behavior. Gracie would have long divorced Edward Lane before he realized what I had done.

As time passed, I thought about calling Anika. That was my friend, and it seemed senseless that she would carry my affair with Gracie to this extreme. After she rallied everyone to come out and support me in court, she was back to not speaking to me. I thought we were better than that. I mean, who did she think she was? She couldn't lay claim to me. I was her boss, and she was my subordinate. Each day I wished she'd walk through those doors so we could kick it again. I missed talking shit to her and bragging about the plethora of women that came and went in my bed. Anika was so stubborn that I wanted to choke some sense into her. Before I got arrested, I was so close to getting her to come back to work. We would talk a few times a week and I could tell that she was entertaining the thought. Now, all that was gone.

My cell phone vibrated and I looked down to see that I'd missed thirteen calls. I scrolled back to see that they all came from Chris. I called him to see what was up.

"What's good?" I asked.

"Turn on the motherfucking news!" he blurted out.

"What? Which channel?"

"Any channel!" He was in a panic and it only took me a few moments to understand why.

I looked at the TV screen and watched as the police taped off Gabriel's art gallery. For a split second I thought he'd been murdered, until I saw him being brought out in handcuffs. He didn't hide himself from the media. He walked proudly as the detectives escorted him to their squad car. As cameramen thrust microphones in his face, he was asked one question.

"How could you do it?"

He stopped and looked at the officer to see if he could answer the question, and then he said, "I'm innocent. I'm being framed!"

"What's going on—" I started to ask.

"Shhhhh, keep watching," Chris demanded.

The news reporter began speaking.

"Gabriel Copa was arrested today in what the FBI has named the biggest fraud in the history of art, for selling fake post-Impressionist works. He's accused of duplicating the certificate of authenticity on early nineteenth-century, modern and Impressionist paintings. He took certificates of authenticity from original paintings and placed them on fakes, and then he would order another certificate for the real paintings from Sotheby's or Christie's auction houses. The auction houses wouldn't give him a problem because he indeed owned the originals.

"Mr. Copa also bought paintings that had no value in order to use the authentic, old picture frames on fakes, even using antique nails to give the fakes a more aged look. He hired a string of recent Mexican immigrants to paint the fakes, and gave them free room and board to duplicate in upward of ten fake paintings per original.

"Mr. Copa grossed his first million from this fraudulent business by selling to overseas buyers. But Mr. Copa's biggest mistake was greed. He began selling his fakes in the United States, and that is how the FBI was able to catch this thief. Copa made more than $14 million with his art scam," the reporter finished.

I was speechless. How could this have happened? Immediately I blamed Chris.

"You vouched for this dude," I yelled into the phone. "I would have never done business with him if it weren't for you!"

"Don't blame this situation on me. You wanted in!" he barked.

"All I know is that I'm gonna break my foot in somebody's ass if I don't get my money back! Do you think that he swindled us? I mean, you're his boy. Better yet, do you think he'd swindle me? I'd hate to find out that the painting on my wall in my living room is worthless, and I just got dicked out of three hundred grand."

"How am I supposed—"

"You should know because you've been riding his ass for the past six months!"

"So what! Oh God, no, my investment . . ." His words trailed off.

"You've been paid on your investments!"

"Don't you get it?! He's a fucking conman. I was paid for my first two investments. Both were very small. This last investment was all the money I owned. I cashed in my 401K-plan, IRAs, and took the equity out of my apartment in order to have enough liquid to get in on this deal."

"Didn't I tell you to wait? That I wanted to do more research on this guy? How could you be so foolish?"

"The same way you walked in and drop three hundred on a painting and you know nothing about art! Greed! We're both guilty of it. Do you think we're the only educated people in America to get swindled? It happens to the best of us...bankers, celebrities, Ivy-league graduates have all been victims. So don't come down on my bail-bondsman ass because I wanted to make a few extra dollars."

"I guess you're right." I thought about what he'd said and nobody forced my hand regarding the painting. Stupidly, I jumped into the deal without any background check on the guy. I was more suspicious of the women I fucked then I was regarding my money. I think one part of the blame is that I had just gotten that large check from Gracie. I was feeling myself as if her money was my money.

"Anthony, listen, man. If anything jumps off, you got to tell them that I didn't have anything to do with it."

"What are you talking about?"

"You know—"

"No, I don't know, so why don't you tell me?"

"I'm just saying that although Gabriel is my boy, he could possibly lie to those federal agents and say that I was down with him."

"Are you crazy? You're as much a victim as I am. Listen, I need to contact the FBI so that they can come and get my painting and investigate the transaction I've done with him. I suggest you do the same."

If the news reporter and my gut were correct, I legitimately didn't have any liquid assets. Anthony Cross was officially broke.

Thirty-Five

Gracie Lane

THE RIPPLE EFFECT OF MY AFFAIR WAS BEGINNING TO rear its ugly head. I stood in front of my mirror in my bathroom, under the fluorescent lighting, and noticed that I had aged over the past couple of weeks. I fingered a few crow's feet around my eyes that weren't there last week. On closer inspection I noticed fine lines on my forehead, and thick creases around my mouth, known to many as laugh lines. I was a worrisome, near 40-year-old who was literally on the brink of a mental breakdown from the stress.

I called the coroner's office for the umpteenth time.

"Hello, this is Gracie Lane. I'm calling to see when you're going to release George Perry, so that we can give him a proper burial?"

"Mrs. Lane, your father's body was released this morning to your brother, Benjamin Perry. Our findings were turned over to the police department. We found thallium in his system. His death certificate reads homicide. Detectives will be in touch with you."

"With me?" I shrieked.

"They asked; I answered. They wanted to know who, if anyone, contacted us about releasing the body. Your name came up several times."

"Because I wanted to bury him!"

"That's not what you said. You said you wanted to get the death certificate for the insurance money."

My body went slack. *How could she have twisted my words?* I wondered.

Today was a bad day for me. Little did I know that it was going to get worse. I sat there wondering whether I should call the insurance agent and get his take on the situation, because I knew that I shouldn't be a suspect. I did not kill George, and insurance policies were only null and void in the case of suicide. Or, if the beneficiary was the prime suspect in the insured's death. Perhaps I should call the police and tell them what I knew.

I decided to probe the insurance company first. As I went to pick up the phone, it rang.

"Hello?" I snapped.

"Mrs. Lane?"

"Yes, who's this?" My patience was growing thinner by the second.

"This is Detective Delgado. I'm Detective Brown's partner. He's off today—"

"Listen, Detective, I've already explained to Detective Brown that I don't plan on pressing charges or testifying, and that the state will have to try Ms. Blair without my help."

"Yes, we have the information, but we have a problem."

"Your problems are your problems," I barked. I'd finally had it with tiptoeing around the cops and allowing them to harass me day in and day out.

"Maybe," he said. He spoke slowly and softly as if my outburst couldn't rile him. "Maybe not. The problem could very well be yours."

"How so?" My curiosity was piqued.

"Ballistics pulled two fingerprints off the kitchen knife. One was traced back to Dakota Blair, the other to a felon. Does the name Marie Perry sound familiar to you?"

The name silenced me.

"Mrs. Lane, are you there?"

"Uhhhh, yes. Someone's at my front door. What was that name again?"

"Marie Perry. She's wanted for murder!"

"No, I don't know that name."

"Okay, thank you."

"Goodbye, Detective."

"Mrs. Lane?"

"Yes?" I asked and exhaled.

"We need you to come into the precinct so that we can run your fingerprints."

"I will do no such thing! I'm not a criminal. I'm a taxpaying citizen."

"I understand that, Mrs. Lane, but I'm not asking. I'm telling you that you need to come down here, so we can clear you. I'm sure you have nothing to hide."

With a tight-lipped resignation, I replied calmly, "Very well."

Click.

My life imploded.

"NOOOOO!" I screamed and let out a haunting wail filled with anguish and fear.

I sobbed for hours, cradling myself on the floor in my kitchen. When Ed walked in he found me crouched near the refrigerator, in a trancelike state, shivering, and mumbling, "No, no, no, no . . ."

I began making plans to leave. I called the illustrious, Jill Stuart, top realtor to the stars and put my apartment on the market. I told her that I wanted a buyer and to close within the next 30 days. I put my apartment on the market for 20 percent less its appraised value. All the wolves would come out for this steal. I decided that I wanted to head west and that it would also be wise to start stashing my money into a Swiss, off shores bank account. It wouldn't take the police long to connect Marie Perry and Gracie Lane so Gracie had to die. All traces of her existence had to go. The only way that would happen is if I put my money in an untraceable account and disappeared from all that I knew. I had accomplished this two decades ago without any money, surely my money would afford me a better escape route.

I knew in my heart that my husband would not run with me, and I loved him too much to ask. How could I subject him to a life on the run? That would be the most selfish thing I'd done in my treasure trove of selfish things. The only thing was that I thought it would have been easier to walk away. I felt the heat hot on my ass, but it wasn't making me jump. I couldn't bear to face reality.

To make matters worse, I felt that my husband might be having an affair. He no longer wanted to make love to me, and it was driving me crazy. He kept blaming it on his recent surgery, saying that his body wasn't built for surgery because he now felt like an old man.

That afternoon, I drank more than the legal level of alcohol and then drove to Anthony's house. I was feeling alone and neglected and wanted to feel some stiff dick, and fuck my blues away.

Again I flirted with his doorman and he allowed me up without first announcing me. I didn't know why it gave me a thrill to get my way like that, but it did. Although I was heavily intoxicated, my walk was steady. By the time I reached Anthony's door, my hormones were blazing. I knocked, only he didn't answer.

"Well hello, Gracieeee," a young man sang.

"How do you know my name? And where's Anthony?"

"He had to stay late tonight at work. He had an emergency surgery. Some woman's stitches burst back open because she didn't follow his orders."

"Are you going to invite me in?"

"Sure, sure, come in," he replied, leading the way farther into Anthony's plush apartment. "My name's Chris. I'm Anthony's friend."

"Pleasure to meet you."

"The pleasure is all mine..."

It never did occur to Chris to call Anthony and tell him to rush home because he had company. He was too busy flirting with me.

"What's your poison?" he asked.

"What's your pleasure?" I retorted.

"Excuse me?" He didn't understand my personal joke.

"Scotch on the rocks."

"No chaser?"

"Not tonight."

I was quite drunk and feeling awfully naughty. I didn't factor into my conscience that Chris was my histress' friend. Maybe I didn't care. We sat close on the sofa, *very* close. Quickly I slid my tongue in his mouth. He tried to resist, but I was too much for him. All the passion I had bottled up inside of me came bursting out. My tongue explored the inside of his mouth and his earlobes, then I moved down to his neck. I sucked gently on his neck until I heard a faint moan. I ground my hips up and down and felt a bulge, which excited me. I got more aggressive and reached inside his boxers. Once my hand touched his penis, it grew to a decent size. It was nothing to brag about, and I almost backed out, but my hormones wouldn't allow me to stop.

Chris started to respond to my gestures and began exploring my body. He gently caressed my back, and then his hands traveled around to my bra. He unclasped it, and my ample breasts spilled out. He opened his mouth and took a mouthful. He sucked until my nipples were like two ripe fruits. We switched positions until we were on Anthony's designer sofa with Chris' body wedged between my legs. I parted my legs slightly, slid up my skirt, and he eased off my silk panties. He looked in my eyes, and lust consumed his face.

"Fuck me," I said. "Show me what you can do."

Chris steadied himself on top of me and gently slid inside. I was so wet, you could hear soft noises as he pushed his dick in and out. With steady, consistent strokes he completely penetrated me. Each deep thrust brought me closer to my climax.

"How it feel?" he crooned in my ear.

I ignored him.

Again, he asked. "It feel good?"

"Please, be quiet," I whispered.

I was grinding my hips to his rhythm, and the feeling was incredible. When the feeling got too intense, I bit down hard on my bottom lip and kept throwing my hips back.

We slid off the sofa and I assumed the doggy-style position. Chris reentered me and began giving me back shots. I gripped the sofa as he pounded into my wet pussy, slapping me on my juicy ass so hard, I screamed out. I loved every minute of the abuse.

"Yeah, this is how you like it! From the back! You like it from the back don't you! You wanna suck my dick how you suck Anthony's—"

"Please, shut the fuck up!" I screamed. This guy was a lousy lay.

Right before I could reach my climax, Chris shuddered and came without warning, collapsing on my back and breathing heavily. Annoyed,

I pushed him off me.

"What was that?" I asked, standing and towering over him.

"That was five solid minutes of good fucking!" he stated boastfully.

"That was three minutes of weak dick! You're too young to be giving me that weak dick!"

"I got mine. Don't be mad if you didn't get yours. I hope you didn't expect me to wait on you!" Chris had already jumped up and adjusted his clothing.

I was furious. I slid on my panties and couldn't resist picking up my glass and tossing my drink in his face.

"How 'bout that?" I asked and stormed off into Anthony's bedroom, closing the door behind me.

"Bitch!" he screamed.

"All day," I retorted.

I showered, climbed into Anthony's bed, and was sound asleep within moments.

Thirty-Six

Anthony Cross

"SO ARE YOU TELLING ME THAT YOU'VE TRACED THE Internet site to my best friend, Christopher Wilkens?"

"Yes, that's correct."

It was after hours and I was in my office with Brian McDonald, the private investigator that I hired to find answers as to who set me up, duplicated my whole DVD collection, and was turning a profit. The news stunned me.

"How long has this been going on?"

"At least eight months. He was uploading small clips of your DVD's to Pornotube.com. Customers can see a 30 second clip and if they like what they see, they can purchase the whole video. All the money is going into an off-shore, joint bank account. Once the money is put in, it's being funneled back out—"

"Let me guess. The other partner is Gabriel Copa?"

"Bingo! I did a little investigating and they both have serious cocaine habits, but Mr. Wilkens also has a large gambling debt owed to the Irish Mafia."

"Irish mob? I didn't think shit like that really existed." I was perplexed. How could my best friend have betrayed me like that?

"It does exist, and the Mafia is more dangerous than any myth could portray."

"Did you see the scandal on the news regarding Gabriel and the art?"

"Yeah, I caught that."

"Well guess who got mixed up in that, too? He got me for $300,000 on a painting."

"Well if it makes you feel any better when I'd made the connection between your friend Chris and Gabriel, I did some investigating and Chris didn't have anything to do with your getting swindled with the paintings. He got swindled as well. It seems as if Gabriel used Chris to bring you and others in on what's considered a Ponzi scheme--"

"Ponzi scheme? Is that similar to a Pyramid scam?"

"Similar but different. A Ponzi scheme is more complex. In a Ponzi scheme they take money from numerous investors promising a large return. Only the money isn't used for a legitimate investment. A few investors see a small return and they think everything is a win-win. Only they don't know that the money they received was from new investors."

"They take from Peter and give to Paul..."

"Correct. The reason they need to pay a few investors a minimal amount of return is to generate a hype around the deal. Once they get all the investment capital they usually skip town and pop up in a new city with the same scam. Gabriel was a professional and didn't mix business with pleasure. If Chris had money then he wasn't going to be exempt. I'll have my report on your desk in two days. Also, I have a friend high up in the police commissioner's office. He'll also get a copy of the report. Steer clear of your friend and don't mention anything. He'll get a knock on his door early next week."

"Thanks, man. Any chance I'll get my money back when all of this is over and done with?"

"Your chances are slim to none. It'll be difficult to recover all the money that was swindled by Gabriel and whatever is recovered, the line for payouts will be so long you won't even get 10 percent back. Most of his take went to expensive cars and lavish living for Mr. Copa."

"Why would Chris conspire with Gabriel to cross me..." I wasn't really asking Brian this question but he answered anyway.

"I have no idea. Only Chris knows."

The news hit me below my gut. I felt betrayed. As I walked Brian out and began to close up the office, I got a knock on the glass door. I looked up and it was Ed, Gracie's husband. Immediately I was aggravated. If he'd burst open a stitch or wanted to bust my balls about his surgery, I swore on my mother that I'd choke the life out of him. I wasn't in the mood for any bullshit tonight.

Aggressively I opened the door.

"What is it?" I asked.

"May I come in?" he asked in a level voice.

"Quickly. I don't have a lot of time. I'm busy and need to get home."

"This won't take long."

The frail-looking man entered my office with his trench coat draped over his forearm. His eyes were cold and distant, and his breathing became erratic.

"I went to my medical doctor last week because I wasn't feeling like myself after the surgery," he began and immediately I knew where he was going with this. "He took a series of tests, and I'm sure you know what the results were."

"Amuse me."

"Amuse you, huh?" If he was upset, his voice showed no indication of that. But the glare in his eyes gave him away. "Well I guess it would be amusing to everyone hearing the story except me. See, I haven't been able to get an erection and make love to my wife in weeks because my plastic surgeon gave me 500 mg of Finasteride to take twice a day. Can you imagine that?"

"Why would I give you that? You must be mistaken."

"I figured you'd say that, and that's what you're supposed to say, because you're protecting your practice. But I'm not a snitch-ass dude. You don't have to worry about me filing some sort of lawsuit, or reporting you to the medical board. But I am going to whip your ass in here tonight. You can believe that. I'm gonna whip your ass for hating! You're not God. If you're a man and you're fucking my wife—fuck my wife! Don't come after me. I work every day and I don't bother anybody. I can get another good woman. Gracie knew from the beginning that I would never tolerate cheating. If you want her, she's yours."

"I *had* your wife. I don't *want* her," I replied. I had to snap on homeboy, who thought he was putting me in my place.

I looked at the six-foot-four male who stood before me. His lanky, undernourished, frail body wasn't going to be any match for me. I bench-pressed 300 lbs., four times a week. It was time I started to throw my weight around and take out some of my anger on him.

"Look, get the fuck out before I throw your black ass out!" I yelled.

I went to grab him by his collar when he seized my hand. In one quick motion he twisted my arm around my back and forcefully slammed me up against the wall. The force of my head hitting the wall resulted in a speed knot over my left eye. Before I could get my bearings, he spun me around and began an aggressive assault, lashing out a litany of punches to my upper body. He was as fast as Ali in his prime. I tried to ward off each punch with half-assed blocks and semi-ducks, but he was just too quick. Almost all his punches landed at their destined locations. He was making weird noises and doing Tae Bo moves and karate chops. Ed was giving me one-and two-piece combinations, upper cuts to the jaw, and then a succession of rib shots. One last punch to my gut leveled me. I fell back over a waiting room area table. I was out for the count. Ed walked over to me and spat in my face.

"Bitch-ass punk!" he yelled.

Could my day get any worse? Finally, I was able to get up and make it to the phone.

"Operator, please send the police here. I've just been assaulted!"

Thirty-Seven

Vengence is mine

BIG MOMMA MORALES WALKED UP THE STATELY STEPS of the Burlington Township Police Department with an undeterred conviction. Her heavy body weight was being supported by her steel walking cane as she took baby steps toward her destination. Dozens of grandchildren hovered around; all at her beck and call. Each one collectively thinking the same thoughts: *I can't wait for her to kick the bucket so that I can get my inheritance.* Big Momma smelled of old money. The expensive sable fur coat was large enough to make three smaller versions out of the skins. She wore gaudy, gold and diamond rings on each finger including her thumbs. Her fat hands could barely close to make a fist.

Everyone in the precinct knew her well. Big Momma had been coming to that precinct consistently for twenty-one years, five months, and eighteen days to inquire about the senseless murder of her grandson, Emmanuel Morales.

Detective Ryser was on his way home from a double shift when he spotted the family's matriarch. He had been handling the case since the original detective had retired 9 years ago. His heart went out to her and he respected her determination.

"Detective when is Marie Perry going to get apprehended. My poor grandson cannot rest until that hussy is behind bars! That trashy-tramp will regret the day she ever said a Morales raped her dirty little ass!"

"Mrs. Morales, we are doing everything in our power to assist in her recapture."

"Do you realize I've spent over one million dollars on private detectives throughout the years searching for clues that will lead us to her arrest! I'm afraid I'm not going to be on this earth much longer. I'm old. And I'm tired. And I want to go on and be with my husband. But I can't until I see that murderer behind bars."

"Well we've got good news from New York. Her fingerprints came back on a knife—"

The whole clan began giving high-fives and sighs of relief. They were sure that as soon as Marie Perry got arrested that their grandmother would die just as she'd been promising for the past decade.

"What? When were you going to tell me! Is she in jail?"

"Let's everyone calm down. She's not in jail, yet. That's why you weren't contacted. But as soon as I know more, I'll fill you in on every detail."

"LET ME SPEAK TO YOUR CAPTAIN!" The canterkerous Big Momma yelled. Detective Ryser wasn't moved. She did the same routine three times a week; every week. Captain O'Mally, who blames his premature balding on Big Momma, came over to placate the situation.

"Yes, dear," he soothed. "What can I do for you?"

The elder lady cut her eyes. She was truly smitten with the Irish captain.

"This here young fella has been withholding important information regarding my grandson's case. Did you know that?"

"Detective Ryser has been putting in a lot of man hours on this case. He feels we're going to make an arrest soon."

"When? Did you know that I've spent well over one million dollars doing the job for the police?"

"I told you years ago to stop giving your good money to those crooks. All of those leads they gave amounted to nothing. All those sightings of Marie Perry in Amsterdam, London, and Prague all turned out to be false leads."

"What about my reward? The $100,000 reward. Do those cops up in New York know that there is a reward for information leading to her cap-

242 Crystal Lacey Winslow

ture?"

"Yes, they know."

"You're looking at me as if you want me to leave!"

"You? Never...you're my favorite lady. But you should go home and I'll personally call you when we get her."

"I hope I'm not dead!"

"You're gonna out live us all," Captain O'Mally replied and gave her a firm hug.

She loved it....

Thirty-Eight

Gracie Lane

IT WAS CLOSE TO ELEVEN AT NIGHT WHEN I HEARD Anthony's key maneuver the locks. It took him at least ten minutes to make it to his bedroom. By this time, I had already slept off my intoxication. Anthony was screaming into his phone, but I couldn't make out his conversation. Soon he walked into his bedroom and was startled by my small figure curled up in his bed.

"Jeez, you scared me," he admonished.

"Where've you been? I've been waiting forever," I said in a baby-like voice.

"How did you get in?"

"Chris was here and allowed me to wait for you."

"That slimy bastard!" he spat. "Are you all right?"

"Yes, I missed you."

He walked farther into the room and clicked on the lights. I gasped at the sight of my lover.

"Baby, what happened to you?" I ran to him, put my arms around him, and began to lightly kiss his face.

"It looks worse than it really is. I don't want to talk about that right now. I got a lot on my mind. Shouldn't you be home, being wifey?"

"I don't want to talk about that, either. Maybe we could talk later."

"Sounds like a plan." He looked deep into my eyes. "I love you, Gracie, and I want you. But I want you to want me, too."

"I do want you, baby," I said and began kissing his lips. "I want you and I don't want to go home. I want to stay with you forever."

Those were the words he'd been waiting to hear.

"Let's get in the shower," he suggested. "I've had a miserable day."

The hot water cascaded down onto our faces as we submerged our bodies underneath the powerful showerhead. The steam was so thick that we could barely see each other. I let the soothing water drench my hair and face as Anthony stood behind me and pressed his hard body against my backside. His masculine hands started lathering my back in circular motions and I got lost in the moment of erotic pleasure. As the soapy rag traveled along the nape of my neck, tracing my hips, my plump ass, and then lingering between my thick thighs, I shuddered. I turned around to face him, and we began kissing passionately. Anthony began to slowly lick my earlobes while massaging my erect nipples with his fingertips.

Anthony pushed me up against the shower wall, got down on his knees, and parted my legs. He put my right leg on his shoulder and opened my nether lips with two fingers. My ripe clitoris entered his warm mouth eagerly. As he began sucking my clit, I held on to the shower walls for support. He traced the creases outlining the walls of my vagina with his tongue, causing me to quiver involuntarily. Anthony nodded as if to say he knew he'd hit the right spot.

Anthony pulled back, stuck his finger into my inflamed pussy, and began twirling. Hot juices seeped out onto his hands. I encouraged him by moaning. He then pulled me up, positioned me in front of him, and bent me over. Spreading my ass cheeks, he began easing his dick into my resisting asshole.

He didn't say a word as he began to aggressively massage my breasts in a circular motion while placing wet kisses on my spine that were driving me crazy. I sucked in my breath. Inch by inch, his fat dick began penetrating my anal cavity. The sensation was exquisite. I began rocking my hips seductively as the sensations began filtering through my body. Finally, he had entered me completely. The pain mixed with pleasure was a little overbearing for me as our slippery bodies became one. As Anthony held tightly on to my hips, pumping in and out, we both moaned in pleasure.

"You . . . like . . . this?" he asked, moaning. "You . . . like . . . this . . . big . . . dick?"

"Oh, yesssss," I agreed. "Yessss, baby, fuck me good."

"Tell me what you want."

"I want you to fuck the shit out of me," I demanded.

"I can do that," he replied through clenched teeth as he began to mercilessly ram his dick in me.

"Yeeessssss," I screamed, still gripping the shower door for support.

"Tell me you love me!" Anthony commanded.

"I . . . love . . . you . . ." I purred.

Anthony continued to guide his fat dick into my backside. The combination was explosive as I felt strong waves of pleasure cascading through my body. I braced myself as my muscles tensed and began to contract. We both exploded and screamed out together.

For long moments, we tried to catch our breaths. Soon Anthony eased out of me and continued to do what he had originally started to do, which was wash my body. He seemed to enjoy washing my fingers, arms, feet, and intimate parts. I was his baby, and at the moment he felt like I was his and only his. When he finished washing my body, he carried me back to his bed, laid me down, and slid his tongue into my mouth. We began kissing softly, which soon progressed to slow, passionate kisses.

My body was yearning desperately for him to enter me again. I arched my back as he aggressively sucked my breasts until my nipples were erect. I wrapped my shapely legs around his trim waist, and he entered my pussy gently this time. As he pumped his dick, I pushed my hips back, meeting each thrust. It felt as if his penis was growing bigger inside me as I dug my nails deep into his masculine shoulders. I began to nibble on his neck before I pushed him over and mounted him.

I expertly rode his dick while his hands guided my waist.

"Fuck this dick," he crooned. I looked down and saw pleasure all over his face. I began sliding up and down on his dick while contracting my Kegel muscles, which drove him crazy.

"Is it good?" I asked.

"Yeah, baby," he said, moaning.

As my pussy began to contract involuntarily, I sped up my rhythm.

"I'm about to cummmm," I yelled as Anthony grabbed me tightly.

We both exploded for the second time. Sweat poured from both our bodies as I collapsed on top of his broad chest.

We'd made love four times from the shower to the bed that night. We were both physically drained and exhausted as we snuggled together and drifted off into a peaceful sleep.

Thirty-Nine

Anthony Cross

IN THE MORNING, GRACIE WAS STILL IN MY BED AND I felt a sense of victory. Could I wake up to her every morning? I thought so. All I knew was that it felt good, and I liked it. I prepared my sleeping beauty breakfast in bed and woke her up by showering her with kisses.

"What's all this?" she asked with a grateful tone as she struggled to get up.

"It's the start to a new beginning," I said and crawled into bed with her. I felt as if it was time for us to have a heart-to-heart talk. There was a lot that I didn't know about her, and I wanted to get to know about her. "Tell me about who you are."

"What do you want to know?"

"Whatever you're ready to tell me."

She exhaled.

"I'll tell you as much as you can stomach."

Her voice was weak and she didn't look me in my eyes. She put her head down in shame and began her story.

"Growing up, I never knew my mother. She left us when I was still very young. Living in a house full of men—my father and two brothers—was hard on a young girl. Especially when my father despised me. My father, who I just recently found out wasn't my biological father, always insisted that I go out into the world and find my own way. If I wanted a pair of shoes, he'd encourage me to go out and get them however I could. If that meant sleeping with the dirty old man at the corner store, so be it.

"I didn't want to whore myself out, so I figured that I'd do as my mother did. I'd marry young and have someone take care of me. I fell in love with Emmanuel. He and I snuck around for years. His family was one of the wealthier families in our area and they thought I was trash. His parents would have never accepted me. He promised me that as soon as we were old enough he'd marry me, and I believed him. When I got pregnant he wanted me to have an abortion, but I refused to kill his baby. I loved him. When he suggested that I sleep with someone else to blame the pregnancy on that person, I was numb. He, too, was whoring me out. But I did as I was told. I didn't know any better.

"It was easy enough to find the perfect scapegoat in my town. His name was Ricky. He didn't come from wealth, but he was a hard worker. I slept with him once and it was a 'miracle.' I was pregnant. He was the proudest man walking the earth. After I gave birth, neither of our parents wanted another mouth to feed, so we had to put the baby in a foster home. Thus, my tell-tale stretch marks." She laughed as tears streamed down her cheeks. I just rubbed her cheeks and encouraged her to keep talking.

"Take your time, baby," I soothed as she began to sob.

"Three years after the birth of my daughter I was still attached to Ricky in the town's eyes, but I was sneaking behind everyone's back with Emmanuel. I had just turned eighteen and Emmanuel still hadn't married me. I sat waiting, like a fool, but he just kept giving me one excuse after the other.

"George, my fake father, had long ago thrown me out, and Ricky had gotten us a place to live. He was such a hard worker, and had finally gotten a job working as an armored car driver. When he asked me to marry him, I said yes. But that was only to force Emmanuel's hand, and to make him realize that he loved me. Instead, Emmanuel encouraged me to marry Ricky, saying that as long as Ricky was there, no one would find out about us, and as soon as he got his inheritance from his parents, I could divorce Ricky and marry him. I know"—she shook her head from side to side as if she didn't know how she could have been so foolish—"how stupid was I?

"Ricky and I weren't married for long before I began sneaking

Emmanuel inside our home, and inside our bed. One day Emmanuel and I were making love when Ricky came home early. When he burst through the door, all I could think of was that he was going to kick me out and I'd be homeless, without anywhere to go. I knew George wouldn't let me come back home. I don't know what made me say it. I really didn't have time to think, but I screamed rape. I mean, I really screamed rape! It was a guttural moan mixed with a high-pitched scream.

"My reaction must have startled Emmanuel, because he never thought to defend himself. He didn't protest or contest what I'd said. He just got dressed quickly and ran out of our apartment. Ricky ran after him and slaughtered him like an animal in the streets. He murdered him in broad daylight with a dozen witnesses. I was in shock. It all happened in the blink of an eye. Ricky was arrested on the spot, and in my young mind he should have been arrested. He'd just killed a man. My man . . .

"Once the town got wind of what happened, they flooded the sheriff's department with calls. The stranger who raped Marie Perry wasn't a stranger at all. His family went there, stating that there wasn't any way Emmanuel could have raped me. They knew all along about our affair and our love child. Ricky was released from jail because his firearm was legal and he was under the impression that he'd shot and murdered an intruder, but I was arrested. They said when I screamed rape, I was negligent. It was no different than screaming 'fire!' in a crowded theater. The day the judge allowed me out of the county jail to await my trial, I ran with only the clothes on my back, and headed this way. The trial was held *in absentia*, which means in my absence, and I was convicted of involuntary manslaughter."

I was stunned. She'd been through so much. It was an awkward moment, and I didn't know what to say. But I had to say something. I kept pushing and wanting to know about her past, and now I knew it all.

"Whatever happened to your daughter?" I finally asked.

"After the incident Ricky, whose name was on her birth certificate as her biological father, took her out of her temporary foster home and raised her as his own child. She ended up working for a Dr. Anthony Cross."

The color drained from my body. The resemblance.

"Anika is your daughter."

Gracie dropped her head again in shame. "I've never been a mother to her. She's so much better than me. All I've ever done was hurt her, as my father hurt me."

She began sobbing her little heart out. She held on to me so tightly that I felt all her emotions. Her revelation drummed in my cloudy head. *Anika* was her daughter....

"I've never told anyone what I've told you . . ." she honestly said.

"Don't worry, I'll help you make this right," I told her. There wasn't any way I'd allow her to spend the rest of her life in jail.

"There's more," she said, reluctantly.

"Go ahead."

"They've found me."

"Who? Who's found you?"

"The police. When Dakota assaulted me the police lifted my finger-prints off the knife and now they're looking for a Marie Perry, wanted felon. Anthony, I have to go. I need to run and get away from here."

"Babe, you can't run. You have to stay and face it or else you'll be running for the rest of your life."

"My life will be over if I don't run!" she screamed, defiantly.

"We can make this right," I soothed, "I'll be here for you. We'll get a lawyer and make them see that you didn't plan on his murder. You had no way of knowing."

"That sounds great in theory but the law doesn't always work like that. I've already been sentenced to seven to fifteen. My only hope is an appeal and request for a new trial. Even with that I'm running the chance of getting convicted on a higher charge. What if a jury came back and found me guilty of negligent homicide! Huh? I could do the rest of my life in jail without the possibility of parole."

She collapsed on the bed, hysterical.

After Gracie had purged her heart out, she was drained. She drifted back to sleep, allowing me quiet time to figure out how I could help her get her life back. She needed me now more than ever, only I didn't know if I could be there for her. Finally, it was sinking in. Maybe Gracie wasn't the one for me. She's been living the last twenty years as a lie. She had all this scandal surrounding her name and I didn't know if I was up to take on her problems. I have my own. Not to mention that my best friend, Chris, had just committed the ultimate betrayal. What was to say Gracie wouldn't hurt me as well?

Forty

Gracie Lane

I WOKE UP IN ANTHONY'S APARTMENT TO SEVERAL voice messages on my cell phone. I began listening and my heart sank. Ed left a message that he had been arrested for fighting with my lover, the doctor, and he wanted me to come bail him out. The next message was from Ed again, several hours later, stating that he was released on his own recognizance, and that he wanted a divorce.

I began getting dressed frantically when Anthony walked in.

"Where are you going?"

"Ed was arrested last night. Did you know that?"

"Arrested for what?"

"He said for fighting with you. You had to have known!" I yelled.

"I didn't know any such thing! Ask him. I wasn't there when he got arrested. He's probably lying."

I looked directly into Anthony's eyes.

"Ed doesn't lie."

I made my way to the front door, and Anthony was right behind me.

"Wait a minute. Let me get dressed and go with you."

"You can't. I have to deal with this on my own. I promise, I'll call you later."

I left Anthony's apartment with a sense of guilt. What the fuck was I doing? Ed directly asking me for a divorce had shaken me up a bit. I was so confused. I felt like rubber being pulled in ten different directions. I had two men in love with me, all vying for my attention and undivided commitment. It was like smoking a cigarette to the butt and having to make the decision to get one last drag, or to throw it out because it had served its purpose.

I entered my home to find Ed flying around the house in a frenzy. His eyes were red and puffy, and it appeared he'd been crying. He was packing some items into a suitcase. He ignored me as I came in. He was upset, which made me upset. After a couple minutes of watching him gather things, and wiping a couple tears away, I finally broke the silence.

"What are you doing?"

"What does it look like?" he hastily snapped.

"It looks like you're packing your things."

"Nope! I'm packing *your* things."

"What's the matter with you? I'm not going anywhere! I got your message about a divorce and we need to sit and talk like adults."

"You are getting the hell out of my sight or I promise I will make you very sorry!" he screamed. Ed was furious and I realized the approach I was using was inappropriate. I needed to calm down and level with him.

"Ed, explain to me why you're packing my things for me to leave. I told you that I'm not having an affair with my doctor. Don't let him come between us."

"I told you that if you ever were unfaithful, I'd divorce you. You gambled with my love, and now you'll have to live with the consequences. You mean nothing to me. You're just another whore. You don't deserve my last name."

"I've never slept with him. I swear on my mother's grave! All this is a misunderstanding. He said he tried to tell you that, but you wouldn't listen."

"How dare you stand in my face and quote what some other man told you! You're cherishing his words like they came straight from the Bible. I'm your HUSBAND! Why do you keep forgetting that?"

"Ed, I'm here, aren't I? How could you accuse me of forgetting about you?"

"How could you leave me in jail, and not even come to support me in court?" He shook his head in disbelief.

"I stayed at the Marriott. I needed time alone to think about our marriage and how much you mean to me," I said calmly.

"Don't lie to me. You were with him, weren't you?" he asked.

"I answered that already. Now stop acting crazy."

"Crazy! Why are you doing this to me? Me? Do you hear how you sound right now? You're cold . . . and distant. You just want me to roll over and accept you for who you are. Turn the other cheek and let you and your male mistress carry on. You selfish bitch!"

Startled by his outburst, I couldn't move. Ed had to physically grab me up by my elbow and toss me and my suitcase out the front door. The neighbors got a front row view as I began pounding and banging on the front door, screaming and crying in hysterics. My dirty laundry was on display—literally and figuratively.

In a rage, I ran down to the front desk and got the master key and went back upstairs to confront my husband. Nobody kicks me out of my motherfucking house! The nerve of him. I came back in ready to battle. He was upstairs when I confronted him.

"Who the fuck do you think you are? If it's over then it's over! But you're getting the fuck out—not me!"

He looked defeated. He was still crying.

"Okay, Gracie, you're right. I'll leave. And I'm sorry…for everything."

Forty-One

Anthony Cross

THAT NIGHT, WHEN GRACIE CAME BACK TO ME, I
was euphoric. I wanted to keep her safe, protect her, and give her the love
she obviously never got from any man in her life. The next morning, she
contacted a high-powered lawyer and then took us on an obscene shopping spree on her American Express Black Card. She had tossed Ed out
and she admitted that she was tired of crying and equally tired of running,
scared. I told her that we were starting over. When I pulled out the charm
bracelet that I had bought for her weeks back, her eyes welled up with
tears. "This symbolizes my love for you."

I guess the new piece of jewelry had sparked something in her, or
maybe it was the looming fear of a long prison term but Gracie was determined to spend a lot of the money she had sitting in her bank accounts.

She'd purchased us both matching fur coats. I watched as she pranced
around in a chinchilla fur designed by Zac Posen. She walked around my
apartment in full diva status. As her chinchilla swept the ground and her
stilettos from Jimmy Choo click-clacked against my parquet floors, I realized how happy I really was. In light of her situation, it felt good to believe
in and pledge your support to someone you loved, and I felt as if she could
be the one. I didn't have a want or desire to call another woman, let alone
sleep with anyone else. I told her that I wanted her to divorce her husband

and marry me—in the face of danger—and I meant every word.

She took me on a major shopping spree to celebrate our new beginning. I had two tailored trench coats from Karl Lagerfeld being delivered to me in the next four weeks, and I couldn't wait to get them. I also racked up numerous items from the Ed Hardy store. She bought herself a natural Russian sable belted swing coat and a Burberry overcoat and matching shoes. We also stopped in Tiffany, and she bought herself a diamond bracelet set in platinum, and the matching, heart pendant necklace. And I picked up a pair of diamond cufflinks set in platinum. But what I loved most was when we went to Tourneau and she replaced my stolen, stainless steel Rolex watch with a platinum version. The watched looked good on my wrist. I felt like a million bucks. She also bought us matching Harry Winston diamond rings set in platinum. We both had them fitted for our pinky fingers. Then we went to Barney's New York and Bergdorf Goodman, and she bought a full wardrobe.

Our day couldn't have been better until I got a call from my doorman.

"Dr. Cross, any moment you're going to be getting a knock on your door for your lady friend. There's no way out. They should be there—the police."

My heart dropped. I looked to Gracie and she had this huge smile plastered on her face as she modeled her new clothing for me.

She detected something in my face.

"What's wrong?" she panicked. "Who was that?"

Before I could answer, the police burst in and grabbed Gracie. They left with her kicking and screaming. I stood there helpless, watching the events unfold before me.

Forty-Two

Anthony Cross
Whatever love means...

AS SOON AS GRACIE WAS PROCESSED AND EXTRADITED back to New Jersey, I made arrangements to visit her. All I kept thinking about on my ride up there was how she was handling being locked up.

The lawyer she'd retained had put in a motion to the court to be released from the case after the State had seized her bank accounts and bank records. The district attorney's office had gotten a court order asking that they exhume her second husband, Phillip's body to run more tests to make sure he died of natural causes and wasn't murdered. They were trying to label her some sort of serial killer; a woman who was manipulative and also a murderess. And the allegations surrounding her father's death were tossed on her criminal jacket as well. Gracie—or shall I say Marie Perry's story went national. The news media had a field day. They had pictures of her when she was in her early twenties side-by-side with pictures of her new face—post plastic surgery. They claimed that she'd gotten plastic surgery in an attempt to escape paying her debt to society and elude the law. Her brothers, Andre and Benjamin came out of the woodwork along with Ed's sister, Tamara. All sold their stories to tabloids showing Gracie in an awful light.

Unless Gracie told me otherwise I'd believe whatever truth she gave me. My funds were a little low at the moment but I was looking to liquidate all my assets, sell my apartment and get her a high-profile lawyer to appeal her case, such as Mark Geragos or Gary Scheck.

Whatever time she got, I was going to ride it out with her. If I didn't, then who would? Surely not her miserable brothers, and most certainly not her husband. The freak had turned her in! How could he look at himself in the mirror? She didn't deserve that as punishment for having an affair.

As Gracie came scampering into the visiting room, I could tell she'd been crying. Her eyes were bloodshot and puffy. Her hair was pulled back into a tight ponytail, and the orange prison jumpsuit seemed to swallow her shapely figure. Even though she looked withered and worn, her eyes had a glint of determination, as if to say, "Don't feel sorry for me. I'll be all right."

I stood to embrace her and she sat down, leaving my arms extended. She dropped her head into her hands and began to sob.

"What are you doing here?" she asked.

"What do you mean? I came to give you my support," I said. "Why? Don't you want me here?"

"Anthony, you shouldn't have come. I don't want anything getting back to Ed. I need him right now."

"Ed? You need Ed right now? He turned you in for reward money—"

"No! He didn't—"

"There was a bounty over your head and he took it!" I exploded and disrupted the visiting room. After getting a glare from one of the COs, I lowered my voice. "Why are you punishing yourself? You don't need him—I'm here for you."

"Here for me?" Gracie laughed, mockingly. "Are you going to make me an offer I can't refuse? Huh? What can you do for me that my husband can't? Are you going to open up these iron bars and let me walk away in to the sunset?"

"Why are you doing this? Why are you pushing me away? I'm finally committing myself to you—a relationship—and you don't want me. I love you Gracie...you don't have to be afraid to love me back."

"Anthony, I'm in a six by six foot cell. That coupled with your being here is insufferable."

Was this the woman that I'd fallen in love with?

She continued. "I've already spoken to a lawyer that Ed hired. He said that I have a good case on appeal and that I may be able to get a judge to set a bail. If that happens I can have my freedom back until my next trial. Hopefully this time I'll have a better ending."

"Are you kidding me? Drop that lawyer. You can't trust someone like Ed. He's a time bomb just waiting to explode. Don't you think he wants revenge for what you've put him through? All of your lies..."

"Anthony, I know you may have ill feelings toward Ed, and that you may be feeling a little slighted, but he is doing what's in my best interests."

"I may be feeling a little slighted?" My voice rose into a little girl's pitch. "He's sending YOU to the can, so I think you should reevaluate that statement."

As I sat listening to her, I wondered how she could take everything so lightly, and not hold Ed responsible for her having to sit in somebody's dirty jail in a tacky, orange jumpsuit. Maybe she was punishing herself for having the affair. I decided to try another approach.

"Gracie, baby, listen, you don't have to feel guilty anymore about us. You don't have to feel that this is just punishment for having an affair."

"Please don't do this, make it about you and me, because it isn't. A man is dead. My husband didn't have anything to do with what happened twenty years ago. He's an honest man, and he's doing what's right."

I listened to the way she spoke of her husband—so fondly, so passionately, so tenderly. Had she always spoken of him in this way and if so, how could I have missed it?

"Even now you choose him over me? After all he's done to you? How could you stay with him?"

"Because he's my husband," she replied, simply.

"Really?" I slowly retorted. "Are you in love with your *husband*?"

She lowered her eyes to the table, exhaled, and then looked me directly in my eyes. In the seconds it took her to answer, thousands of questions went through my head. My heart dropped and my stomach fluttered. Jeez, for the first time in life someone was breaking up with me. I didn't like it. I didn't like it one bit.

"I'd be lying if I said no."

There it was. As simple as elementary school. The one question I never asked throughout our whole relationship was the one thing that could have saved me from all this pain I was currently feeling.

"What about us? I thought that we were going to get married. I thought that you loved me."

"Either I deceived you or you made an inaccurate assumption but I never said love nor did I ever suggest marriage. We were just having a good time. You knew I was married when you met me. I never lied...you knew."

I *knew* I was defeated. I *knew* I had to throw in the towel. I *knew* I had been played. I couldn't grovel and beg for her one minute more. I was a man, and I just realized she'd been playing me like a bitch. I decided to take a good look at the woman I'd fallen in love with, and drink in her looks for the last time. I would never see her again. I stared deeply into her eyes and she seemed to age instantly. Now she looked every bit of her 39 years. Tell-tale signs peeked out at me— microscopic gray hairs, tiny crow's feet, wrinkled and veined hands.

Holding back my pain, I got up and kissed her on her creased forehead.

"Take care of yourself, kid," I told her.

"You do the same."

I looked back over my shoulders with one last burning question. "Did you do it?"

"I already told you what happened. I didn't have any idea that he would be murdered."

"Not Emmanuel. I'm talking about Phillip, your second husband. Did you kill him?"

"You've been reading too many tabloids."

Was that an answer to my question?

I walked out of the correctional facility with mixed emotions. The visit had besmirched any fond memories of our affair. I wondered if she felt at least half of what turmoil she'd caused. I'd reached my emotional peak. I thought that we had more than loveless sex. I was a wounded man with an ego. The pain hurt deeply as I tried to come to terms with my past actions. Was I really in love with Gracie? Or was it the chase and challenge of pursuing another man's wife? I didn't know.

I might not ever know.

I hopped in my ride and did the only thing I knew how.

"Hey, Anika, what's up, baby?"

"What do you want?"

"You...I want you..."

To my peeps:

If I had to rewrite my life--I wouldn't. Life is about learning--yourself, friends, and family. And also seeking out truth. Your truth. I'm not perfect but I'm strong. I'm a survivor and a fighter. *No weapon formed against me shall prosper.*

Lacey
XXX

MELODRAMA PUBLISHING'S 2007 CATALOG

PLEASE SEE WEB SITE FOR 2008 CATALOG

www.melodramapublishing.com

SEPTEMBER 2007
JEALOUSY
LINDA BRICKHOUSE

In Chaka Dubois' world, careful planning was the difference between a poor man and a rich soldier. Nothing however, prepared him for the betrayal that claimed his life, which sets off a roller-coaster chain of events. Secrets meant to die with him rise from the grave, turning friend against friend, when the mystery begins: who killed Chaka, and why? Experience the chaos, fears, and perverse passions as friendships are tested and lovers become enemies. Did Chaka earn the destruction that hovered and eventually killed him or was he merely a victim of pure jealousy?

Experience the bitter taste of *Jealousy* as it sets out to destroy everything in its path.

DECEMBER 2007
THE MADAM
JACKI SIMMONS

Jade Wilcox is a queen bee at the top of her game. She's the number-one celebrity agent in the country, she's got a great man, and everyone she knows is an A-Lister. But nothing lasts forever.

Everyone knows that sex sells, so when her near-bankrupt boss uses that idea to his advantage, it means a world of change is headed for Jade. Her fairy-tale life is about to turn into a nightmare as she fills shoes she'd never thought she'd wear: those of a madam, a mother hen to a flock of high-priced call girls. As she struggles to juggle both sides of her life, Jade must keep herself and her girls on the right side of the law without losing her own life or anyone else's. This becomes harder and harder to do because the smallest triggers become everyone's motivation for murder. Jade has her eye on the finish line, but can she get there before she becomes a victim of the world she's worked so hard to become a part of?

OCTOBER 2007
LIFE AFTER WIFEY
BY KIKI SWINSON

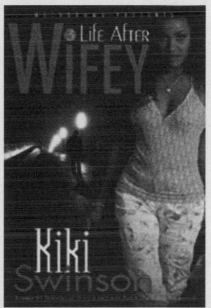

Nikki is in possession of a lot of chilling information that could not only shed light on some unanswered questions, but could also put a lot of dangerous people behind bars for life — including her new boyfriend, Syncere, from New Jersey.

Well aware that she is sleeping with the enemy, Nikki knows she must step up her game and take some precautionary measures to protect herself if she plans to seek out Kira's shooter. What better place to start on her journey than with the man she shares her bed with?

In *Life After Wifey*, Nikki is going to put herself in some very compromising situations but through it all, she knows that she must never implicate herself and Kira in the plans that ended Ricky and Russell's lives. Nikki must suit up with everything Kira has ever taught her about the streets and then prepare for the worst.

DECEMBER 2007
IN MY 'HOOD II
BY ENDY

You thought there would be no one left in the hood after the horrible chain of murders that occurred in *In My 'Hood*. But the 'hood don't stop living; the saga only continues with a new breed of street dwellers to take their place.

Nettie's back to wreak havoc on the city of Newark by targeting the HNIC, Leroy "Big Roy" Jenkins. But she is not alone. She recruits Ishmael's old squad, along with a few people of her own and takes *getting money by any means necessary* to a new level. But there's a new cat on the block and his name is Wild. The name is self-explanatory and he has the same vision in sight: to conquer and destroy Leroy. Nettie and Wild join forces to create the illest crew Essex County has seen in decades.

DECEMBER 2007
HISTRESS
CRYSTAL LACEY WINSLOW

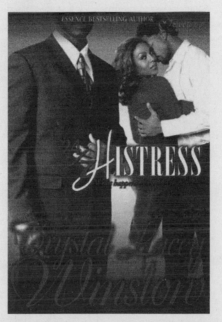

Anthony Cross is a highly successful, well educated, young, up and coming plastic surgeon. He has a string of sexy, young, single women at his fingertips. So why is he sweating Mrs. Gracie Lane? She was a challenge: a married woman who was still in love with her husband. The married, mysterious temptress eventually becomes his stress with her incessant lies, secret past and constant mood swings. Why can't he let her go? That question will haunt Anthony as his boys try to talk sense into him: *Married women are good for one thing...booty calls!* Anthony's heart —or is it his ego? — won't let her go. When he and Gracie's worlds collide, Anthony, the self-proclaimed bachelor, realizes that Gracie's in control and he's become her HISTRESS!

DECEMBER 2007
DEN OF SIN
STORM

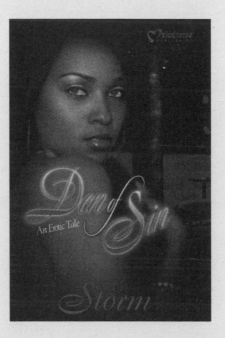

Sex, Secrets, Drama – Nadia Weber – Beautiful. Sexy. Scandalous.
A self-proclaimed sex fiend, Nadia's seen it all and screwed the rest.
Swearing off sex with married men for cash, she sets her freaky sights on
her co-worker – a gorgeous playboy with his own secrets and private
fantasies. They get together in The Den, where anything and everything
goes. Then a stranger rocks Nadia's world and she finally meets her
sexual match – in the dark, literally. Now Nadia must rely on friends and
family to get her past lonely and confusing days where everything she
loves and thinks she knows are threatened.

ORDER FORM
(PHOTO COPY)
MELODRAMA PUBLISHING
P. O. BOX 522
BELLPORT, NY 11713-0522
(646) 879-6315
www.melodramapublishing.com
melodramapub@aol.com
Please send me the following book(s):
LIFE, LOVE & LONELINESS ISBN: 0-9717021-0-1
THE CRISS CROSS ISBN: 0-9717021-2-8
WIFEY ISBN: 0-9717021-3-6
I'M STILL WIFEY ISBN: 0-9717021-5-2
A TWISTED TALE OF KARMA ISBN: 0-9717021-4-4
MENACE II SOCIETY ISBN: 0-9717021-7-9
SEX, SIN & BROOKLYN ISBN: 0-9717021-6-0
CROSS ROADS ISBN: 0-9717021-8-7
IN MY HOOD ISBN: 0-9717021-9-5
STRIPPED ISBN: 1-934157-00-7
EVA FIRST LADY OF SIN ISBN: 1-934157-01-5
THE CANDY SHOP ISBN: 1-934157-02-3
HISTRESS ISBN: 1-934157-03-1
LIFE AFTER WIFEY ISBN: 1-934157-04-X
THE MADAM ISBN: 1-934157-05-8
IN MY HOOD II ISBN:1-934157-06-6
JEALOUSY ISBN:1-934157-07-4
DEN OF SIN ISBN: 1-934157-08-2

ALL ABOVE BOOKS ARE PRICED AT **$15.00**

UP CLOSE AND PERSONAL ISBN: 0-9717021-1-X
THE POETRY BOOK IS PRICED AT $9.95
SEE OUR WEB SITE FOR ADDITIONAL TITLES

QUANTITY `@ 15.00 (U.S.) = _____`

Shipping/Handling* = _____

Total Enclosed = _____

**PLEASE ATTACH, NAME, ADDRESS, TELEPHONE
NUMBER(for emergencies)**

***Please enclose $4.50 to cover shipping/handling
($6.00 if total more than $30.00 AND under $50.00)**

FOR BULK ORDERS PLEASE CALL THE PUBLISHER.
To pay by check or money order, please make it payable to:
MELODRAMA PUBLISHING.

Send your payment with the order form to the above address, or order
on the web.
Prices subject to change without notice. Please allow 2-3 weeks for
delivery.

WWW.MELODRAMAPUBLISHING.COM